THE TRENCH COAT CHRONICLES

THE TRENCH COAT CHRONICLES

Edited by
Ann Stolinsky and Ruth Littner
Gemini Wordsmiths

CELESTIAL ECHO PRESS
ROSLYN, PA, USA
2020

Celestial Echo Press
An imprint of Gemini Wordsmiths
P. O. Box 1191
Roslyn, PA 19001
geminiwordsmiths.com/publishing

Cover art and design: Don Dyen

Acquisitions and editing: Gemini Wordsmiths

Dedication

French novelist Honore de Balzac once wrote, "Behind every great fortune lies a great crime." And we believe him. Some of the stories you will read in this anthology include criminals motivated by riches and fortune. Some of the stories have perpetrators with more pure agendas. But as Jacques Barzun quipped, "The danger that may really threaten crime fiction is that soon there will be more writers than readers." We don't believe *him*.

We know you, along with millions of other book lovers, will continue to enjoy reading stories throughout the ages. It's because crime stories evoke the "bad boy" in all of us, the hidden, mysterious desire to vicariously commit the crime — and get away with it. And we love to read about those criminals. "We don't give our criminals much punishment, but we sure give 'em plenty of publicity." Thanks, Will Rogers. We agree, and we promote.

This murder mystery anthology is dedicated to Sam Spade, Hercule Poirot, and Dick Tracy, as well as to all the writers of hard-boiled detective stories of years past, many of whom formed the basis for the crime mysteries we read today.

Enjoy this wide variety of storylines, each of which include criminals, victims — and trench coats.

Contents

Praise for *The Trench Coat Chronicles*

"This collection of clever shorts features trench coats worn by cunning murderers and world-weary detectives, wrapped up in mysteries both wild and domestic. A treat for fans of mystery and imagination."

Dennis Tafoya, author of *Dope Thief, The Wolves of Fairmount Park,* and *The Poor Boy's Game*

~~~~~~

"The Trench Coat Chronicles is an eclectic collection of stories that mixes mystery and suspense while exploring the detective who-done-it in new and fascinating ways."

Janice Gable Bashman, author of *Predator* and *Wanted Undead or Alive.* JaniceGableBashman.com

~~~~~~

"From a whimsical murder mystery in a world where rabbits mimic people, to a chance encounter with a vintage motorcycle and its young rider on a lonely road in the middle of the night, to long overdue reckoning in the fog shrouded English moors, this collection of short stories, all incorporating a trench coat in their theme, has something to catch the attention of and delight every reader."

Nick Russell, *New York Times* bestselling author of the *Big Lake* mystery series
goodreads.com/author/list/659478.Nick_Russell

Foreword

Kelly Simmons

Ah, the sturdy trench coat. A traditional mainstay not only in classic wardrobes, but classic literature. Plenty of pockets to hide things in. Water repellent and sometimes, villain repellent. An icon for beloved detectives, inspectors, and spies for generations. (Not to mention flashers, femme fatales, and minor characters who just need to keep dry in the rain.)

The Trench Coat Chronicles, cleverly conceived and superbly assembled and edited, offers the reader far more than a clever way to tie stories together. It provides myriad ideas of how to defy stereotypes, upend the murder mystery genre, and, perhaps, even make wardrobe a character. With varied writing styles from conventional noir to cozy mystery to feminist detective, there is much in this collection to delight and admire.

Engaging for readers, and inspiring to writers. What more could a short story anthology possibly offer, short of being packaged with whiskey?

So, settle in for a fun ride. Enjoy the variety of colorful settings and interesting characters. Smile as you watch each coat emerge and work its story magic.

We promise, the next time it rains and you open your closet? You'll never look at those epaulets and belt the same way again.

And who knows what's next from this talented editing team? I, for one, will be advocating for *The Go-Go Boot Collection*.

Kelly Simmons is an international selling author of suspenseful women's fiction.

Visit her at kellysimmonsbooks.com.

Kinurie Mist

DJ Tyrer

Alasdair shuddered as he stood in the doorway of his cottage. The thick moorland mist reminded him of the gas. He could almost hear the *peep!* of the officer's whistle, the shouts, the rattle of gunfire, the rumbling thunder of counter-battery fire.

He screwed his eyes tight shut and willed the memories away. The fog remained, horrible and gas-like when he opened them again, but silent now.

Not for the first time, Alasdair regretted taking the position here, but really, what was the choice? Jobs were as rare as compassionate factory owners these days and he was lucky the Captain had owed him a favour.

Still, he would've preferred a country estate whose hills were less often draped in mocking mist.

If only the grouse could care for themselves, he'd stay within the stone walls of his cottage and make the day a holiday. If only he could've found another post. ...

Movement brought him out of his self-berating reverie and he blinked as he looked into the murk.

For a moment, Alasdair thought it must just have been the motion of the vapor, coiling in upon itself, that had caught his attention. Then, he saw it. A figure.

Alasdair cursed. A dark shape, half-hidden in the fog, outline blurry like ink that had run, the figure was almost formless — and, yet …

He stepped back inside his cottage and reached, clumsily, for the door, desperate to shut out the vision.

The figure was a familiar one. One he recalled from the fog of gas over ten years before.

"You're dead," he whispered as the figure drew near.

Though little more than a shadow in the mist, Alasdair had no doubt who stood before him.

"Leave me alone! I never did you no wrong!"

The figure stepped up to the cottage doorway.

"You shouldn't have lied, Alasdair."

The cart clattered to a halt outside the grey hulking edifice of the baronial-style hall in a scene that wouldn't have looked out of place before the war.

Angus Shand dropped down with a crunch onto the gravel, his long overcoat flapping about him. Shreds of mist scattered away from his feet, agitated by his presence.

Some would doubtless refer to such a day as 'bracing' or even 'wholesome,' but in his opinion, it was merely cold and damp, and the scent in the air had the unpleasant hint of sodden wool and mouldy wallpaper. Angus pulled his coat tight about himself. It might be natural, but he would've rather known the smell of city smoke and seen the welcoming front door of a house that didn't look as if it might once have hosted a chilly Robert the Bruce or Macbeth, and been neither maintained nor aired since.

The cart driver tossed down Angus's travelling case. Angus caught it with ease as the doors to the hall swung open and a ruddy-faced man in tweed with wild whiskers stepped out to greet him.

"You must be Shand," he said in a loud, but raspy voice that Angus recognised from over the telephone.

"Aye, that I must, sir. Angus Shand, at your service."

"Captain Campbell." There was no proffered hand to shake, no exchange of pleasantries, merely a curt gesture for Angus to enter his home. After all, he was nothing more than hired help. Hired help that, he suspected, Campbell would much rather have done without. Indeed, in his shabby grey trench coat, he probably looked more like a vagrant than a man of any worth.

Nodding in acknowledgement, Angus paused to brush away the droplets that had condensed upon his beard, and then shook the drips from his coat, before following his employer inside.

"A bad business. A damnable bad business."

Angus nodded again and entered a bleak drawing room behind his employer. He wasn't invited to sit.

"Whisky?"

He doubted the Captain wanted him to answer in the positive, but there was a line between gruffness and being a bad host that even a man such as he wouldn't cross, even with an employee. After all, Angus wasn't a mere tradesman, but more akin to a doctor or a man of the cloth.

"Please," he said. "A small libation would be just the thing to revive body and soul after my ride from the railway station."

Campbell grunted and grudgingly poured him a neat shot and slid it along the side-table.

"Thank you."

Kinurie House was a good long cart ride up muddy lanes from the nearest station. Angus felt as if the chill and the damp had, in spite of his trench coat, penetrated right through into his marrow on the journey. Still, he was here for a reason and a sip of the whisky was certainly revivifying.

He nodded at the Captain.

"There was a murder?"

Campbell's face reddened with an apoplectic expression at the word.

"We don't know it *is* murder."

"Yet, you called me in."

"A colleague of mine, from my days in service to His Majesty, said you are a discreet and reliable fellow. I trust he was correct?"

"Indubitably, sir. I have handled several such cases for gentlemen like yourself in order to avoid unwanted attention from both the police and the press."

Captain Campbell snorted. "Vultures."

"Indeed." Angus wasn't certain to which august body the man was referring, but men such as Captain Campbell, men of status and reputation, always had good reason to avoid scrutiny from either. *Captain Campbell more than most.*

"There has been a death," Angus said, laying down the now-empty glass and beginning again. "An unfortunate and mysterious one."

It wasn't a question, but his employer nodded.

"One of my employees." The Captain had said as much across the telephone wires.

"And you haven't involved the police?"

"Only the local constable. He's deferential and a couple of drams smoothed his acceptance of the death as nothing but an accident or ill fate. Doctor Drummond, likewise. They nodded it through, no questions asked."

"Yet, *you* have questions …"

"Yes, dammit!" Captain Campbell sighed and poured himself another whisky without offering Angus one.

"Who died — and why does it have you worried?"

The Captain downed his shot and was silent for a moment.

"It was a man named Alasdair McKeith. My ghillie. He died in his cottage on the estate. His neck was broken. His eyes …" Campbell's voice trailed off.

"His eyes?" prompted Angus.

"Wide with fear, as if he'd seen a ghost."

"The shock of snapping his neck? Terror in the moments before death claimed him?"

"Perhaps. Perhaps." Captain Campbell shifted nervously. "Yet, that isn't how it struck me."

"You think he was murdered and saw it coming?"

"Possibly."

"Very well. I shall need to take a look at his cottage, although I doubt there are any clues that escaped the notice of an erudite and perspicacious man such as yourself."

"It isn't far."

"Then, let us go now. We can continue our conversation as we walk."

The mist thickened as they followed a lightly gravelled path across the moor, transforming it into a fog as dense as any peasouper.

The Captain patted a stout wooden post as they passed.

"Should you be out here alone and the mist grow too thick to see, these can guide your way. Every two yards. Look for their outline and you shan't become lost, lad."

"Thank you for the advice, sir. Now, to return to my questions."

"Yes?"

"Had McKeith worked for you long?"

"He was in my employ for about six years, but previously he served under me as a lance corporal in the army."

"So, you knew him well?"

"As well as any master can know his man. We didn't socialise, save for the odd dram when discussing the grouse, but I knew him to be a reliable fellow."

"Any enemies?"

"McKeith? Every ghillie has enemies — it's his job to make the lives of poachers hell."

"Forgive me if I'm ploughing in the wrong direction," said Angus, "I am, after all, a city boy, but would a poacher break a ghillie's neck or stage an accident? Wouldn't they just take a pot shot at him? I've read in the newspapers …"

The Captain's silhouette shrugged at him through the fog.

"That would be more likely, but I cannot say for certain. That *is* why I hired you."

Angus chuckled. "Very true. But he had no other enemies? Nothing from his army days? He was never involved in anything illegal?"

Captain Campbell was silent for a moment, then said, "Nothing that I know of."

"And yourself?"

"Sorry?"

"Do you have any enemies, someone who might have wished to strike at you by killing your man? Someone who wished to embarrass you, maybe?"

Again, Campbell was silent for a time, the only sound the soft crunch of gravel beneath their boots, before he again replied in the negative.

"Then," said Angus, "it would seem it was most likely a poacher — unless, of course, it was a ghost."

"A ghost?"

"I was referring to his look of wide-eyed terror."

"Oh, yes, of course." Captain Campbell gave a weak, raspy laugh. Angus supposed that, out here in the grey mist, it was easy to start believing in ghosts and echoes of the past returned to haunt you.

"Ah, it looks as if we are here," he said, looking past his employer. Ahead of them, the late-ghillie's cottage was visible as a dark, ill-defined shape through the murk.

They approached it and the Captain took out an old iron key and unlocked the door.

"It is as it was when he was found."

Angus nodded and followed him into the shadowy interior, taking out an electric torch and shining it about, examining the single room that McKeith had called home.

"The door was open when he was found?"

Campbell nodded. "Yes. He was lying before it, as if he'd been staring out into the mist when he was attacked."

"Then, it seems likely whoever attacked him came from out of the mist, in that direction."

"If you say so, lad."

"I do." The Captain accepted his assertion; he seemed to Angus the sort of man with enough sense not to quibble with the expert advice he was paying for. That was good.

"Then, we should seek answers in that direction." He shone the torch-beam at the Captain as if interrogating a prisoner. "Did you and your men look for tracks? Did you find anything?"

"We did, but no. I assumed whoever did it took the path, as we just did."

"I doubt it. No, I believe they came over the moor. To do otherwise would've brought them too close to the hall."

"But there were no footprints."

"The grass is scraggy but springy and a footprint might not take. Besides, I'm sure a poacher would know how to move without leaving a trail. Or …"

"Or?"

Angus lowered the electric torch and gave his employer a thin smile.

"Or, it might have been a ghost. I'm led to believe they leave no trace in passing."

Captain Campbell returned the thin smile, but there was uneasiness in his eyes, not mirth.

Pulling his coat about him against the cold, Angus stepped out into the mist.

"Let's take a look and see what we can find."

"A bad idea," said Campbell. "In all this, we're liable to get lost and stumble into a bog and never be seen again."

"Ah, yes, I've heard of them pulling ancient bodies out of the peat in Ireland. I shouldn't want to find myself as a museum exhibit in a dozen centuries time!"

He shone the torch-beam back into the cottage.

"There's a length of rope there—tie it to the door handle and toss it here. That way, we shan't become lost."

He caught the rope and tied it about his waist, then slipped the coil over his elbow to feed out as they went.

"Just stay near me, Captain."

His employer nodded and placed his hand upon the taut rope as a guide.

"Here." He passed Angus a walking stick. "Test the ground as you go."

"I will."

Probing ahead of them, Angus led the way across the mist-shrouded moor.

Behind him, Campbell snorted. "This is hopeless."

"On the contrary, sir, I believe this is the route your killer took to McKeith's cottage."

Whistling, Angus strode on as if taking a constitutional around a city park and not a trek over rough moorland.

"Wait up, lad; you're leaving me behind, dammit."

"Just follow the rope, sir."

Compared to his employer's damp splashing footsteps, Angus moved with confident ease, outpacing him without effort.

"Nearly there," he called back.

"Where?"

Angus didn't answer, just watched through the mist as Captain Campbell approached the silhouette before him and listened with a wry smile as the man cursed at the discovery it was a stunted moorland tree and not his employee.

"Dammit, where are you, Shand? What the hell kind of game are you playing?"

"Just my little joke, sir."

It had taken him no more than a moment to tie the rope about the tree and slip it from his waist, before vanishing into the thick mist.

He approached the Captain and heard him curse again.

"Anything wrong, sir?" Angus asked. There were several feet still between them, but he could make out the Captain well enough.

"For a moment, I thought ..."

"Thought what, sir?"

"Nothing. Nothing. Your talk of ghosts had me imagining things."

"You thought you saw a ghost, sir?"

Captain Campbell wheezed a sound intended as a chuckle. "For a moment."

"I reminded you of someone? A shade from your past? Lieutenant McKenzie, perhaps?"

"How did—? I mean, I don't know what you're talking about."

"Really, sir? I would've thought you would recall the name of an old colleague? Or did you perform a *damnatio memoriae* of those who were considered cowards?"

"I don't know what—"

"Oh, but you do, sir." Angus took a step towards him and Captain Campbell took an involuntary one back. "You *do* know. You were there when he died: struck in the back by a German bullet as he cut and ran, yes?"

The reply was a slow wheeze: "Yes."

"Liar! You shot him in the back as he led the advance, then turned his body so that the shot looked as if it came from the German trenches. In the chaos, who would think to suspect murder? Not when that vile word—*cowardice*—was uttered. Hush it over and move along, eh?"

"That's not true!"

"Quite out of character, those who knew him said, yet who could argue with the facts?"

"Who are you …?"

"Only McKeith was there, and a sergeant named Dalziel. You paid them off and even got McKeith a position when he needed it, to keep them quiet. Nobody else knew."

"Who are you?"

"But I had my suspicions, spoke to those who knew him and eventually, I spoke to Dalziel."

Angus took another step forward, forcing Campbell back.

"He gave you up, told me everything — about your business in looted goods and smuggled whisky and gin. Told me how Lieutenant McKenzie found out and refused to be bought.

"Told me how you murdered him and besmirched his name and reputation to save your own."

"*Who are you?*"

"I was eight when you killed my father. Mother remarried and I was given a new name to blot out the shame attached to the one I was born to. But I could never believe my father was a coward."

Captain Campbell groaned.

"I thought you might recognise this." Angus tugged at the trench coat he wore. "It was my father's. But, when the rank insignia have been torn off, and you've scrubbed the coat a dozen times to remove the mud and blood and patched the bullet holes, it no longer looks like an officer's coat, just a shabby off-grey."

"It was only business, lad. Had your father taken payment ..."

"Sold his honour, you mean? Aye, he'd have lived, but at such a price. And, no, don't think to buy me off. I value my honour just as highly as he did.

"Besides," Angus laughed, bitterly, "I cashed your cheque, so have done quite well out of today, regardless. As you can see, I had good reason to ask for payment in advance."

"Please, don't kill me."

Angus snorted. "Don't beg, Captain, it only demeans you."

With swift steps, he advanced on him and Captain Campbell turned and ran, just as Angus had planned.

The fool should've followed the rope, not that he had much hope of escape, but terror and guilt made men do foolish things. Things such as run headlong into a bog.

Angus doubted anyone would even find the man's body and, if they did, there would be nothing to indicate that Angus was to blame for Campbell's death. As he had calculated, when reconnoitring the area before killing McKeith, his father's murderer had effectively killed himself.

"Thank you for covering up McKeith's death," he called into the mist after Campbell.

The Captain's desire to avoid scandal had not only allowed Angus to lead him to his doom, thanks to the introduction made by a Dalziel desperate to salve his conscience, but meant that there was no evidence of his earlier act of revenge.

It was all very clean.

Angus pulled his father's coat tight about him, then untied the rope from the tree and began to follow it back to the cottage.

It was over, done. His father was avenged and he could leave the damp moorland behind for the comfort of a modest town house.

For just a moment, in the eerie silence of the mist, he wondered if his father's ghost was watching, satisfied.

DJ Tyrer is the person behind Atlantean Publishing, and has had stories in *Disturbance* (Laurel Highlands Publishing), *Mysteries of Suspense* (Zimbell House Publishing), *History and Mystery, Oh My!* (Mystery and Horror, LLC), and *Love 'em, Shoot 'em* (Wolfsinger Publications), and has a novella available via Amazon, *The Yellow House* (Dunhams Manor Press). https://djtyrer.blogspot.co.uk

Raguel

Chris Chan

I was babysitting my girlfriend's much-younger brother Bernard the other day, and halfway through a game of Scrabble, Bernard scrunched up his forehead, stared at my sleeve, and asked, "Funderburke, why do you like your leather trench coat so much?"

Someone who knows more about fashion than I do told me once that technically it's a walking coat due to the knee-length hem and the absence of a belt, but I didn't feel like quibbling over terminology. "What makes you ask about that, Bernard?"

"I was just thinking about it. You wear it everywhere, and even when you're in the house you rarely take it off, even at meals. Why is that? As soon as I get home from school, I take off my parka and hang it up. Is there something special about that coat?"

"Definitely." I ran a finger along one of my lapels and sighed. "Raguel reminds me of one of my first cases as a private investigator. I managed to clear the name of a teenager who was falsely accused of murdering his own father."

"Why haven't you told me that story before? And why do you call your trench coat Raguel?"

"I like naming some of my favorite possessions. No real reason for it, but I've done it ever since I was a kid. And as for why I haven't told you the story. … I suppose I just haven't gotten around to it yet. This story just slipped through the cracks." This last bit wasn't exactly true. Some of the details just weren't suitable for a kid Bernard's age. Still, I figured I could bowdlerize it a bit.

"Well, it all started a couple of years ago, when I was still working at that little agency, about a month after I started working as a P.I. My boss was out seeing his doctor about his alcoholic hepatitis—"

"What's that?"

Darn it, my attempt to tell this story at a first-grade level was blowing up in my face already. I decided to level with Bernard. He'd know if I was sugarcoating it. "It means he drank too much liquor and hurt his liver. Anyway, I was the only one in the office since the receptionist went home early with a headache." As a responsible adult, I prudently neglected to tell Bernard the cause of our receptionist's headache. "The phone rang, I picked it up, and I heard a woman sobbing.

"'Please help me! My son is going to be arrested for killing his father. And he didn't do it, I know it!'"

I spent about five minutes calming the woman down, until I was finally able to ask her for the details. The murder occurred at a seedy motel about two miles from the office, and the woman, Mrs. Feeback, begged me to hurry before the police dragged her son away in handcuffs.

I tugged on the battered old parka I'd had since high school. At the time, I didn't have the funds to replace it, and the expensive coat I'd bought for myself a year earlier when I thought my financial future would be far more affluent, had been destroyed during an altercation with an irate divorce lawyer. ... But that's a different story. I found my way there with only one wrong turn, and when I arrived at the motel, I saw a sobbing woman shrieking at a pair of police officers, and a frightened-looking kid in his mid-teens sitting in the cop car's back seat.

It was easy to summarize those events in an age-appropriate way for Bernard. But now I was moving into trickier waters. Bernard noticed my hesitation and pressed me to continue.

"I introduced myself, although it took some coaxing to get Mrs. Feeback calm enough to speak to me. The police officers were relieved that I was able to get her to stop screaming at them, so they let me talk to her without any interruption. That's when I learned that she and her husband had recently separated, and that she'd brought her son, Myron, to the motel so he could talk to his dad about some ... personal matters. She thought it would only take fifteen or twenty minutes, so she decided to sit in the car and wait. Ten minutes later, Myron texted her and told her to hurry inside and help him. When Mrs. Feeback wanted to know what was wrong, he replied that his father was dead and all of these strangers thought he killed him."

"I don't understand," Bernard frowned. "Why did they think he did it? Did they see Myron attack his father?"

"Not exactly. Myron's father, Mr. Feeback, was staying in room 398. I should sketch this out for you." I tore a piece of paper off the Scrabble scorepad and started drawing the motel corridor. "This is the hallway. Room 398 is the second room from the end. Room 400 is the last one. There are odd-numbered rooms on the opposite side, but the only one you need to know is this one, 395. Some local high school students were having a party there, and a couple of them had gotten a little sick, so a maid was there cleaning up the mess."

"Why were teenagers partying at the motel?"

"They didn't say. Maybe Chuck E. Cheese was all booked up so they just picked the nearest available venue." I quickly changed the subject, because Bernard is very intelligent and if he started asking questions we'd be getting into age-inappropriate details.

I need to describe the motel in question. I will not name the actual motel, not because I fear legal reprisals over denigrating their business, but because I worry that people reading this will be so horrified and intrigued by this location that they'll visit the place out of some perverse curiosity, thereby catching some incurable communicable disease simply by touching a doorknob.

There are three types of people who stay at this motel. The first type is jurors who are being sequestered during a trial. The second type is people on business trips whose employers book rooms for them there because it's the cheapest place to stay in the area other than a cardboard box on the street. The third, and by far the most common type, is people who are up to no good and don't have the money to do their dirty deeds anywhere nicer. We're talking about adulterous spouses, people diving into drug-fueled bacchanals, johns and prostitutes, and teenagers looking for a cheap place to do everything they shouldn't away from the watchful eyes of their parents.

Six members of this last group were staying in room 395. Since they had enough money between them to rent the room for a few hours (yes, paying by the hour is an option at this establishment) and enough bottles of hard liquor between them to keep a downtown bar running all night on St. Patrick's Day (no, I don't know how they obtained all that alcohol), they were kicking back and getting blasted. Apparently, two of them simultaneously realized they couldn't handle their booze as well as they'd hoped, so they both lunged for what they believed was the door to the bathroom, only to find out midway through the process of being violently ill that they had actually rushed out into the hallway and were now staining a carpet which, quite frankly, had seen much worse in its day.

Of course, when I described that carpet to Bernard, I simply described it as "filthy."

I need to put this motel into context. It's legendary for all the wrong reasons. It's situated in a generally respectable commercial district with a panoramic view of the freeway. Not too long ago, I grabbed a quick lunch at a gyro shop there. As I chatted with the server behind the counter, I gestured at the motel through the plate glass window, and mentioned the crime that'd occurred there a while back. The server grinned at me and said that when police officers stop by to refuel with a delicious blend of beef and lamb, they often regale him with stories of drug deals, crazed hookers, alcohol abusers behaving badly, and assorted criminals hiding from the law who patronize that establishment. You would think that given its horrifically seedy reputation, the authorities would burn the place down and salt the earth where the structure once stood, but in fact, it helps the police to have a centralized location for all this activity that would give the great Dante Alighieri enough material for a sequel to *The Inferno*. Instead of ne'er-do-wells spreading their debauchery across the entire area, they keep it mostly to one centralized location—the motel of the damned. The sex, drugs, illegality, and assorted weird stuff stay in one place, and the allegedly respectable citizens can go about their lives with an "out of sight, out of mind" attitude.

Needless to say, I shared none of these details with Bernard.

"Mrs. Feeback was still pretty upset, understandably so, but shortly after the officers drove Myron away, I managed to calm her down a bit so she could provide me with more details. Myron had gone up to visit his father, who had moved out of the family home a week earlier after multiple arguments with his wife." I neglected to tell Bernard that the reason for these arguments was a young woman known as Trixie who was just a few years older than Myron.

"Apparently, Mr. Feeback had texted his son to let him know he'd just gotten off work and had arrived at the motel. Mrs. Feeback immediately drove Myron from their home to the motel, which took about three minutes. When Myron arrived at his father's room, he found the door unlocked and his father lying dead on the bed. He'd been stabbed with his own pocketknife. Myron just stood there for a while, too stunned to move, and, according to Mrs. Feeback, one of the maids wandered in, saw the carnage, started screaming, and called 911. The police arrived, asked a few questions, and soon concluded that Myron was the only person who could've killed his father."

"Why is that?"

"That's exactly what I asked Mrs. Feeback, Bernard. That's when she pointed to a teenager who was stumbling out of the motel's main entrance, and told me that he'd spoken to the police, and after hearing what he had to say, the police arrested Myron. I helped Mrs. Feeback back to her car, assured myself that she would be fine on her own, crossed the parking lot, and introduced myself to the youth in question, an amiable but acne-plagued fellow named Arnie." I purposefully neglected to mention that Arnie was none too steady on his feet due to the alcohol wafting from his breath.

"How old was this guy?" Bernard asked.

"About seventeen, give or take a year. I told him I was a private detective and asked if he'd mind telling me a bit about what he saw inside the motel. He agreed to help, and launched into a lengthy account of his experiences that evening."

I knew right away I wasn't looking at the class valedictorian. I don't want to sound cruel or uncharitable, but if all of this guy's high school classmates were assembled together at their five-year reunion, and someone asked "Where's Arnie?" and someone else announced that he'd passed away eighteen months earlier after overdosing on Tide pods, everybody in the room would just nod silently and think to themselves, "That sounds about right."

After a few moments of careful reflection, I decided not to quote Arnie's ramblings verbatim to Bernard. Not only did Arnie's dialogue require substantial bowdlerization, but he was the sort of talker who never used one word where twenty would do. So, I edited him down a lot.

"Over the course of ten increasingly annoying and befuddling minutes, I managed to extract the following information from Arnie. First of all, he and his friends decided that after a long week of goofing off at school, they'd earned the right to kick back and party in the privacy of a dirty motel room. After he and his friend came down with some sudden stomach trouble in the hallway, they noticed a man who they'd later identify as Mr. Feeback walking into Room 398. One of the maids showed up to clean the mess five minutes later, and, while she more than earned her minimum wage while the recovering Arnie and his friend watched, Myron walked past them, knocked on the door of Room 398, found it was unlocked, entered, and a few seconds later ran out, screaming that his father was dead."

"A few seconds later?" Bernard looked puzzled. "Was Myron supposed to have entered the room while three witnesses watched, stabbed his father without so much as a 'Hi, how are you?' and ran out, hoping that no one would realize that he was the most likely suspect?"

"That's what I thought!" It's nice to deal with a smart kid. "Myron and his father didn't have time to argue, so it's not like a hostile situation could've escalated into a stabbing. But here's the twist. According to the witnesses, no one else went into the room after Mr. Feeback except for Myron. Therefore, since the nature of the wound ruled out suicide, Myron was supposedly the only one who could've done it."

"Almost a locked-room mystery, though the door was open," Bernard noted.

Bernard has a habit of sneaking into the living room and hiding behind the sofa when the adults were watching television shows he was too young to see. He probably picked up the phrase "locked room mystery" when they were watching some crime show.

"Exactly! The obvious suspect had to be Myron. But I saw Myron in the police car, and I saw no blood on him. So maybe, I told myself, there was another way for someone to get into that room. After I convinced Arnie not to drive himself home, put him on a conveniently arriving bus, and said a quick prayer that he'd be sufficiently alert to get off at the correct stop. I went into the motel. Fortunately, the front desk clerk was staring at her phone, so I slipped through the foyer, up the stairs to the third floor, but was immediately turned away by the police forensic team, who told me that the area was currently off-limits."

"So, what did you do?"

"I muttered a quick 'excuse me,' turned right around, and decided to check out a different floor. I figured that the layout of the motel was pretty standardized, so I hurried to Room 298, presuming that the room would be exactly the same as the one directly above it. I didn't know if it was occupied, so I knocked, and when there was no reply, I turned the unlocked doorknob and let myself inside 298." That was not exactly a lie. I left out a critical step, where I found the room locked and opened it using my library card. I didn't think that was the sort of detail I ought to share with Bernard.

"I went inside room 298 and immediately wished I hadn't. If I ever needed major surgery, and my only options for where it would be performed were either this motel room or a gas station restroom, I'd be going under the knife grateful for the hospitality of Shell Oil. The carpet was sticky and oddly squishy. If you were foolish enough to lie down on the quilt covering the bed, you'd best take a handful of antibiotics at your earliest convenience. The television screen was cracked, and there were unidentifiable yet nauseating stains on the walls that even my own dark and twisted imagination couldn't conceive of their origin. There was a little wooden table with two matching chairs in one corner, where guests could have their meals, though why anybody would want to eat in such a setting was beyond me. Looking around, I saw no connecting doors to other rooms, and the windows weren't designed to open. No chance that anyone could've come in and out aside from the main door.

"Summoning up all my courage, I forced myself to enter the bathroom, even as I felt myself developing germaphobia with every step. I saw no other potential means of entrance or exit there. I was about to admit defeat when I looked up and noticed that two of the big tiles that lined the ceiling had a bit too wide a gap between them. I was about to stand on the toilet to get closer, but the commode in question had no lid, just a grimy seat. Picturing the many ways that something could go wrong, I instead brought a wooden chair from the main room, stepped up, and realized that the tiles were made of Styrofoam or something similar, and could easily be lifted up and moved to the side. Sticking the top of my head into the newly created hole, I could see a small gap leading toward the next room.

"Before I had time to celebrate my discovery, I heard a voice behind me, asking me who I was and what I was doing." I deleted some four-letter words from the question, once again for Bernard's benefit.

"Who was it?"

"A police officer. I talked as quickly as my mouth allowed, but the cop was a perceptive fellow, and he soon saw my point about there being an alternative way of getting into the room. I was compelled to answer a lot of questions and sit for a long time in the motel lobby under the watchful eye of an enormous policewoman, but soon everybody accepted my theory, that someone could've come into Room 398 by entering through the ceiling of Room 400's bathroom, though it would've had to be someone small and light."

"Who was in Room 400?"

"A four-foot-eight, seventy-five-pound woman named Lixie Trayne. I don't believe that was her real name, but she had an extensive criminal record." I didn't tell Bernard her true occupation, nor the fact that she shared the room with a much larger man who was passed out from popping too many pills.

"Apparently, Lixie knew the motel well, and realized that she could sneak between rooms through the ceiling. She'd pound on the connecting wall, and if nobody pounded back or complained, she'd slip over and see if there was anything lying around she could steal. That day, her timing was bad. Mr. Feeback caught her rummaging through his possessions, but before he could shout at her she grabbed the pocketknife on the dresser and silenced him. Then she grabbed his watch and wallet and made her way back to Room 400. She would've escaped soon afterward, but then Myron arrived and raised the alarm, leaving her with no choice but to hide in 400 and try to wait it out.

"The police weren't mad at me, though one guy informed me that they would've figured it out themselves pretty quickly. I didn't argue. They'd tried to ask Lixie questions as a potential witness, but she'd refused to open the door and they didn't have enough probable cause to open it until they were able to utilize my discovery to their advantage."

"So, it all worked out for Myron and his mother?" Bernard asked.

"Yep, Myron was released right away. Unfortunately for me, the Feebacks were just about broke, and they needed every cent they could scrounge to pay for the funeral. I didn't think I was going to get paid. And I didn't. Not exactly. But one of the reasons why Mr. and Mrs. Feeback fought is because Mr. Feeback was in the habit of buying luxury items online they couldn't afford, like pricey clothing. He'd tell his wife he needed to look sharp to succeed at work, and one item he'd recently bought was ... take a guess ..."

"A leather trench coat."

"Bingo! He'd bought it from an online auction site that didn't take returns, and as it turns out, Mr. Feeback and I are about the same size. Mrs. Feeback offered me the trench coat in lieu of my fee, and as it was new, unworn, and really nice, I accepted. As soon as I tried it on I knew I'd found my signature look. It fit me perfectly, and if I flatter myself, it looks great on me. It's smooth like silk, soft like butter, and has a removable insulated lining so I can wear it year-round. Not only that, but it reminds me of my main goal in life—helping out kids in trouble. This was my first time as a P.I. that I was able to help a kid accused of some crime he hadn't done, and that gives my coat a special significance."

"But what does 'Raguel' mean?"

"In religious tradition, Raguel is the archangel of justice, vengeance, redemption, and equity. All qualities that I hold in high regard, and calling my coat by that name reminds me of my mission. Plus, when I wear this coat, I feel like an avenging angel."

28 

Chris Chan is a writer and educator from Milwaukee, Wisconsin. He is a researcher and "International Goodwill Ambassador" for Agatha Christie, Ltd. He is the author of the Funderburke mystery series. His first book, *Sherlock & Irene: The Secret Truth Behind "A Scandal in Bohemia"* was published by MX Publishing.

A Murder on Ganymede

Rebecca Buchanan

"May I interest you in some Neptunian blue wine, Detective Silveira?"

Regiane turned smoothly, hands clasped behind her back. She smiled politely. "No, thank you, Chief Administrator Psukulski." She dipped her head towards him in greeting, taking note of, and then ignoring, the fluted glass he held in each hand. Thirteen primary, secondary, and tertiary assistants followed in his wake, their wrist pads primed, their faces a mixture of curious and bored as they readied to follow any order issued by the overseer of the Jovian system.

Psukulski shrugged and took a swig of wine. He waved the other glass around. "What is this one, again?"

"Chief Administrator?"

"This one. Some kind of jungle, yes?"

Regiane cleared her throat. "There are sixty-two arboretums scattered throughout Ida City. Each features the biome of a different region of Earth. This is the Atlantic Biome of eastern South America." She tilted her head towards the carefully cultivated trees, shrubs, and flowers which burst out of the ground all around them, pathways looping round: *Justicia polita, Begonia angularis, Canna coccinea, Lamanonia ternata.*

She did not need to access SolNet to know them all on sight.

High in the trees, gregarious *guira guira* called back and forth to one another. A nocturnal *Nyctibius grandis* poked its head out of its nest, fluffed, and disappeared again. A fiery winged *Topaza pyra* whizzed past Regiane's head, dodged around a drone, and dove into the foliage.

Four-hundred-and-twenty-seven citizens of Ida City, their attire as bright as that of the *Topaza pyra*, currently wandered those swooping pathways, laughing, talking, sipping alcoholic beverages. Drones of various sizes and shapes circled through the crowd and overhead, offering refreshments and reminders of the wonders that awaited them when the Terran Cultural Exhibition finally opened in just two hours and eighteen minutes.

The artificial breeze created by the fans lifted her hair, brushed her cheek, carrying the scent of *Cinnamomum cassia*.

She inhaled. A fragment of her pre-augment life rose up. *Bolinhos de Chuva*, fresh every morning in her grandfather's kitchen—

"As I said: jungle." Psukulski nodded definitively, looking around. Then he straightened, his eyes narrowing. He waved a nearly empty glass at Regiane. "Don't move!"

He sprinted away, his small army of assistants scrambling to follow.

Regiane sighed long and low under her breath, and just barely suppressed the urge to roll her eyes. Instead, she tilted her head back.

The Great Red Spot.

The Trench Coat Chronicles

The ancient storm was a roiling, swirling mass, visible even to the bare human eye through the overhead dome. With a thought, she dimmed the ambient noise of the arboretum: people, drones, birds, insects, water fountains, fans, and heaters, and lessened the low hum of the gravitational field. With a second thought, she accessed SolNet. All available information about the Great Red Spot flitted across the implant in her right iris, golden letters superimposed over her view of Jupiter, five of its moons, and the darkness of space all around.

A shuttle slipped into view, crossing over the face of Jupiter. She calculated its course, determined that it was en route to Io, then tapped into Ganymede's NavNet and verified the ship's registry and destination. Satisfied, she exited the NavNet to continue her study of the tumbling, multicolored clouds of Jupiter.

The Great Red Spot was dying, of course, as all things were. In the centuries since it had first been observed by humanity, it had steadily decreased in size, its winds slowing, bits of it sloughing away to be lost among the wide bands of white and brown and red and copper clouds.

It was still a monster, though. Even dying, it could tear her augmented form apart in seconds.

She added these musings to the data packet on SolNet and closed down her link. She reset her auditory sensors and returned her attention to the arboretum.

"Detective!"

A fresh glass in each hand, his arms looped through those of the woman and man to either side of him, Chief Administrator Psukulski trotted over to her. The mob of thirteen primary, secondary, and tertiary assistants trundled along behind, jockeying one another as they tried to stay on the pathway.

"Detective Regiane Silveira, recently appointed Security and Investigations Officer for Ganymede District." Psukulski blinked rapidly, seeming to forget what he was saying for a moment. "Uh … my companions need no introduction?"

Regiane nodded her head towards the woman and man in turn. "Administrator Keaton. Administrator Isley. Welcome to Ida City. I trust that your flights from Io and Europa were uneventful."

Administrator Keaton smiled broadly. Her dress sparkled and tiny crystals rotated in a circlet around her dark head, flashing blue and green and yellow. "Completely boring—though surprisingly, Administrator Kovacs was not present to greet us—"

"Yes, where *is* he?" Psukulski asked, wobbling on his feet.

"The District Administrator *should* have met us," Isley agreed.

"—Still, Isley and I were just discussing which exhibits we wish to view—as we will only have this one evening to enjoy them. Personally, I am quite eager to explore the Hall of Fashion. Isley wants to see Agriculture." With the last word, Keaton's voice tipped up and vibrated, carrying a note of disbelief.

Isley flushed. His suit rippled when he rolled his shoulders, the collar decorated with swirling patterns of colorful seeds.

"An excellent choice, Administrator Isley," Regiane commented. "Without the necessary advances in genetic engineering, humanity never would have been able to leave Earth and begin colonization of the rest of the System. I understand that horticulturalists on Europa have been making advances in high-yield, low-grav cereals."

Keaton's chin drew in and her eyes narrowed, while Chief Administrator Psukulski *hhmm*ed and took another sip. Isley straightened his back, darting a look at Keaton. "That is so, Detective. We hope to begin field tests very soon."

"I apologize for the intrusion. Detective Silveira?"

Regiane smiled at the sound of that soft voice and turned smoothly, hands still behind her back. "Yes, Sub-Administrator Bouchard?" —

—and stopped. Her smile flattened into a frown. "Petra, your heart rate and breathing are accelerated thirty percent above normal. What has happened?" Behind her, she heard Chief Administrator Psukulski and the two Administrators subtly shift forward.

She lifted a hand, not touching Petra's back, but leading her further down the path.

Petra followed along without protest. She tucked a twisty curl behind one ear. Her eyes flicked around. She fiddled with her wrist pad. Finally, leaning towards Regiane, she whispered, "A murder. There has been *a murder.*"

The corpse had once been Jean-Michel Yamamoto, director of the Terran Cultural Exhibition. They had spoken eight times and met in person three times while Yamamoto and his team transported the Exhibition from Ares City on Mars and assembled it on Ganymede—a massive undertaking. Fifty-six-thousand-two-hundred-twenty-one different pieces, dating from Earth's pre-history and earliest civilizations, through the great empires of the Industrial Age, the rise of the Digital Age, and into the Age of Expansion, when humanity finally united and set out to explore and colonize the rest of the Solar System.

Twenty years to carry Earth's treasures throughout the System, for the enjoyment and education of her scattered children. Paintings, sculptures, pottery, books, clothing, jewelry, musical instruments and musical scores, furniture, vehicles, antique weapons, and technology. Treasures that could be seen and touched and experienced directly, rather than virtually, through SolNet.

Yamamoto had been energetic, detail oriented, and enthusiastic. He had been devoted to the Exhibition.

Regiane felt her jaw tighten.

Now he was gone, and all that was left of him was a corpse: a rapidly decaying collection of proteins, lipids, hydroxyapatite, and carbohydrates that lay sprawled among the artifacts of the Hall of Cinematic History. A circular, bright-red stain spread across his chest, soaking into the cream of his shirt.

"From the Proto-Indo-European *mrtró* meaning 'to die,'" she murmured. "Descended from the Middle English *mordre* and the Old French *murdre*."

Administrator Kovacs, looming from six-point-five meters away, growled low under his breath. "I do not require a linguistics lesson, Detective."

She tilted her head. His circulation, respiration, and perspiration readings flitted in gold across her iris implant. Five standard weeks since she had arrived in Ida City, and her opinion of Kovacs had not improved since their first meeting. "You prefer ignorance?" she asked, and watched as all three jumped in irritation.

Behind Kovacs, Petra mouthed, *"No,"* and very slowly shook her head.

Silently conceding, Regiane turned her attention back to the corpse. With a thought, she tapped into the IdaNet and used her passcode to pull up all of the security feeds from the Exhibition over the last three hours—city residents, maintenance workers, and Exhibition staff moved up and down hallways, through doorways, up and down ladders and lifts, in and out of transports, hundreds of people. While those ran at four-times speed over her right iris, she examined the corpse with her left, noting temperature, rate of cellular decay, the shape and depth of the mortal wound, the tear on his right sleeve, and the shallow bruises on his right hand and cheek.

"He was murdered between 18:15 hours and 18:36 hours. The mortal wound is a slim, precise, and symmetrical incision through the left atrium and aorta, with virtually no tearing. Not a stiletto, more like a long needle. Approximately fifteen centimeters in length. The microscopic droplets of blood here—" she pointed at the floor and drew an arcing line away from the corpse, " —and the bruising indicate that the murderer stood to Yamamoto's right. I will have the exact time of death and the identity of his murderer in a moment." She glimpsed at Petra tapping notes into her wrist pad, then flicked the security feed forward in time.

"No, you won't," Kovacs muttered.

The feed scrolling across her implant went black at 18:01. And stayed black. No audio, visual, atmospheric, or chemical information. When it flicked on again at 18:31, it showed Kovacs standing in the eighth level of the Hall of Cinematic History, Yamamoto already a corpse at his feet.

She pulled the other feeds forward, one by one. All black for the same length of time, all coming back online at the exact same moment, down to the quarter of a second.

"They came back online automatically, at the precise thirty-minute mark."

Petra paused in her typing. "They were not reactivated by passcode?"

Regiane shook her head and stood slowly, funneling power into the fingertips of her left hand. "Did you kill him, Administrator?"

Kovacs scoffed. "For what possible reason?"

"I do not know," she admitted. Her fingers tingled. "But there are only four people with the necessary clearance to turn off the security feeds for the Exhibition: you, Sub-Administrator Bouchard, Director Yamamoto, and myself." She paused, accessing all of the cameras, sensors, and drones outside the Exhibition, moving farther out in narrow circles. "You already knew that the feeds inside the

Exhibition had been cancelled. You checked them before you sent Sub-Administrator Bouchard for me. Why?"

His lips thinned. "Yamamoto had been acting oddly when I spoke with him earlier today. I wanted to check with him before the Exhibition opened to the public. He was dead when I arrived."

More information flitted across her iris: infrared scans, atmospheric figures, audio data. At 18:10, she found Kovacs leaving the gathering in the Atlantic Biome arboretum. She followed his progress until he entered the field of dead security feeds in the Exhibition Hall at 18:17.

Theoretically, that left Kovacs fourteen minutes to have murdered Yamamoto before the cameras came back on at 18:31.

"You had the opportunity, certainly, but no motive is apparent. Hosting the Terran Cultural Exhibition is a great honor. There was serious competition between Ida City and the administrative districts of Europa and Io. A disruption—especially one as serious as murder—would be a personal embarrassment for you. Given what I have determined of your psychology, you *are* capable of murder, if you think it to your advantage. But if you had done so, you would have concealed your crime to maintain or advance your authority, not brought it to my attention."

Kovacs' jaw twitched.

Regiane turned away from him, fixing her gaze on Petra.

Petra's eyes widened as her pulse and respiration ticked up. "No," she said, her voice shaking just a bit. "I did not kill him. And I did not turn off the security feeds. I do not know who did."

More information sliding across her iris at five, six, seven times speed. Moving in concentric circles, farther and farther from the Exhibition.

There. Petra exiting the central administrative offices at 18:28 hours. She caught a transport and headed straight for the Atlantic Biome. There she found Regiane speaking with Psukulski, Keaton, and Isley, and together they traveled to the Hall.

"I went to find you as soon as Administrator Kovacs contacted me," Petra was saying. There was a pause. "Though he apparently took his time doing so."

Kovacs turned and glared at Petra. She faced him, her expression carefully blank.

"He was hoping to identify the murderer and deal with the matter quietly." Regiane did not bother to hide the note of disgust in her voice. "When that plan failed, he sent you to fetch me, no doubt hoping that *you* could be imposed upon to influence *me* to be as quiet as possible."

Petra's blank expression hardened.

Regiane drained the extra power from her hand. She pushed away the disgust in her voice, softening her tone. "You, in contrast, do not display any of the psychological traits necessary to commit murder."

She spun slowly in a circle, moving away from the corpse to begin a detailed analysis of the rest of the Hall, scanning, sniffing, listening. The Hall spread around and above and below them in a dozen tiers, each level dedicated to a different era. The eighth level contained an axe and a broken door, a refitted white emergency vehicle, a white karate gi, a superhero costume of red and blue, an anatomically incorrect frog puppet, an impractical fake sword, and a badly worn brown trench coat with a wide, upright collar, among six hundred and twenty-three other artifacts.

She paused in front of the trench coat.

"Detective," she whispered. "Originally derived from the adjective, meaning 'fitted for or skilled in detecting.' Evolved into the noun, meaning 'one employed or engaged in detecting lawbreakers. ...'"

Her left iris narrowed, focusing.

She knelt, reaching out with her hand. She brushed the brown cloth, feeling its coarse, ancient threads beneath her fingers. When she pulled her hand away, a tiny sliver of crystal clung to her skin.

Petra leaned over her shoulder. "What is it?"

Regiane sent a fractional pulse of energy through her hand and into the sliver. It glowed blue, then green, then yellow.

"A clue."

"No murderer has escaped justice for the past two-hundred-and-sixty-seven years, Administrator Keaton. Do you know why?"

Keaton's shoulders stiffened beneath her sparkling dress and her chin lifted. Beside her, Chief Administrator Psukulski blinked blearily over a nearly empty flute of blue wine. Isley, six meters away and deep in conversation with a group of bioengineers, fell silent and edged closer.

Around them, the ambient noise of conversation dropped to almost nothing. A *guira guira* called out.

Regiane held out her right palm, the sliver of crystal glittering. She sent another pulse of energy through it—blue, green, yellow—and a simple activation code. The crystals spinning around Keaton's head stopped. In a neat line, they whirled towards Regiane's palm. One by one by one, they fused together into a slim, crystalline needle.

A single microscopic droplet of blood stained the sharp tip.

"Because it is impossible. There is always a clue, always evidence, always proof. And a Detective will always find it. A Detective will *always* deliver justice." She paused, shunting power into the fingertips of her left hand. She narrowed the focus of her right iris, charting Keaton's respiration and pulse, calculating the angle and speed at which the Administrator would flee. With the left, she examined the sensor data of the Biome from the previous three hours at eight, nine, ten times speed. "Yamamoto deactivated the sensors himself. He did not want there to be any record of his meeting with you. Not for his sake, but yours. Was it a bribery attempt?"

Keaton's jaw tightened. She backed up a step.

"No," Regiane continued. "Sabotage?"

The Administrator's head whipped around, and her eyes fixed on Regiane for a moment before she looked away again.

"Sabotage, then. Born of petty jealousy? Or did you hope to force the Exhibition to relocate to Europa? Both?"

A flush crept above the collar of Keaton's sparkling gown, up her throat and across her cheeks. She shifted a half step to the left.

"Both. Yamamoto uncovered your plan and tried to stop you." The Biome's sensor data paused, breaking up into two separate entries. "You departed the Biome at 18:06 and returned at 18:22. You are not present on any sensors during those fourteen minutes. Where did you go?"

"That would be the dress," Psukulski announced into the silence. He waggled his fingers. "All those pretty sparkles aren't just *pretty*. Some sort of, er, what are they called?"

"Sensor blinds."

Psukulski snapped his fingers. "Yes, Detective, that's it. Thank you."

"Administrator Keaton, you stand accused of murder. Motive, opportunity, and means have been established in the presence of your peers. Do you wish to speak in your own defense?"

A soft click. A flash.

Regiane's eyes and ears went dark.

She lunged, left hand outstretched, following the precalculated angle and speed. She felt sparkly cloth beneath her fingers, sleek, sharp-edged slivers. Power flooded out of her hand. Cloth sizzled, arced.

She could see again, hear again. Shouting. People panicking, running. Petra was calling her name.

Blood ran from Keaton's nose and eyes and ears. Her mouth opened, silent, and she fell. She dropped to the ground, sprawling across the pathway, and was still.

Psukulski sighed, his shoulders drooping. "And now I need to find a new Administrator for Io."

High in the trees, a *Nyctibius grandis* moaned.

Regiane sat on a bench in the darkened arboretum, watching the storm that was the Great Red Spot roll through the skies of Jupiter. Shuttles crossed in front of the gas giant, carrying cargo and citizens destined for every corner of the Solar System. She plotted their individual courses, checked their registries. Six were inbound for Ida City; many of the passengers would be pilgrims traveling to experience the Exhibition.

Alone, Chief Administrator Psukulski dropped onto the bench on the far side of the pathway.

"What else?" Regiane asked. When he tipped his head, eyebrows lifted in apparent confusion, she continued. "In addition to murder, what other crimes did Keaton commit?"

"Now that is very difficult to say. She was an *Administrator*, after all. *Suspicion about* and *proof against* someone at that level of government, well, those are two very different things. But a woman who was willing to commit sabotage and murder to spite a political rival—"

"Did you know that she would kill Director Yamamoto?" Her fingertips tingled.

Psukulski leaned forward, elbows braced on his knees, all traces of his exaggerated drunkenness gone. "No. I did not. No more than I knew that you would be killed when I sent you to investigate certain incidents on Callisto."

Soft footsteps coming up the path.

Regiane drained the power from her hand.

Psukulski rose and straightened his suit. "Kovacs, I think. Best to keep him close, and how better than by appointing him as Keaton's replacement?" He smiled. "And that will leave Ganymede in much better hands, don't you agree?"

He dipped his head towards Petra in farewell and wandered away.

Shoes in one hand, a basket of *Bolinhos de Chuva* in the other, Petra settled onto the bench beside her. She dug her toes into the soft grass and bumped Regiane's shoulder.

"Did I look like that, I wonder?" Regiane asked.

"Pardon?"

"Like Yamamoto. Like his corpse. I was dead for thirty-seven minutes while the augments were implanted. All cardiovascular and neurological functions ceased. When I was … activated, when I awoke, there was little of the first Regiane Silveira left. Just fragments."

Petra dropped her shoes and wrapped her fingers around Regiane's hand, squeezing. She lifted their joined hands and kissed Regiane's knuckles, one by one.

"You are not afraid to be with a dead woman who can kill with a touch?"

"You are a Detective. You will never hurt me. I will never be afraid to touch you."

Her respiration, pulse, and perspiration never changed. They remained steady as Petra settled their joined hands in her lap and leaned her head against Regiane's shoulder.

"No, Administrator Bouchard," Regiane said. "I will never hurt you."

And they sat quietly beneath the Great Red Spot, among the trees and the singing birds, for a very long time.

Rebecca Buchanan is the editor of the Pagan literary ezine, *Eternal Haunted Summer*, and a regular contributor to *evOke: witchcraft*paganism*lifestyle*. She has released three short-story collections and one poetry collection. Her poem, "Heliobacterium daphnephilum" was awarded the Rhysling Award 2020 (long category).

Chasing Popeye

Antaeus

As I had done every day at dusk for the last five months, I drove the pickup down the hill toward the lake. In its bed were an ice saw, a lantern, and a deep-sea fishing pole. The reflective tarp that covered everything redirected the setting sun and hid what was under it from prying eyes.

Jasper Finnigan, the owner of the town's only general store, stepped out onto the front porch and waved as I drove up. "Evening, Missus Lancaster," he called out.

I smiled and nodded in acknowledgment as I navigated the last step. "Evening Mister Finnigan.

The shopkeeper opened the door for me, and we both went inside. I could hear the crackling of the fire inside the cast-iron stove as it consumed the wood. The heat it generated kept the store as warm as toast against the cold New England winter.

I wore three layers of thermal clothing, and a lined trench coat that shed water like a duck. A dozen steps into the store, and I started sweating like a condemned woman standing on the gallows in the midsummer heat.

My perv radar went off, so I turned and caught the merchant staring at my butt. *Pig. As if you could see anything under all these layers.*

Caught with his mind in the gutter, the old perv

blurted out, "The usual order Missus Lancaster?"

I wanted to kick Jasper in the gonads, but instead, I smiled. I didn't want to act out of character—not yet anyway. "Like I said yesterday, Jasper, I think we've known each other long enough to where you can call me Elsa."

The merchant turned a light shade of red. "Now, now, Missus Lancaster, that wouldn't be right. In the eyes of the law, you're still a married woman. Even if your husband has been missing for all these months. If a bachelor like me started to call you by your first name, people would talk."

I held back my laughter. *Yeah, you wish, old man.*

Out loud, I said, "Yes, it'll be the same as yesterday, and the day before that, and for the last five months."

Jasper slipped behind the counter just as I stepped up to it. "I guess you'll be wanting some hot coffee to fill your thermos with, right?"

No, you idiot, I'm here because I find you so attractive.

"Yup, pretty much," I said instead.

Jasper removed a box from under the counter. "Here ya go, El—er, Missus Lancaster. I put it on your tab. There's a bucket of bait, some lantern fuel, and a ham and cheese sandwich in there. The coffee is hot, and I made a fresh pot an hour ago. Go on over and fill your thermos; it's on me."

I stuck the chocolate bar Jasper always snuck in with the order into my pocket. *You're not getting into my pants for a bar of chocolate, you nasty old man.*

After filling my thermos bottle to the top with the dark but fragrant brew, I walked back to the counter. Jasper leaned on his elbows and asked me the same question he'd been asking me for the last one hundred and forty-nine days. "Why are you doing this, Missus Lancaster? Is it for the reward money? Ain't no one collected the thousand-dollar reward for old Popeye in ten years. They say ten men have gone out on the lake and tried, and he's taken ten men down to the bottom of the lake with him."

I gave him the same answer for the 149th time, "I don't need the reward money, I'm doing it because I need to know, that's why."

Jasper just nodded his head like he understood. In the five months I'd been coming in here, he never once asked me what it was I needed to know.

I swear that man only has one oar in the water, I thought as I walked out the door.

After putting the coffee and sandwich into my thermal case, I tossed the box with the bait under the tarp and climbed into the truck's cab. *No sense stinking up the cab, and the winter cold will keep it fresh.*

I'm what some people would call a petite woman, and my feet barely reach the truck's pedals even with the seat all the way forward. My husband, Roy, was a tall man, and he insisted on owning a big truck. I knew what the other women said behind my back: "The bigger the truck, the smaller the man where it counted." Yah, well, he wore a size fourteen shoe, you bunch of old biddies. *What-cha think of that?*

I don't give a damn what those nosy old women say. As far as I know, the only other woman who really knew what Roy had in his pants was his concubine, Rita Letch. Roy and his lover didn't realize it, but after Jerry, the motel owner, accidentally walked in on them, he ran right up to my house and told me about it. Jerry said they looked like two puppies fighting under a blanket. The damn bitch, Rita, made no secret of their affair, so the whole town knew about it. As for Roy, he was stupid enough to think I didn't know.

Screw her and screw them. They're just gossiping like old biddies in a tearoom. What they think or say doesn't matter one bit. The only thing that matters now is me finding Roy's body.

Five months ago, Roy and two of his buddies had been fishing from the pier. They wanted to get some fishing in before the cold snap came and froze the lake. When it got dark, his buddies left, but Roy said he wanted to stay awhile longer. He never came home. That night a nor'easter hit, and the lake has been frozen solid ever since.

Some of the gossips said it was Old Popeye that had pulled Roy under. Old Popeye being a one-eyed catfish supposedly twelve feet long. Others said Roy and Rita Letch ran off together because she had disappeared that same night.

Let them talk, they don't know shit. What the old bitches think doesn't count for nothing. The only thing that matters is what Sheriff Tomson believes, and he's leaning toward the Popeye theory.

Most of the townsfolk thought I was an oddity — a woman in limbo, not single nor available for courting, but not legally a widow. To them, I was just a crazy woman on a mission to kill Popeye, gut him, find what was left of my husband, and collect the reward.

48

The Trench Coat Chronicles

I backed the truck into my usual spot about a mile downstream from the pier where Roy had gone missing. I'm not stupid. I'd spent my days during the winter months going over current-flow charts of the lake. At night I'd cut a good-sized hole in the ice and fish where I though my prize would show up. Now that the lake and the streams feeding it had thawed, the denizens of the deep would be waking up and moving this way.

Tonight has to be the night. I'll catch him tonight for sure.

Once I had set up camp, I cast my line and sat shivering in the cold night air. Distant voices caught my attention. I fished the binoculars from my backpack and looked across the lake. Two little boys at the edge of the lake were shouting and pointing. The sun was setting red.

Red sun in the morning, sailors take warning. The red sun at night is a sailor's delight — another good omen.

Oh, to be young again, like those boys. To start over and not make the same mistakes. To choose a different path, one that didn't lead to sitting out here in the freezing cold, like I've had to do all winter.

I shrugged and settled in. My father was a preacher man, and he used to say, "Elsa, there are consequences for everything you do in life. Some are worse than others, and you should always try to choose the lesser ones if you can."

Then he'd make me choose the switch he was going to use to beat my bare butt. Later that same night, after Momma was asleep, he'd crawl into my bed and rub my backside to "make it better." That went on from the time I was seven until I was eleven. He and mom died in a tragic housefire a week after my eleventh birthday. I left Kentucky then, and never looked back.

My long, sensitive fingers were wrapped around the fishing pole. I wore special gloves that cost a small fortune, but they fit me like a second skin and kept my hands warm, too. They would allow me to feel the slightest tug on the line. Then I'd set the large Treble Hooks fastened to the 500-pound-test fishing line.

I watched the sky as the clouds rolled in from the mountains. It looked like rain. The cold North wind chilled me as I sipped coffee from my thermos. It sent a shiver through my body, so I wrapped the trench coat tighter around me. I set my jaw, determined to see this task through no matter what nature threw at me.

"Go ahead, God, throw your worst at me. I can take whatever you've got!" *I will endure, I MUST endure.*

Around three in the morning, I was struggling to stay awake. One minute my head was dipping up and down like a dashboard bobblehead doll, the next, I was wide awake. It was like someone had stuck my finger in an electric socket. Even half-asleep, my fingers felt the slight tug on the line, and I reflexively set the hooks. I shook my head to clear the cobwebs, and the fight was on.

Come on, come on, please let this be him. I need this to be him.

I yanked violently on the line and felt my catch pull back—hard. The current was strong, and so was whatever was at the other end. Maybe I'd hooked Old Popeye after all. My feet were slipping on the snow, and I was being pulled relentlessly toward the frigid water.

It's only ten feet to the water. Now it's just eight feet. Come on, come on, dig in, girl, don't let him pull you in.

I may be a petite woman, but I'm strong, healthy, and determined. I dug my boot heels into the wet dirt, an' pulled back with all my strength. I started walking backward, and my catch began to slowly move toward the shore again.

Don't give up now, Elsa; you've come too far and fought too hard for this. You keep on fighting, girl. That's it, just a little bit further now. You're gonna make it!

When I reached the trees, I wrapped the fishing line partly around a young sapling and pulled with all the strength that was left in me. It was a little easier now, and slowly, inch by inch, the black body emerged from the lake. Its carcass was long, maybe too long to be Roy. *Damn, I hope I haven't hooked Old Popeye.*

One more tug and the body popped out of the water and slid along the snow-covered bank.

Well, butter my butt and call me a biscuit. It's not a giant catfish — it's a six-foot-seven man.

"Gotcha!"

The adrenaline rush provided renewed energy, as I pulled Roy's body further up the bank and looked at him by lantern light. The fish had feasted on his flesh, and most of his face and neck were gone. Only his spinal bones and some leathery looking tendons kept his caved-in head attached to his body.

His fingers are gone, so they'll want to identify him through his dental records. At first glance, the sheriff would probably say Roy died when his head hit the rocks at the bottom of the pier. Until the coroner found the piece of clawhammer embedded in his skull, that is.

The hunk of metal was still there, so I pulled it out and threw it into the truck. Then I reached for the ice saw.

I've endured months of gossipy women, and people knocking on my door, bringing me soup and sympathy. If that wasn't enough punishment, I had to spend five months sitting out here on the bank of a frozen lake in the biting winter cold. All these consequences, because the jerk fell forward instead of backward.

Once Roy's head was tucked safely under the tarp, I drove home.

Someone walking their dog would find his body washed up on shore in the morning. Even after all those months in the water, Roy's fishing license was still pinned to his vest, legible thanks to lamination. That'll tell them all they need to know. The hooks caught his jacket, so a few more holes will mean nothing.

When I reached the house, I dumped Roy's head in the dried-up well behind the house. His concubine's body was already there waiting for him. In a few weeks, I'll have someone take down the sides and fill the hole with cement.

The next morning, I sat at the kitchen window, coffee in hand, waiting for the sheriff's call. Jasper Finnigan was on my mind. He's not a handsome man by any stretch, and he doesn't know whether to scratch his watch or wind his butt, but he has money. I knew that from working as a teller at the bank. Best of all, he's hot for me.

Once I was officially declared a widow, I'd be free to marry whomever I wanted. It doesn't take much to seduce guys like Jasper. Men are so easy. A touch here, a touch there, and an unspoken promise of more are all it takes.

We'll be married in six months — the bachelor and the widow, what a lovely couple. There wouldn't be any children, and in a few years, Jasper will have an accident. I'll be devastated. Poor Elsa, people will say, losing two husbands in such a short time. Will it be more than her frail body can bear? Of course, I'll have to sell everything, move to another town, and start over. That doesn't matter, though, because it won't be the first time. My parents were the first ones, and I've been a widow six times now with no consequences. *This woman learns from her mistakes and knows how to travel light.*

At the age of seven, Antaeus worked in a bar cleaning toilets. His first poem was written on toilet paper. Antaeus is the author of *The Prepared Citizen*, a three-book series on how to react to and avoid dangerous situations. Antaeus now uses real paper to write on.

Pearls Before ...

Charles Barouch and Ann Stolinsky

When I read mystery stories, I see two kinds of detectives: well-off and investigating as a hobby, vs. professional and broke. I don't fit either mold: I'm not a professional even though I've been paid for it, and it is not my day job. Yet I'm too poor for the hobby-detective thing I read in those other stories. If I had to explain my success in one sentence, give you the key thing that got me started, it would be, "My boyfriend thinks he's funny."

Four months ago was the start of it. Morning of my twenty-sixth birthday and I'm looking at the three nice dresses I own. My boyfriend was dead-asleep and snoring. I heard a knock on my front door. It was Aunt Linda. Eleven in the morning on a Sunday and it was Aunt Linda, who never fails to bring drama.

"You're going to kill me," Linda blurted. "Murder me, on your birthday. And I deserve it." Linda pushed past me into the living room.

"Please, come in, Aunt Linda."

My boyfriend shambled into the living room and joined us. He'd taken a moment to pull on yesterday's clothes. Linda's earnest distress was an interesting contrast to his yawns and mumbles. It was like they were acting out two unrelated scenes.

"The pearls," she sighed.

The Trench Coat Chronicles

So, there was a some-number-of-great-greats grandmother who was given a beautiful pair of pearl earrings and a matching necklace. Eventually, the set went to my mother, and when she died last year, I got them. My mom wanted to make my inheritance more personalized, so she added a heart charm, etched with my initials, to the necklace. I don't live in a great neighborhood, so I'd asked my mom's little sister, Aunt Linda, to hold onto them. It meant a lot to her.

What she confessed, on my birthday, was that she wasn't just holding them for me. She had taken to wearing them—frequently. She'd worn them today to early Mass and they were now missing. I was furious. These pearls were a big deal in the family. I was named for them, that's how important they were to my family. Besides, they were pretty much all I got from my mom, aside from bills, when she died. And Aunt Linda had been wearing them around. And she'd lost them.

I took her car keys and retraced her steps. I checked the car carefully. I ultimately ended up back at her house. The pearls were sitting in the jewelry box. Earrings and necklace, safe.

I went home and told her she didn't lose them; she'd forgotten to put them on. That was unlike Aunt Linda. She would put on makeup on the chance that someone might ring the doorbell. She'd been late to mom's funeral because she'd smeared her nail polish and had to fix it and let it dry.

I found out that she'd just been dumped by the guy she was dating. I had never met him, but I was mad at him. He broke up by text. It really threw her. That was the end of the mystery and should have been the end of the story, but, as I said, my boyfriend, Jules, thinks he's funny.

At my party that night, Jules had been pulling aside guests, in ones and twos, and telling the ever-expanding story of my detective work. One of his co-workers, Aida, bought in so strongly, she chased me down and demanded I take her case.

It was my party but somehow, instead of dancing with my friends, I was stuck in the kitchen with this relentless woman. In trying to get out of the conversation, I gradually heard more and more from her about my exploits tracking down an international jewel thief for the heiress who was missing her diamond-encrusted pearl earrings. At least the pearls had made it to the current version of the story. Not much else of the truth had made it that far.

"Pearl, you simply have to help me with my husband. I'm sure he's cheating," Aida begged.

"Why do you think that?"

The battle was lost. I was actually in the conversation with the hope that going through it might yield an exit.

"Things in my bedroom aren't where I leave them. Rumpled sheets on the bed," she said, distraught.

"Great," I said.

"Great? What is great about it?" She glared at me, her face the color of a sunburn.

"No, the cheating is terrible, but if you know *where* he's cheating and it is in your house, you can just get a nanny cam."

"Nanny cam?"

"People who don't trust their nannies get these little cameras and hide them so they can see that their kid is being treated right. That office store on Beech, I think I saw a display in there," I explained.

She thanked me and, best of all, she left.

If Aida were a normal person, that might have been the end of it. Instead, two weeks later, my boyfriend comes to my place after work with Aida. Aida told me she caught her husband, pressed two hundred dollars into my hands for my help, and then told me she'd tell everyone about me. She told me another co-worker needed my help. My funny boyfriend had passed on my exploits to everyone in his office. Nice guy. Nice, funny guy.

When she left, Jules said he'd be right back and ran to his car. He returned with a dress-sized box from my favorite dress store. I'm mostly a jeans-and-a-nice-blouse girl, but we do go out fancy sometimes and there are occasional parties, so I was excited. I like having some dresses in the closet when I open the door, even if they don't make it out of the closet often.

He'd been empty-handed at my party. What he'd ordered hadn't come in yet. So, this was huge to me. It meant he'd listened when I'd shown him those dresses on the website. I wondered if it would be the blue one. That was the nicest and was in the middle of the three prices.

"You have to promise to try it on for me," he said, then winked.

I knew what that meant. He wanted me to get undressed. He didn't care how it looked on me.

Considering that we'd been together for over a year, I was glad that undressed-me was still exciting to him.

I nodded and opened the box.

It wasn't a dress in the box. It was a very feminine take on a trench coat. As a "just because" gift, it would have been too expensive but thoughtful. As a birthday gift that I had to wait for, I was livid. Instead of apologizing, he pulled a deerstalker hat – a Sherlock Holmes hat – out from behind his back, and a clay pipe.

Funny guy. He's lucky I didn't kill him on the spot. I sent him home and I threw the pipe and the hat into the box before closing it.

I put the box on the top shelf in my closet and slammed the door shut, determined to forget about this birthday.

I threw my pocketbook on the table when I got home the next day, threw my coat on the floor, and stomped into the kitchen. I never throw things around; I'm very organized.

Jules hadn't called all day. That stupid SOB didn't call all day.

Then I heard a knock on the door. I figured he'd come to apologize in person. He just got a plus in my estimation.

It was him but he wasn't alone. The woman with him looked like she was making an effort to not burst into tears. She looked up and I was surprised. It was Nancy Wilson, I hadn't seen her in more than a decade, but it was her. Her family lived next door until I was eleven. Her younger sister and I had been thick as thieves for most of grade school. How did he find her and what had happened to put her in such a state?

"This is Nancy, Aida's friend," he said.

It really is a small world. The smallest. I put that aside and opened the door wide. She was a mess.

She couldn't sit, she couldn't stand. I graciously asked if she wanted some tea. She collapsed onto a dining room chair and nodded. I headed to the kitchen and put the kettle on. I walked back in while I waited for it to heat up.

"I think my daughter has been murdered."

It was emotionless. I got the feeling she'd said it so often that she didn't dare allow herself a reaction to her own words. I couldn't imagine what she was going through.

"Why did you come to me?"

"Because Jules said you'd helped others. Aida said you could help. And I need help. The police are useless."

I found it funny that I recognized Nancy immediately but she didn't seem to know me. I guess it's the difference between my seeing my friend's cool, much-older, older sister and her not seeing her little sister's annoying little friend. That, and the horrible circumstance.

Two cups of tea later and I had heard the sad story. Nancy's daughter was in an abusive relationship. Nancy hadn't heard from her for a week. Her daughter, Ruby, always called her on Saturdays. Always. Nancy went to the house where Ruby lived with her boyfriend. No one answered the door, and no cars were in the driveway. Nancy called Ruby's cellphone, and heard it echoing inside the house. "Please," Nancy begged. "You've got to help me."

Jules looked at me with those puppy-dog eyes that I can't resist. He also pouted, to really make his point. I wanted to laugh at him but there was no humor in the room.

"Hey, babe, can't you help Nancy?"

What did I know about finding lost people? Or about possible murders? Still, this was Nancy. Her daughter was the niece of the girl I trusted with all of my childhood secrets.

I didn't answer him. Instead I got up and went to see what food I could offer her. The tea had helped but she still looked like a wreck.

When I came back in, Jules had the damn trench coat box out. I wanted to be angry but Nancy seemed to be almost smiling as she looked at it. And, I overheard what he said to her.

"I generally suck at getting gifts. I don't know why Pearl puts up with me. But when I saw this, I canceled the blue dress I had ordered for her. Anyone could get her a dress. This was something that reminds me of her, something that connects to her," Jules said.

I didn't see it that way but knowing that he did changed everything. I walked in, put down the tray with the sandwiches and put on the coat. Gotta admit, I liked the way it looked. I had a bit of fun with it, putting the hat on too, and sticking the pipe in my mouth.

Seeing a hint of a twinkle in Nancy's eyes ... I didn't think I could help her with what she'd asked but at least I could do this.

I asked her for the details: her daughter's name, address, boyfriend's name, phone number, etc. All the things that detectives on TV ask for. I figured I'd go to the cops and report this for her and that would be the end of my involvement.

Nancy pecked me on the cheek, then grabbed my hands with both of hers. A sad smile and a nod told me all I needed to know about what it meant to her that I was going to try.

Nancy was right. My visit to the police the next day proved fruitless. In fact, I was peppered with questions about my interest in Nancy's daughter. How long had I known her? Did I know the boyfriend? No questions I really could answer to their satisfaction, and they didn't attempt to answer mine to my satisfaction, either.

Driving home, I came to a decision. Jules and I had to help her. He wasn't getting out of this.

Jules has a lot of friends. I'm amazed at how many people he knows. So, when he told me he knew a locksmith, I just nodded.

"Call him and tell him to meet us at Ruby's house tomorrow."

Jules complied.

His friend Kevin got the back door open in record time. No one saw us; Ruby's house backed up to the creek. Kevin left after being paid, assuring us he'd say nothing.

Jules and I held hands, then walked in. And yes, I wore the damn trench coat. Again, Jules' idea of funny. He begged me to wear the hat and carry the pipe, too, but I drew the line there.

The door opened into the kitchen. A strong odor of laundry detergent assaulted us as we walked in cautiously. The laundry "room" was part of the kitchen. We walked through, into the living room, to find Ruby on the floor, dead. We amateur detectives couldn't find any signs of a struggle. The air conditioning was turned up high; we imagined that was because it would inhibit the body from smelling. Yes, we watch too many detectives shows on TV.

We both stopped short as we saw a bunch of pearls, identical to mine, next to Ruby. The string was broken, and they were loose. But I knew, I just knew, these were my pearls. *What the hell?*

The sun shining through the window highlighted something on the floor near the sofa. I knew I shouldn't touch anything, but … it was my charm! The one with my initials etched on the back. Confirmation of my suspicion—these were my pearls.

"Police will have to take us seriously now," I said.

"We aren't supposed to be here. The police won't look any further than us," Jules said.

"I have an idea."

Jules followed me out of the house. When we got into our car, a block away, I called the police and told them I'd gone to see if Ruby was all right and saw someone leaving out her back door. It wasn't brilliant, but it put us there for innocent reasons and got their attention.

Jules wanted to leave but I insisted that would be more suspicious. And Nancy would back us up if the cops didn't believe us. Now that I'd completed the call, the reality was hitting me. Ruby was dead. I was going to have to tell Nancy that her daughter was dead.

I leaned on my boyfriend and started crying. I couldn't tell for sure, but I think some of the crying and shaking was him, too. At some point, might have been quick, I was pretty well out of it, the police arrived.

We got questioned, a lot. Nancy got called down and I convinced the police to not give her details over the phone. I didn't want her driving in that state. It was bad enough that the police called her down to Ruby's house at all. The reality… I wanted to be there for her when she heard. No one should have to deal with that alone.

Just as Nancy arrived, the officers, who were still questioning us, stepped away to deal with a loud, angry older man who'd stormed up to them. I took the opportunity to intercept Nancy.

"That's her boyfriend, Tom," Nancy sniffled, pointing at the man who was arguing with the cops.

He was old enough to be her father, easily old enough. I looked for some sign of what would attract anyone to him. I was seeing him at, presumably, his worst but even so. Angry looked normal on him. Like a default state. I don't know what made me see it that way, but I did.

My cell rang as I unlocked my door. Aunt Linda. I didn't know if I could deal with her drama right then, but I answered it anyway.

"They've been stolen," she yelled into the phone. "Stolen! That damn Tom called …"

"Aunt Linda, calm down. I've had a really rough day."

"Sorry, sweetie, but I wanted to tell you right away. Confess." I could tell her breathing became more regular. "That damn Tom called me last week. I didn't want to tell anyone, after all that I went through and everyone's compassion. He called, and he came over. And we … you know…"

Yes, I could figure out that part.

"Why are you telling me?"

"I looked in my jewelry box today. I was going to wear your pearls. They're gone. No one else has been in my house, except you when you found them on your birthday. It had to have been Tom! I mean, he was in my bedroom …"

"Aunt Linda, we'll talk about this later."

I related to Jules Aunt Linda's current tale of woe and her real loss of my pearls. I also told him I think my pearls were next to Ruby because Ruby's boyfriend and Aunt Linda's were one and the same. All I had to go on was the name and the general description, and the fact the pearls near Ruby were mine, but my detective's gut was telling me I'm right. That damn Tom killed Nancy's daughter and left my pearls at the scene of the murder.

Like I said, Jules knows people. One of Jules' friends put hidden cameras in a few rooms in my place and was monitoring them. So we set up a gathering at my house, inviting Aunt Linda. We told her to bring Tom. We also invited Nancy.

Nancy arrived first. We tried hard to comfort her. Then Aunt Linda knocked on the door. Nancy looked confused.

Aunt Linda didn't barge in like usual. She seemed … subdued … as she and Tom walked in. Is this how she reacts when she's with a man? Disgusting. I closed the door behind them. She stood in front of Tom, then turned to introduce him to us. Nancy jumped up, ran to the living room, screaming.

"What's he doing here?"

"What the hell are you doing here?" Tom bellowed.

Jules let me play the detective.

"Nancy, when we saw Ruby's body, my pearls were next to her, broken. I knew they were mine, handed down for generations in my family. Aunt Linda had been the custodian of my pearls."

I took a breath and looked around. I liked this dramatic tension, enjoyed being the detective despite the tragic nature of the situation.

"Aunt Linda, you said the pearls had been stolen. That led me to believe your Tom was also Ruby's Tom."

Tom frantically booked it for the door. As he ran, he jumped over Aunt Linda's pocketbook, on the floor. A pearl jumped out of his coat pocket.

Jules tackled him. Tom wasn't having it. He pushed Jules off him and again bolted for the door. That's when I realized I didn't have everything exactly right. I was in over my head. There was nothing for it. I had to play the hand I dealt myself.

"I'll call the police," Jules said, after restraining Tom again.

I agreed and did my best to keep my shaking to myself. I sat on the couch and counted the seconds until the police arrived. When they did, I suggested that they interview us separately. Because this was tied to Ruby's murder, they agreed.

My stomach unclenched a little. With the police here, we were all safe for now. But, once they had our stories, they'd leave. That meant the killer would leave with them. I had to make sure that didn't happen.

Jules went first. That was good. It gave me time to calm Aunt Linda and Nancy. I made sure I was the last interview. The officer taking our statements wasn't a detective but that was OK. I was.

"Before we start, I know who killed Ruby."

"The others have told me about Tom. Please, let's just do this by the numbers. The sooner we get this done, the sooner we can give your house back," Officer Klein said.

"Tom isn't the killer. I was fooled into believing it but I understand now. And it is a matter of life and death that you understand."

I laid it out for him as simply and quickly as I could. It broke my heart, but I did it. When I was done, the police took Aunt Linda into custody. She started to proclaim her innocence, but I stopped her.

"You found out Tom was cheating on you. You couldn't stand it. So, you confronted Ruby. I don't believe you intended to kill her but once you did, you decided to frame Tom."

"Lies!" Linda shouted.

She started to protest again, and I cut her off.

"Once I was involved, once Nancy involved me, you needed a way to make me believe it was Tom. So, you tainted my birthright for your own ends."

Jules took me into his arms as they left. Nancy just sat there in stunned silence. When she finally looked up, she asked if I was sure.

"If his motive was the pearls, he wouldn't have left them at the scene. He wouldn't have come here with pearls in his pocket. Aunt Linda and he were the only ones who had access to the pearls and access to Tom's coat. If it wasn't him, there's only one choice left. The murder scene only makes sense if Aunt Linda was the killer."

Nancy thanked us, then, crying, headed for the door. She turned back.

"I can't thank you enough."

Jules and I nodded. As the door closed behind her, Jules took me in his arms.

"Hey babe, not today, but maybe tomorrow, could you model the trench coat for me?"

I smacked him.

Charles Barouch is an author, editor, lecturer, and lifelong learner.

You can find some of his works at hdwp.com/r/cdb.

Ann is a partner in Gemini Wordsmiths and Celestial Echo Press. She is Ruth Littner's twin. Except Ruth is a year older than Ann. And a foot taller. And not related. Several of Ann's short stories have been published in various anthologies. Ann co-published *The Twofer Compendium,* an anthology based on the theme of twins. She is a graduate of Bram Stoker award-winning author Jonathan Maberry's short story writing class. Jon McGoran and Don Lafferty were the other teachers. Ann is a member of the Writers Coffeehouse in Willow Grove, PA, and two writing critique groups.

Sunset at the Circus

Ruth Littner

Even as the sun's blaze faded into evening, there was little relief from the heat. The lions' ears flicked off flies. The acrobats deftly grabbed cans of cheap beer from the fridge, simultaneously wiping sweat from their brows and the cans. The Ringmaster slogged toward his air-conditioned trailer when a shriek pierced the soupy air.

"She's *gone!*" Hubert whimpered, mournfully. "How could this happen?" Hubert crumpled into the hay pile, limbs limp, sobbing. "She's … she's … so … *substantial* … so … *Brobdingnagian!* How could she get out?"

"You don't have to throw your stupid education at us all the time, Bert," Tonya sneered, cracking her gum. "I don't even know what you're saying."

"She's *gone.* Peel is missing. Disappeared. Mislaid. Lost. Absent. AWOL. Astray. Outtahere. Do … you … understand, Tonya? The … elephant … is … missing!" Hubert's clipped speech dripped with his sarcastic drawl.

"This is the fourth animal this week," Reginald bristled. "Last week, the monkeys, Kofi and Penny, disappeared along with the horse, Suzy. This week, Aryeh, our showstopping lion, Ze'ev the wolf, Hazeer the pig, and now, Peel the elephant, have disappeared. We may have to shut down if we don't have enough acts. Kids wanna see them animals more than all the other acts."

"You're a ringmaster," Hubert replied civilly, although silently correcting his grammar. "Can you use your contacts to figure this out?"

"No. We have to keep this quiet. We'll have to call the ATF to help us."

Hubert and Reginald escorted both members of the Animal Task Force into a blue tent. The stakes were high. The first to push in, Rolfe the Fire Eater, sat quietly after downing a bottle of water. Tuffy the Tramp Clown sauntered in, eyes skyward, whistling air, hands clasped behind his back.

"Hey Tuffy, you look guilty of — *something*," Hubert alleged, motioning the closest seat, an overturned bucket. Tuffy sat, silent.

"Do youse know anything about these disappearing animals? It's costing me big alfalfa each time this happens," Reginald the Ringmaster bemoaned. "Or have any good ideas about how to solve this?" The four concurrently grabbed their chins, furrowed their brows, and murmured, "hm."

"I have an idea!" Rolfe volunteered, voice scratchy. "Let's ask my wife, Rita the Fire Eater, to keep an eye on the animals overnight while the rest of us sleep. She'll walk the length of the field and watch for any weird movement, light, sound, or ... *thing*."

"Any other ideas?" Hubert searched the faces. Nada.

"All in favor?" Hubert, Reginald, and Rolfe raised their hands. "Majority rules!"

Rita could juggle fire. Children and adults alike gaped, astonished by her dexterity and ability to control the batons bearing shimmering, dangerous flames. She could spin the emblazoned torches, then swallow the nub ends as they spewed sparks and fear, no doubt cauterizing her throat.

But she could not guard animals. She could not even remain sober as she guarded animals. She could not guard animals more than three nights. She would not live to see the morning light on the fourth day, astonishing as she was. Rita had been murdered.

The ATF reconvened in a red tent with actual wooden chairs. Around this tent, the stakes were even higher. Rolfe looked sadder than Tuffy the Tramp Clown could on a good day, with a really, really good makeup frown. Hubert sucked on a sippy cup of chocolate milk. Tuffy traipsed in, late. Again.

"I think you're involved, Tuffy the Tramp Clown!" accused Reginald, as he stood straight up, elbows akimbo. His body lurched left, but his shiny black top hat remained exactly as it always was, slightly jaunty. "I think you are stealing these animals. You want the attention! You're jealous of me!" He turned sharply. "Or is it *you*, Hubert?!" He turned back again. "No! It's you, Tuffy! Jack Yuse!"

Hubert blew milk out of his nose at this misused *j'accuse*. All he could think was, *ineffectual dolt.*

"*What*? What evidence do you have? Why are you saying this?" Tuffy slumped so low in his seat, his knees knocked into his nose and pushed it left. "Guard him!" Reginald commanded to Hubert and Rolfe, who proceeded to do nothing. Reginald ran into the three-ringed tent, through the tied-back entrance flap. He brushed by Francine the Bearded Lady, Andrew the Human Cannonball, and Eleanor Roosevelt, the chihuahua clad in a pink tutu, the chihuahua that could jump through fourteen hoops in a row. Eleanor Roosevelt yipped and nipped as Reginald flew by.

"I need two strong men! Now!"

Two Strong Men followed Reginald back to the red tent and grabbed Tuffy by the underarms. They shoved him into a downtown wagon and drove him directly to Clown Jail.

Things appeared hopeless. Hopeless for the circus because animals were disappearing now at a rate of almost one per night. Hopeless for Reginald because after two more nights of continued theft he figured out that Tuffy the Tramp Clown could *not* be the culprit, since he was in Clown Jail at the time of the new animal thefts, and hopeless for Tuffy, still stuck in jail. Tuffy became depressed but did not adjust his makeup frown, which should be the opposite of whatever he was feeling.

Tuffy reminisced about his childhood and winced. He was a third-generation Tramp Clown, a fourth-generation circus child. He'd started his first year as a barker. He'd lived with, and witnessed, abuse. Abuse of his family, abuse by his family, abuse of his coworkers, and abuse of the animals. He remembered the sadness, the pain, the loneliness. Tuffy wept inside, careful not to mess up his greasepaint.

On the third morning in Clown Jail, Tuffy pulled himself together. He had reason to smile.

Miss Daisy the White Face Clown brought him breakfast. *If she is anything like her greasepaint, she's gorgeous.* Miss Daisy brought him lunch. And Miss Daisy brought him dinner. All these meals were meagre and tasteless, but Tuffy did not care. He struck up a conversation with Miss Daisy.

"Why are you in here?" he asked.

"I'm doing community service," she replied. And he asked her no further questions.

Then Daisy asked him about his woes.

"I may be able to help," she offered.

"How's that?"

"I have an uncle, a really, really old uncle, who runs MAGA. He'll bail you out, help you figure out who is stealing your animals, and find out who killed Rita the Fire Eater. I'll call him."

D.T. the Jester Clown (also known as the Fool Clown), arrived at the Clown Jail after breakfast the next morning. Wearing orange greasepaint and dressed in a foolish robe, he cracked as he sat. *Was that his knee?* D.T., Daisy, and Tuffy discussed the events, and afterward, D.T. bailed Tuffy out of jail. As they drove back to the circus in style in a huge limo-type car D.T. had named Ground Force One, Tuffy thanked D.T. for paying his bail. He shared some memories about wanting to help the animals when he was very little, but D.T. stared out the window as he drove, looking nonplussed.

Reginald, contrite but stoic, greeted the crew after Tuffy introduced everyone.

"I have an idea," started D.T., "about how to solve these crimes. I run an outfit called MAGA. I think me and my team can help you find who you're looking for."

"Great. Let us reconvene the ATF tomorrow," said Reginald, "and Daisy, you, and your employees will be our guests. At that time, please present your plan to find the culprits. We will meet in the Big Top, where everyone can sit comfortably."

"I will present a yuuuge plan, one never heard before in the history of plans. Me and my crew will arrive at dawn. We shall have the cases solved by lunch. Who knew it would be so easy to solve all these crimes? See you in the morning with my team."

Reginald, resplendent in cropped red jacket, black jodhpurs, shiny, high black boots, and pencil-thin mustache, held his stovepipe hat in his hand as he welcomed the ATF and Daisy.

"Ladies and gentlemen! Welcome to the Big Top!" his voice boomed.

Daisy could barely contain her nausea. The overwhelming stench of multiple animal poos mixed with gunpowder and perspiration made her woozy.

"I hear a car," Daisy said, thanking her universe that her uncle and his team had arrived. She ran outside to look for Ground Force One but spied a solitary black Volkswagen Beetle pulling up to the tent. On the side of the door, in bold orange, was written: Merry Andrew Gumshoe Agency (MAGA). Her uncle stepped out of the driver's side door and moved through the tent door flap.

Oh, no! He forgot the team. How will we get this done?

Then, from the back seat and the front passenger seat, one by one, 16 clowns of all sorts — two White Face, two Auguste, two Tramp, two Character, two Jester, two Rodeo, two Mime, and even two Creepy Clowns — squished out of the Beetle. Each one wore a beige trench coat.

They surrounded Daisy. She shied, anxious, drawing into herself. From above, the group looked like a dying flower — Daisy in the center, the 16 petals chaotically angled, all tan but with splotches of greasepaint color.

"We're here to help in any way we can," they said in what sounded like singing in rounds. High voices, low voices, even two exceptionally creepy voices. Daisy channeled visions of Munchkin Land. And then as if one choreographed unit, the entire flower moved toward the

Big Top. In single file they entered the tent, each personally greeted by Eleanor Roosevelt.

Once seated inside, they undid their belts, unbuttoned their trench coats, and made themselves comfortable. A mélange of color, odor, and sound painted the stands. D.T. stood up.

"Let's begin!"

"Let me tell you what I've done already this year," began D.T. It was August so the clowns settled in for a long list of alleged accomplishments. Both Rodeo Clowns snored as D.T. droned on and on. He hadn't yet passed April's accomplishments.

"Now!" D.T. snapped. "I'm up to today." It was two hours later. "And this is how I plan to catch a thief and a killer. And they may be the same criminal."

"It's really not that bad a plan," the ATF agreed. "Maybe it'll work."

"So why would anyone want to steal animals from the circus? Let's start with the presumption that this is a really, really bad person. I mean, *animals*? *Cute* animals? Animals with talent? Whaddya think, to resell them? *To eat them?*"

"Well," said one of the crime-fighting MAGA clowns, "I'll review the videotape."

"What's videotape?" asked a millennial clown.

"This is a circus," said another MAGA clown, shaking her head. "There are no cameras."

"So, who would have killed Rita? Who would have stolen the animals?"

Later, D.T. and Miss Daisy, along with the cohort of 16 clowns, trekked to the scene of the crime, the grassy knoll where Rita had bought it.

"Oy," grumbled D.T. "My trick knee. It hurts."

"You have a trick knee? You should be in the circus."

"Let's study the evidence here. I found a wet brown paper bag with some glass in it. I'll let you know what that is."

"I found some peanuts. Peanuts?"

"This is a really large crop circle," another clown noted. "What would do that?"

"I see tracks," said another clown.

"Jeep tracks? Deep tracks?"

"Multiple. All shapes, all toes. No shoes."

"Here's a ripped piece of paper with dirt and words on it."

"Egad!" cried D.T. "I have just solved the crimes!"

They trudged back to the Big Top, a gleeful cadre of pandemonium.

D.T. the Jester Clown whistled harshly at the 16 clowns. The clowns instantly paired up like the animals in the ark, but animals wearing trench coats. Next D.T. summoned Reginald the Ringmaster, Andrew the Human Cannonball, Francine the Bearded Lady, Hubert, Rolfe the

Fire Eater (who was pressing a photo of Rita to his chest), Miss Daisy, Tuffy, Tonya, and Eleanor Roosevelt, and herded them into the Big Top. Other curious performers joined them. Each took a seat except Reginald, who stood in the center ring of the three rings. Rolfe sat in his own row. No one really wanted to sit next to Rolfe, especially in August; his body always exuded so much heat.

The tent buzzed with excitement. Miss Daisy grabbed Tuffy's hand. Tuffy blushed but no one could see his pink cheeks.

"Ladies and gentlemen! Children of all—" D.T. rushed to Reginald's side, snatched the mic out of Reginald's hand and mumbled, "Shut up, Reginald." Reginald scoffed, lowered his head—his hat tumbling to the dirt floor—and trudged to an empty seat in a walk of shame.

With mic in hand, D.T. pushed his fingers together several times, like Mr. Burns. Then he stared into the crowd. D.T. raised the mic to his crimson-painted, oversized lips.

"I have just solved the crime," he repeated. "I know who killed Rita and I know who stole the animals." The crowd roared with excitement. "You must know that I am the greatest crime-solver who ever lived. No one in the history of crime-solving has ever solved so many crimes or did it so well or—"

"Get on with it!" The crowd thundered with laughter.

Hubert, eyebrows arched, turned his head toward Andrew the Human Cannonball, seated next to him.

"Why must the crowd bombinate every time there is news?" Andrew's eyes glazed over. He had suffered so many concussions during his repeated 475-foot journeys that he could barely understand English at its most colloquial.

"Huh?"

The crowd hushed again, each clown and performer shushing the next.

"Let's review the evidence from the murder scene. First, here we have a brown paper bag, inside it a crushed bottle of Svedka. Next, cement imprints of all of the footprints and tracks we found at the scene of the crime. And finally, a note written in charcoal, which looks like a warning. It reads, 'Dis is jusd the baginnin. Led us go ore eech 1 of youse bys it.' The handwriting appears primitive and there are misspellings.

"I thought and thought about this note. And then I remembered what Tuffy told me about his childhood memory of animal abuse.

"From this scientific review of evidence and intellectual recollection of discussion, I have concluded the following: The animals were not stolen. They escaped with the help of each other. First, the monkeys got out. With their dexterous opposable thumbs, they were able to grab the cage keys and let the other animals out." A collective gasp moved throughout the audience. The knife-throwers leaned in.

"They had devised an elaborate plan to release all the animals but *someone*—" At this, every head—curly haired, hatted, bald, and shiny—turned toward Rolfe with sympathetic expressions. Many of the female clowns whimpered and grabbed their hearts. Miss Daisy made the heart symbol with her white-gloved hands and thrust them toward Rolfe.

"—*someone* started patrolling the fields, making it impossible for them to proceed." The crowd murmured in unison, sympathetic to the situation.

"So, who killed Rita?" the seal-trainer shouted from the fifth row.

"Yeah, what happened then?"

"You're killing us, Smalls! Tell us what happened!"

"*Who dunnit?*"

D.T. clutched his chest in the most dramatic fashion. He glanced up, then rolled his eyes and fell forward, his face slapping against the prone mic. The impact broke his nose.

"Get the medic!" shouted Tuffy. No one moved so he ran toward the Help Tent himself.

This is all my fault. His gait quickened. His heartrate quickened. *No one was supposed to get hurt. No one.* His heart pounded now. *Now Rita's dead and D.T. looks pretty banged up.* Greasepaint ran down his cheeks, revealing channels of beige skin. He stumbled and pitched forward, arms flailing like, well, like a clown. Once down, he drew himself into a fetal position. From that vantage point, he saw an unused tent that had recently been moved. From the ground, he could see feet. Not just feet, but paws as well. He definitely saw elephant feet.

At that exact moment, sirens wailed. Two police cars, an ambulance, and two fire trucks raced past the animal pavilions, past the midway, past the porta potties, past the amusement rides, past the fried Oreo stand, past the performers' sleeping quarters, and past the empty tents, and stopped directly in front of Tuffy. A clowny caricature of a cop stepped out.

"Our detectives looked into this case when you were brought into Clown Jail. They reported back to us just now," the Sergeant declared in an unnecessarily loud voice. "We know you're not guilty of killing Rita. The State will not be pressing charges and therefore you are free from any charges. Whoever posted your bail will be reimbursed."

Tuffy was gobsmacked. His mouth wide open, he pointed toward the Big Top where D.T. lay.

"D.T. down," was all he could manage. "Medics."

The crowd poured out of the structure, impeding the medical help from getting inside and reviving D.T. They were furious. They were grumbling and whining and sneering. D.T. had collapsed before revealing the killer.

Once again, Tuffy pulled himself together. He rose and ran around the back of the tent into the emergency exit and squatted nearby the EMTs working on D.T. He picked up the evidence bag and examined its comments.

"Voila!"

"May I have your attention *please!*" Tuffy shouted after donning Reginald's shiny black stovepipe hat. Everyone had poured back into the Big Top, now including all the other performers, and the police and firefighters. The EMTs were on their way to the hospital with D.T.

"We are all safe. There is no killer to fear. No killer running around on the loose. These animals have feelings, you know. They know when there is abuse. They know they should be feeling better. They know when they are mistreated. I know that, too. I saw it firsthand. I saw it when I was just a child. I was so happy when they started to disappear—I felt that wherever they were, they were somewhere where they were better off." Tuffy had a captive audience.

"Then the ATF decided to send a sentry to avoid any more losses and I was sad, so I wrote that note. I made it appear as if Tonya had written it, kind of illegible and childlike. But that was supposed to be the end of it. Just a threat.

"But I'm guessing the animals wanted revenge. All of these tracks and footprints reveal that the animals approached Rita the Fire Eater. They wanted her—along with all of their handlers—to be more careful, less mean, more gentle, less abusive.

"But Rita had drunk the Kool-Aid, or rather the Svedka, and didn't hear them coming. They encircled her. Then the elephant came down hard. He crushed the bottle but rolled by accident. This cut off her breath, and she asphyxiated."

A huge sigh resonated within the tent.

"I'm so happy that there's no killer!" one clown offered.

"I'm disappointed that it was a accident," said another, hoping there would have been more drama. Hubert tsk-tsked when he heard this sentence structure.

"Well, case closed," said Tuffy. And he decided to find a way to release the animals.

The sixteen clowns stuffed themselves back into the little Beetle except the last one, who snagged his trench coat belt on the door. Tuffy moved into the driver's seat. Now Chief of the Merry Andrew Gumshoe Agency (yes, Merry Andrew is a real clown thing), life went back to how it was before. For the most part, anyway. Rolfe buried Rita. Hubert tutored Tonya in grammar and syntax in exchange for, well, in exchange for *something*. Tuffy and Miss Daisy got engaged. Andrew the Human Cannonball and Francine the Bearded Lady started a boardgame night. Mostly it was Chutes and Ladders and Candy Land. And Eleanor Roosevelt was given seven new tutus in different colors, one for each day she had to work. They worked her like a dog.

MAGA became successful even without the guidance and leadership of D.T. And Tuffy purchased a 10,000-acre farm in upstate New York where he figured all of the animals would roam free and live happily ever after.

Things looked normal, because as Tonya said, "Irregardless of circumstances, the show must go on. Right, huh?" She winked at Hubert and cracked her gum. Hubert winced in pain.

And exactly one month after the incident, just at sunset, Peel, Kofi, Penny, Ze'ev, Hazeer, and Aryeh met in the hidden tent where the stakes were high. They did not want to go to upstate New York. …

Ruth Littner, daughter of Holocaust survivors, penned *Living with Ghosts*, a story of loss and survival. She is a member of the Authors Guild, National Association of Memoir Writers, and the Writers Coffeehouse. She is a graduate of *NY Times* best-selling author Jonathan Maberry's Short Story Class. She edited four books that are in the Rock and Roll Hall of Fame and four of her short stories have been published. She has an M.A. from Goddard College, and a B.A. in English from SUNY at Buffalo. Ruth lives a drab, ordinary life in Pennsylvania with her adorable husband and ornery cats. *Or is it her ornery husband and adorable cats*? Ruth is a partner in Gemini Wordsmiths and Celestial Echo Press with Ann Stolinsky. They both still deny their twininess. Visit her at ruthlittner.com.

The Blowpipe Killer

Viktor Rain

Rain fell hard on the windowsill. Night's cold breeze blew through the open window, a rejuvenating stream of fresh air. Sirens wailed in the distance. The city never slept. A tireless microcosm of grime and dirt, deformed and twisted, slithering its million-legged body in search of a new victim. An angry beast, a stained mattress covered in bright satin sheets.

We offer you tomorrow, the fancy neon banner at the city's outskirts said, flashing its pretty lights like a midnight concubine on West End Boulevard. Yet it was the serpent of Eve spitting ornate words, seductive whispers to trap the gluttonous.

The new tomorrow dressed in a body bag. Zipped, tagged, indexed, and forgotten.

"What's wrong, boss?" Dan asked, rubbing the circles around his eyes.

He looked like a ghost, his sinewy frame covered by a loose shirt. It had been white once, a piece of pure fabric sitting on the shelf of some fancy fashion outlet. Overpriced and useless, sold by a pretty girl in a black dress, her lips full and welcoming.

"When was the last time you slept?" Mark asked, pouring himself a glass of water.

The Trench Coat Chronicles

The young inspector shrugged and reached for the bottle of rum under his desk. The salvation of any youngling, the amber spirit to caress the tired soul, a spiritual mother, always there, bright and warm, prepared to go where no other human would even dare to, only to soothe the pains of the heart.

"Monday, I think. What day is it?" Dan asked, downing a mouthful.

"Thursday. It's been a while, hasn't it?"

Dan sketched a weary smile and eyed the open window. Bright lights flickered in the distance, the pulse of human flesh intertwined in its eternal dance of evolution and interaction. Beautiful creatures all of them, at least when in one piece.

It was pleasant, the silence. The boy had learned quite fast: few words, lots of action. A young, tender heart, almost idealistic at first. A man of plans and schemes, of revolution and reform, but after three years on the job there he stood, silent, watching the jungle outside with cloudy eyes.

"How's Anna?" he asked, offering the bottle.

"You know I don't drink that shit," Mark replied, sipping his water. "My mind's cloudy enough as it is."

He paused and caressed the handle of his pistol. A comforting partner, one who was always there.

"She's left the city with that banker of hers."

Dan chuckled and took another sip, sinking in his chair.

"They are calling again, aren't they?"

The phone buzzed and jingled. Mark picked up the receiver and frowned at the inspector.

"How did you know?"

"The sirens, old man. It's time for him to strike again. The second Thursday of the month, isn't it?"

Mark bit his lip and squeezed his eyes shut. Sloppy, careless, chaotic. His thread of thought was unfocused, like a teenage boy in a brothel — off-track.

"Mark Downing," he grumbled, lighting up a cigarette. "Him again?"

The phone buzzed in his ear and he nodded, darting out of his chair. He shot a glance at Dan, who followed, but not before saying goodbye to mother with a long kiss on her glassy mouth.

Mark dressed in his trench coat, feeling as if he were putting on the skin of another man. It was warm and comforting, his shell, a personal sanctuary built amid the chaos. He checked its ragged sleeves and smiled. It was like a good woman, her beauty unaltered by the passage of time.

She laid in her bed, wearing nothing but a black thong and a lace bra. A beautiful girl perhaps in her twenties, her face perfect underneath smokey eyes and fire-red lipstick. Her long legs were bound tight with a rope, dried trickles of blood contoured on her ankles.

She had been dead for a while. Long enough for the blood to dry, but not long enough for her body to spoil.

It was the usual method, alcohol spiced with a dash of batrachotoxin, the poison of frogs. A quick death, ten minutes of suffocation and convulsions, with no postmortem marks besides residual chemicals in the victim's blood.

And the rope. The rope was always there.

Mark walked around the hotel room, his predatory eyes scanning, searching for anything out of place. But there was nothing there except boring order, perfect stability, the bleak blandness of a cheap rental, with its little shampoos and soap samples, its immaculate white towels and impersonal decor. The epitome of conformity and commonness.

"He rented under the name of Mark Downing, didn't he?" Dan asked, his hands wrapped around the receptionist's gentle fingers.

The boy had his charm, and he was wicked enough to turn a death scene into an opportunity to expand his stable of shocked, feeble young fawns.

The girl nodded, her blonde hair reflecting rusty glints from the bulb above.

"It's OK now; go downstairs."

She wiped her wet eyes and vanished behind the door.

Mark sniffed and walked to the bed, his eyes measuring the soulless flesh below. She fit the pattern: young, brunette, slim, wide waist. The hips of fertility. Gently, his fingers parted her full lips, reaching inside.

And it was there, as in previous murders. Locked in a plastic bag protecting a folded piece of paper, the type of bag dealers used to ration their stash. He rubbed the bridge of his nose and grumbled like a frustrated ox revisiting his breeding days.

'Chief Inspector Downing,

I am writing these words as the woman you now gaze upon is succumbing to the temptation of death. I admire her struggle, as her attachment to this rotten world is strong, like the root of an oak. A blossoming soul she is.

As her body shivers, desecrated by the ripples of the world beyond, I can't help but wonder if you've ever felt this rush. As an entity of the law, I am inclined to believe that you have dabbled in the art of death.

The pure soul of our filthy world, the pillar of justice ... nothing else but a man with his hands soaked in innocent blood.

I want to hear from you, Trench Coat Downing, I want you to unleash the savage within, for we both know that our primal side is an egg fertilized by the most potent sperm.

The sperm of power.

And there is no greater power than that of controlling life itself, is there?

I believe that both of us are sick of this little game of ours. The cat and the mouse, always on the hunt, always on the run.

How about we settle our little dispute like the savages we are?

You are the only one who can stop this cycle of death and reincarnation I bring, for I, just like you, am an aspect of the impending spiral; we are but actors directed by the voice of fate, ordered around to enact its most basic need: cyclicity.

When the goat will shine, the waters will tumble, and as the tide will rise and fall, the man who ends the third quarter of the Apostles will become a host of metal and concrete for the next girl to die. It is written in the Triad of Honors.

Because I am writing this and I hear no door slamming, I see no dark trench coat looming in the frame of this bleak hotel room door, I assess, as any logical man would, that you have yet again failed to solve my riddle.

This is the fate of siblings, my brother, to run around in circles without reaching the true embrace they so much desire.

All in all, you've taken something of mine, a very precious toy, so now I'll be taking something of yours.'

He crumpled the paper in his clenched fist, heart pounding like a war drum. It was him all right, *The Blowpipe Killer*. A perfect embodiment of the city: obsessive, driven, murderous, and precise.

"Another riddle?" Dan asked, fixing his rubber gloves.

He was a professional, by the book. a smug accountant dressed up in a velvet suit, his expensive briefcase dangling by his side.

Mark nodded and handed him the paper. The young inspector unfolded it with the grace of a princess at a royal dinner, his eyes dashing across the parchment.

A smart lad, top of the class. He would have enjoyed a bright future had he not chosen the detective life. But a road once abandoned was forever closed.

"I think I know this one," he said, sitting by the beautiful dead. "Look, he mentions the shining goat ..."

"So?" Mark said. "How does this help?"

"It's the astrological sign of Capricorn, the month of September. I think our friend implies that he'll skip August. Perhaps he's planning a nice vacation by the beach, eh?"

Mark didn't laugh.

"And the rest? What does it mean?"

"Now boss, I may be smart, but I need to sit down, have a drink, and meditate on it. I can't just cook answers like an oven."

A deep sax cried below, its soothing tunes struggling to cover the rattle of rain. The plaintive ballad roused from *Studio Jazzuette*, a classy restaurant for rich boys and girls glittering in their elegant clothes and expensive cars. But most of them had a lot of filth swept under the carpet. Mark had seen their world up close; he had been a part of it for far too long to ignore it. But he lacked something of value.

Real power.

"Let's go boy, we'll let the local police deal with this mess," he said, sauntering to the door, his dark trench coat fluttering like the closing curtain on a theater stage.

"Are you sure this is the spot?" Mark asked, picking his teeth. A little piece of beef had stuck in a decayed tooth and it was starting to taste bitter. It was stuffed down pretty tight, stubborn enough to ignore his anxious tongue licks. But where flesh failed, metal conquered, just like in a fight.

"Warehouse AJ, boss, I'm pretty sure of it," Dan said, fixing the brim of his almost-black hat.

It was the second Thursday of September, the month represented by the sign of Capricorn. Mark had read about

Capricorns among the stars. The whole astrology business was phony—but what wasn't?

Stubborn fellows, a disturbing genetic crossbreed of goat and fish, translated as an astral splintered self; mule-like determination of a horned beast in perfect sync with the flow-like state of a river trout. Slow but nimble, patient, but erratic, a magnanimous tyrant, the Capricorn was. A paradox. A cornucopia of imagination, reason, decisiveness.

"Hm. … A capricornucopia."

"'Scuse me, boss? What did you say?" Dan asked, reading *The Blowpipe* case file for the hundredth time.

"Nothing, I'm just blabbering."

"Don't you want to know how I've reached this conclusion?" Dan asked again, grinning.

It was a rare occurrence his tongue itching, so Mark just nodded. Young boys needed their dazzling moments, those moments of self-importance everyone yearned for. Self-validation, auto-glorification, necessities.

"Go ahead."

Dan's eyes sparkled like a puppy's eyes.

"You remember the Apostle thing that bugged me for the past three weeks. I just couldn't understand the semantics of it all. The meaning was all jumbled. At first I thought it might be an anecdote, so I ran a full graphical and phonetical analysis on it to see if there were any encoded meanings in its structure."

"Cut to the chase," Mark said, lighting up a cigarette.

"Finally, it hit me four days ago."

"When you trashed your brains with that stripper of yours, right?"

Dan stared at his feet, shoulders dropping.

"I'm not judging you, boy. We all did that when we were your age. Go on then, what about the Apostles."

"Yes, yes! The Apostles," Dan replied, reverting to his joyous self. "He mentioned the host of metal and concrete, which clearly meant something industrial, right? Like a hall, a factory, or whatever. That was easy enough. But the key, the true substance of it all, was in that ninth Apostle of his.

"I've tried to attach some meaning to it, but nothing seemed to fit. Only natural, because I was looking at it from the wrong angle. You see, boss, I thought that the rising and falling tide was linked to the Capricorn, not to the Apostles."

"Cut to the chase," Mark growled again, a mushroom of smoke enveloping his aged features.

"'The man who ends the third quarter of the Apostles will become a host of metal and concrete for the next girl to die,' he wrote. How many Apostles are there, boss?"

"Twelve."

"Indeed, twelve. Now, I've read the Bible and isolated the first three passages where all the Apostles are mentioned."

"Why only the first three?" Mark asked.

"He said that it is written in the *Triad of Honors*, so I think this is what he meant. And look now, the man who ends the third quarter is the ninth Apostle, right?"

Mark nodded.

"Good. In the book of Matthew, chapter ten, verses two to four, the ninth disciple is James, the son of Alphaeus. And the next two mentions are identical, the ninth Apostle, James, the son of Alphaeus ..." he said, trailing off.

"And? What should I make of this?"

"How many warehouses do we have at the docks?"

"How should I know?" Mark growled, his impatience starting to show.

"Twelve of them, boss. I've looked at the blueprints of the place, and there are twelve of them."

Mark started counting and laughed. Twelve they were, cubical, bland, lacking the touch of humanity, just like the rest of it all.

"But this is the sixth one," the Chief Inspector said, straightening the creases of his trench coat. "Why are we here then?"

"Ah, this was the hardest part still. For the past three days, I've had some lads from local keep an eye on the ninth warehouse, or the fourth, depending on how you look at it. Just think how absurd it would have been for us to miss our friend for such a technicality. Still, the lads saw nothing coming in or out, but last night, one of them mentioned that the lights in one of the other warehouses flickered open for a few minutes.

"But which warehouse, I wondered," he said, displaying a smug grin. "You know how locals are; he must have been drunk or something, so the answer, as always, was hard to obtain."

"And then …" Mark said, scratching his scalp, "how come you're so sure that this is the right one?"

"I've looked at the blueprints, boss. It's warehouse six, also known as warehouse AJ. Alphaeus, father of James. Blowpipe said that 'the waters will tumble, the tide will come and go,' so two semantic references to reversion, to a chess castling, you know? So, James, son of Alphaeus, became Alphaeus, father of James, a full shift in the relational direction among the two. … Warehouse AJ, our ninth Apostle."

"For the past three years you've had crazy theories like this, but you were wrong every time."

Dan nodded and reached for his bottle, drowning his dinner in rum.

"I know I'm right this time, boss. There is a pattern in all this, it's in his behavior. He made it easier this time, he wants you to find him. I've noticed that his references, while at first dark and pretentious in the aspect of cultural knowledge, became easier and broader in their reach. I'm sure he's in here, boss."

"You're a good boy, Dan. And that brain of yours … don't drink it to death."

The lights clicked open. Old stage bulbs, like those of antique theater halls, silvery and blinding. Mark reached for his gun and took cover, shoving Dan to a side. It was his turn to shine now. The boy, brilliant as he was, had the combat skills of a paraplegic goose.

"Stay there," Mark whispered, scanning the warehouse.

A huge chamber stacked with blue and green containers on the sides, metallic poles supporting its tall ceiling. It creaked and bellowed like a living thing, a huge industrial worm that had swallowed them whole but was unable to digest them.

The lights above joined and brightened up a corner at the other end. A brunette girl, wearing nothing but lingerie, was strapped to a chair, her pale skin glowing like spotless marble in the sun.

Blowpipe had been there.

Mark dashed from cover to cover like a prowling panther, his fifty years of age all but gone. He was an athlete, a professional boxer, a soldier on the front, the rush of adrenaline rewiring his lazy synapses.

The pleasure came back as it always did. Heart pumping, sight blurring, hearing enhanced … the beauty of dopamine, the soothing chant fear always brought. He was a sucker for fear, an addict, a suckling piglet twitching for food.

He was just a few steps away from the girl. Her eyes glimmered, showing life, but she made no sound. A silent muse in distress, guarded by a poisonous dragon, waiting for Prince Mark Charming to save her and make her his Queen. If only life had been a fairytale. …

It came like a thunder splitting the skies above. Ears ringing, he dropped on the ground, his lungs refusing to inhale. He looked at Dan and a sharp pain stabbed him in the chest. A pain he had long since forgotten, the agony of the soul.

The boy's head was a popped cherry, as he laid sprawled on the ground like a ragdoll, a headless stag watering from a dark pond. He was still there though—there was no way for him to be dead—his brains were still inside his cranium, processing, tinkering, not pink chunks on the concrete.

He got up and ran for the girl. The second bang came, and he flew to the ground, the front part of his shoulder exploding like a watermelon. It had to be a .308 caliber, as no other bullet could have done that much damage.

A pair of steps echoed to his right. Blowpipe was there, walking elegantly, like a businessman prancing around in public. He threw the rifle away and leaned in, his face brightening. It was a young face, that of a man around his mid-twenties, shaved and creamed, soft like the face of a woman.

He smiled and caressed Mark's cheek with a gentle touch.

"Do you remember me, Chief Inspector?" he asked, his voice deep.

Mark shook his head, struggling not to scream.

"Hm, I thought you wouldn't, but I had my hopes. Does the name James Oldbrand ring any bell to you?"

A synapse connected. He had seen that face before in court. The little brother of the meth-head he had shot point blank in the face. He was older, a real man, not the wimpy city runt he used to be.

"Yes, my feral friend, it's me. You've remembered, I see it in your eyes. I will keep it short, Chief Inspector, as I pride myself to be a practical man. You've taken something away from me, something very important, a core component of my early life."

"I didn't …" Mark croaked, clenching his shoulder.

"Shh, my friend. Although I made sure you wouldn't die, there's still a chance if you force yourself. I find it to be pragmatic of me, elegant I daresay, to take something away from you. Your surrogate son for instance," he said, pointing to Dan. "I've followed you for many years waiting to see you form a strong bond. I must say that your divorce turned you into a tough shell to break, but this boy here … this boy! Brilliant, was he not?

"Now, of course, my friend, a surrogate son is not even close to a blood brother, but there's more, isn't there? Your reputation, your sanity, they are all gone now, and they will never return."

He walked to the girl and plunged a thin needle in her shoulder, his lips curving up in satisfaction.

"I wonder what the Bureau will say when they find you here, your MIT-brained partner all but … scrambled, another dead girl by your side …"

"The local police are here," Mark said, laughing.

"On a stakeout, I know. They're dead, don't worry, but they died more gracefully," he replied, eyeing the needle. "Now, I'm afraid I must leave, my feral friend, for I am expected on the other side of the world to enjoy the blessing of a quiet, plentiful life. I wish you all the best, Chief Inspector."

He pressed a piece of cloth on Mark's face and walked away, his lacquered shoes clacking on the floor.

Mark's lids grew heavy and he rolled to the side, the dark outline of Dan's body a headless silhouette. As the girl started convulsing behind him, he fell unconscious, wishing for his brain to be splattered on the floor.

If only he could have switched fates.

Viktor Rain is a science fiction and fantasy writer, who also dabbles in the arts of noir genre and gritty detective fiction. Born in a historic city in the heart of the mountains, his dream has always been to find a career in the arts, and after a tumultuous youth in which he studied music, sculpting, wood-carving, drawing, and digital modelling. He finally settled into writing and hasn't stopped since.

The Trench Coat Chronicles

102

The Last Case

Alanna Robertson-Webb

Lacy Goodman's trench coat lay crumpled in a pool of ink, the rejected sleeves so coated in the coal-colored liquid that ol' Kris Kringle himself would've tried to shove it in a stocking. Detective Edward Moksha let a sigh escape, his fingers absentmindedly rubbing his temples as Officer Jameson rattled on.

The young author, a local celebrity, never went anywhere without that damn coat, and the whole town knew it. It was the only thing that showed this was her flat, the only shred of evidence that showed she had ever set foot in such a dump.

"No witnesses, no non-vic prints, no blood. Even the neighbors claim they didn't hear a peep, but with how trashed the joint is ..."

The policeman shrugged, gesturing at the mess in the studio apartment. Eddy's dispassionate gaze encompassed the carnage, which ranged from overturned furniture to shredded books and large ink splatters. He turned to face the incompetent policeman, a deep scowl knitting together his slicked-down eyebrows.

"Look, Charlie, why'd ya call me in? No blood plus no evidence equals no crime, and I thought ya was a better copper than this. Unless ya got more for me, or need me as some sorta witness, then this just looks like some bad housekeepin' ta me."

The officer's eyes, more white than blue, darted around the room, as beads of sweat slithered down his portly neck.

"Well, uh, see, there's something I didn't tell the Chief, since he wouldn't believe me. But you, you know how things sometimes get extra weird around here, right?"

Eddy took a deep breath, his fingers tapping a harsh tempo on his thigh. He didn't have time to beat around the bush, and Charlie was maxing his patience.

"Come on, out with it! I ain't got all day."

"I think a monster got her!"

"Beg pardon?"

"You heard me, Eddy, I think a monster got the vic. Under the bed there's claw marks, and brown fur. I think something hid under there and snatched her."

Eddy rolled his eyes, a huff reverberating from his barrel chest.

"Charlie, she probably has a dog."

"No, she doesn't."

"And ya know this how?"

"Well, uh, my, um, sister … well, let's just say she's really, uh, *close* to Lacy. Plus, the marks are massive, not house-dog-sized. So, unless she had a pet wolf ..."

"Did the Chief already interview Brit as a potential witness?"

"No, he doesn't even know they're acquainted."

Something like anger flashed across Eddy's eyes, a look that made Charlie subconsciously take a step back from the detective.

"Roger that. No worries, I'll talk to 'er and see what she knows."

"Come on Brit, my little honeypot, butt me."

Eddy lounged against the club's doorframe, watching the shapely blonde as she sashayed up to him. She passed him her cigarette, her doe-eyes turning accusingly on him.

"Eddy, when you gonna bust me outta here, like you promised? I hate being 'round these zozzled flappers, and my shift ended almost an hour ago …"

The burn of needle-like claws against her ribcage shushed her, and Eddy casually tapped the cigarette so that the ashes sprinkled across her hibiscus-hued Mary Janes. He pressed his claws in a little harder, just enough for her to feel them slip beneath her epidermis, and then he released her before she could cry out.

"What was that, baby cakes? You was sayin' somethin'?"

"N-no, nuthi-n' Eddy, I didn't say nuthin'."

"Attagirl Brit, that's what I thought. Go see a man about a dog, Corpse Reviver style, then we'll blouse. Now move it!"

He stuffed a crumpled dollar into her hand, noting gleefully that his prey was trembling as she broke eye contact with him. He gave her a firm shove, a chuckle slithering out of him. He had to give this one an award or something. Not many humans had been able to hide his secret for as long as he had. Too bad he had eaten her lady friend, or else he might have been able to keep Brit around awhile.

She slunk back with his drink a few minutes later, silently handing him the change. Eddy tossed the gin-infused concoction back in one gulp, his fangs scraping the polished glass as he stuffed the jingling coins in his pocket. The alcohol wouldn't affect him, but it would help get rid of the dry itchiness he felt when he stayed out of his wolf form too long.

He grabbed Brit's arm, leading her out onto the rain-splattered street. His Model T Highboy Coupe was a welcome cover from the frigid deluge, even for a nonhuman, and it didn't take long before they were cruising into the heavily wooded outskirts of the city. Soon the paved roads gave way to rut-riddled dirt, then the streetlights dwindled out. Eddy stopped about five miles out of town, killing the ignition just as the rain stopped.

"All right Britty Baby, run."

"What? Eddy, where's Lacy? You said we was gonna pick her up ..."

"Oh, that? She ain't comin'. Now run, or I'll pow ya in the kisser."

"*What!?* Were you raised in a barn or something? That ain't how yous talk to a lady!"

"Nah doll face, werewolves ain't raised in barns. We do get raised to play with our food before eating it though, so scram!"

"I ain't runnin' just for your sick pleasure! You need to be in a looney bin!"

"*Run or die.*"

Eddy leaned in; his lips close enough to Brit's that she felt the heat from his breath waft across her chin. Every syllable dripped with malice, and his eyes were a glowing topaz in the inky darkness. Gone was the gentleman who had taken her to nice restaurants, and who had handed her a dozen roses at the end of their first date. Something inside the human screamed at her to run, but her curiosity outweighed her common sense.

"Why, Eddy? Why get me to bring you the junkies to eat from the homeless shelter, just to off me? I've kept your secret, kept youse fed. I'm more valuable alive!"

"You got a little too close to the woman I loved, so you're done for. Super simple, eh? After this I'm boardin' the next train outta this podunk town, so at least you can die knowin' dear Charlie will be safe from me."

His once Sinatra-smooth voice was raspy, little flakes of skin showering down onto Brit's flower-patterned dress. Like clothing seams bursting, Eddy's skin began to rip, and out tore a monster. All she had time to take in were the six-inch fangs spouting from his gums, then everything went black as his teeth connected with her jugular.

Alanna Robertson-Webb is an up-and-coming author who enjoys long weekends of LARPing, is terrified of sharks, and finds immense fun in being the chief editor at Eerie River Publishing.

The Truth

Joel Burcat

Even a dishonest man can tell the truth. Jimmy McCarthy was a dishonest man. The nuns at St. Anne's Elementary School had drilled into his head the importance of telling the truth: *the truth will set you free*. If he would only tell the truth it might not guarantee a good day, but his afterlife would be assured. He didn't pay too much attention to what he learned at St. Anne's, but from time to time it came in handy.

He'd been wondering where he was going to get a thousand bucks to pay off some bad bets at Liberty Bell Park Racetrack and not paying too much attention to the yellow lights on Frankford Avenue, when two of Philly's finest pulled him over. He was driving his black 1964 Oldsmobile Cutlass sans license plate. He claimed he had no idea what happened to the plate and the cops, naturally, didn't believe him. Let's just say Jimmy had a little personal history with the law.

Jimmy sat in a small windowless interrogation room in a precinct house in the Kensington section of Philly. His trench coat had been thoroughly searched and now lay tossed over a chair. A large "NO SMOKING" sign was one of the few decorations in the room. It hung on a wall over a full ashtray. The room smelled of stale cigarettes, anxiety, and Clorox. The heavy wooden table in front of him had rings on top of rings, stained from coffee cups and scratches from prior occupants. Someone had scratched III twenty times. Jimmy hoped that wasn't one for each hour. Framed portraits of Mayor Rizzo and President Nixon faced him from the opposite wall.

The cops had put him in there to wait for the detectives at 9:30 in the morning and now it was eleven. They wanted to soften him up, make him sweat, so no one had so much as offered him a cup of coffee for that hour and a half. It was very impolite, but this was standard police tactics. The cops knew it, Jimmy knew it.

Thirtyish, dark hair, and clean-cut, Jimmy wore a decent lightweight striped wool suit, and the underwear, shirt, and necktie he'd worn since yesterday. He *was* sweating, but from the lack of ventilation in the room, not nerves. As he waited impatiently, he twirled his gold cufflinks, the fanciest jewelry that he owned.

At 11:05 Detectives Murphy and Angelo entered the interrogation room. Murphy carried a beat-up manila folder. A wrinkled suit hung limply from his shoulders. A white shirt and striped necktie rounded out his ensemble. It was not a *rep* tie; it was a striped tie. He also wore a scowl. That was his resting face. Always a scowl. Like his face might break if he ever smiled.

Angelo wore brown polyester pants and a blue blazer. The last time he'd been able to button the blazer was the year Nixon was inaugurated, a good three years earlier. His top shirt button was open so he could breathe. The paisley necktie escaping from under his bulbous neck sported a new spot from the drippy fried egg sandwich he'd eaten that morning. He had a pleasant enough round face, wobbly jowls, and less hair today than yesterday.

Jimmy was no choirboy, Boy Scout, angel, any of those. He had spent some quality time with Murphy and Angelo's colleagues in the past. He was kind of a utility ballplayer for a certain underclass of crook; an unkind person might say he was a low-life. Not a made man or a full member of any outfit. Although the opportunity had presented itself from time to time, to his credit he never did the rough stuff which would have speeded up his initiation, advancement, and compensation. If you needed someone to help with a job though, maybe the third or fourth guy in a crew — reliable, honest in a crooked way — then he was your man.

He knew the drill with the cops. Don't talk first and don't say anything more than you had to. He also knew it was possible there was a tape recorder hooked up to a microphone illegally recording his words. *Yo, Philly.*

Angelo spoke first. "Hey Jimmy, did you catch the Phils last night? They managed to win again. That new kid, Mike Schmidt, hit a homer. He looks like he'll be OK." Angelo smiled a big toothy smile. *OK, Angelo established he's the good cop. That means Murphy will be the bad cop.*

Jimmy nodded.

"You live in South Philly?" Angelo asked. "How come I don't see you around the neighborhood?"

Jimmy shook his head. They knew who he was, his address and police record, so no problem answering this question. "Nah, I live below South Street. South, but not all the way in South Philly."

"Let's cut the crap and get down to this," Murphy the bad cop said, swatting the folder on the table. "We got you driving around without a license plate. The only one who does that is a guy on his way to do a crime, or maybe a guy on his way *back* from doing a crime. Do you want to tell us which one it was? Save us a lot of time and we can get to lunch at a decent hour."

Jimmy made eye contact and thought for a minute. "You left out a category. The other is where some douchebag stole your plate. That's the answer behind curtain number three."

Murphy looked up at the ceiling and shook his head. "You're telling me someone *stole* your license plate?"

A few potential responses ran through Jimmy's head. *You're pretty smart for a dumb cop.* Or, *How many times did you have to repeat kindergarten at the police academy to learn that?* Finally, *Yes, I'd like to report a crime.* He decided the last alternative was both the truth and least likely to get him punched in the face.

"Yeah, I'd like to file a criminal report," Jimmy said truthfully.

"Bullshit," Murphy said. His hand slapped the folder. Angelo's face collapsed from the smile that had just started into a frown. "You took the plate off your car hoping no one would be able to report your car if they saw you driving away from a job. There was a robbery this morning. Over on Sansom Street. Isadore Silver's The King of Rings: Just Rings & Necklaces & Bracelets, Plus Other Fine Jewelry and shit. Old man Silver got a pretty good bump on the head as he entered the store at eight this morning. The crooks pushed their way in just after he disarmed the security system, tied him up, and made off with twenty thousand dollars' worth of jewelry. Some kid walking to junior high school saw the whole thing go down. He said he saw a big-assed car drive off. Same color as yours. No license plate, same as yours. Three white guys inside. That was you driving the getaway car, right?"

This was easy. Jimmy was in Fishtown this morning. He'd spent the night with his girlfriend, April, who was married to his best friend, Sean O'Brien. Sean was a salesman. They'd been friends since first grade at St. Anne's. Sean was a mean kid, rough, the opposite of Jimmy. Nevertheless, Jimmy and Sean had always been friends. Sean was somewhere down south till Friday, North Carolina or South Carolina. Jimmy couldn't remember any geography south of Baltimore.

Jimmy's marriage fell apart over a year ago. Just a few months later April called Jimmy to help her change a lightbulb while Sean was in North Carolina. April was young, thin, and pretty, with long reddish hair. It was wavy in the Irish way. He'd be delighted to help her he said, and shaved and changed his underwear and shirt before he went over. The lightbulb hung from the ceiling in their bedroom. She steadied his legs while he stood on the chair replacing the bulb, and by the time he was done screwing the fixture back into the ceiling, she was stroking his thighs. Ten minutes later, the light fixture wasn't the only thing Jimmy was screwing.

Since then, the day after Sean left on his sales trips, April would have Jimmy over for dinner. And breakfast. He happened to glance at Sean's clock radio next to the bed at 7:59 a.m., the moment he climbed on top of April for the third time since last night, so he knew exactly where he was when the crime went down.

This presented a moral dilemma for Jimmy. He and April had been doing it for months now and Sean was none the wiser. He liked the arrangement and so did April. Things were so comfortable that after he won the trifecta at Liberty Bell Park one night, he'd bought her a tiny ten-karat gold cross on a gold chain, which she loved. If Sean ever asked, Jimmy told her to be sure to say she'd found it in an old box of her communion trinkets.

If he told these cops he was with April, they'd interview her and he'd be off scot-free. Also, he had no doubt word would get back to Sean. Cops talked. He didn't want that for April. He really liked the girl and didn't want her to get into any trouble with her old man. And, although he was having fun with Sean's wife, he really didn't want to mess things up for Sean, either. They were old friends, good friends. Fishing buddies. Eventually, this thing with April would end and she'd go back to Sean full time. Have a houseful of kids. None of this should matter, he didn't do the job. He shouldn't have to put April on the spot.

Again, he went with the truth. "No. Wasn't driving any getaway car or doing any robbery. I wasn't on Sansom Street. I was still in bed at eight. It wasn't me."

Detective Angelo, his new cop friend, leaned forward. "Look Jimmy, we checked. We asked a few of your neighbors on Seventh Street and no one saw your car this morning. Someone said they thought they saw you drive off last night about five, but your car wasn't parked anywhere on your block last night or this morning. Let's make it easy on everyone and tell the truth."

Jimmy thought for a minute. He'd been in Fishtown from about five the night before until nine this morning. He'd had a little dinner and a lot of April and never left the house. His car was parked in the same place all night, on Columbia Avenue around the corner from Sean and April's row house. Some bastard stole his license plate, probably up in Fishtown while he was doing April. The truth was, he didn't do the crime.

"I wasn't on Sansom Street this morning or anytime in the past few months, I didn't do a robbery or drive a getaway car, and some dickhead stole my license plate. That's the truth."

Murphy slammed his hand onto the table loud enough that it caused the portraits of Rizzo and Nixon on the cracked wall behind him to go crooked and stay that way. "Bullshit. You did this. You drove the getaway car. You're going down for the robbery, the aggravated assault, all of it. That's ten years in Graterford. You want that? You're a frickin' moron for not telling us the truth and turning over your accomplices. We can deal on this, Jimmy, but you have to cooperate."

Jimmy knew he could clear this up in a minute, but it would cost. Jimmy scrubbed his hand down his face; he was clean-shaven since he'd used Sean's razor and Barbasol after April finally dismissed him from the bed. If he told them exactly what he'd been doing, he'd screw everything up for April and Sean. He pressed his lips together and shook his head. *I just can't do it.*

Murphy leaned his head back on the creaky wooden chair. "Let's try this. We think it's you, Jimmy. It's not like your record is squeaky clean. You've done time. Rizzo wants us to get all the scumbags off the streets and as far as we're concerned, you're a scumbag. We think you were driving the black getaway car, the one without the plate. For months now, some crew has been knocking off jewelry stores, liquor stores, corner stores, and anyone with a lot of cash all over Philly, even the Main Line. Tuesday, Wednesday, Thursday mornings. Three white guys, black getaway car, the same MO. We think Pat Donaldson hit Izzy Silver over the head. Was it Donaldson?"

Jimmy didn't know anyone named Pat Donaldson. He didn't know anyone named Don Patterson. He didn't know if the guy had committed the crime. He didn't even know if there *was* a crime. This was bullshit. He remembered something his lawyer, that shyster Feldstein, once said to him: "If all else fails, fall back on the truth."

"Not to my knowledge."

Murphy and Angelo looked at each other. Murphy nodded slowly, glancing at his partner. "We've heard that one before. So, you're saying it *was* Donaldson?"

"I'm saying I don't know."

"Uh huh," Murphy said, nodding. "I get it. Now we're getting somewhere." He made a note on his pad.

"Silver said there were two guys in the store. We're pretty sure the second guy was Shamy Duffy. We think he was the brains behind the heist. It was him, right?"

Jimmy actually *did* know Duffy. They'd grown up in the Port Richmond section of Philly and attended St. Anne's school together. A tough kid. Shamy started doing crime when he was twelve or thirteen, shoplifting. By the time he was sixteen he was stealing cars, doing burglaries and even robberies. Jimmy knew Duffy had spent some time in state prison. Jimmy had no doubt Duffy was the kind of crook who *could have* participated in this robbery, but he had no idea whether or not he did. Better not to mention him.

"Not to my knowledge," he said, shaking his head.

Murphy and Angelo nodded. Murphy, slowly, Angelo like a chicken pecking for feed. Murphy made another note on his pad. The two detectives looked at each other and Murphy's lips began to arch up into the closest thing to a smile since the Phillies beat the Brooklyn Dodgers on October 1, 1950.

"We got it. Look, Jimmy, we appreciate your help," Angelo said. "We're going to be able to put this one on the books before quitting time today, thanks to you." He looked at Murphy, who nodded at him, one tight nod. "Honestly, we don't care who was driving the getaway car. We're going to look the other way on that. This time, anyway. We wanted the brains and brawn, not the wheels."

"Like I said, I wasn't there, I was in bed, I didn't do it, I have no idea who did it."

Angelo winked at him. It was an exaggerated stage wink, the kind a third-rate actor might use in one of those vaudeville and titty theaters on Market Street.

"Yeah, yeah, we get it." He looked at Angelo and the two of them nodded to each other. "We have some good news for you," said Murphy.

"The Sansom Street Store Owners' Association authorized a twenty-five-hundred-dollar cash reward for information leading to the arrest of the crooks." Murphy said. "We appreciate your help."

Murphy opened the folder and slid an envelope across the table. Jimmy opened the envelope and could see it was full of $100 bills. He quickly riffled through the stack of money.

"There's only fifteen-hundred dollars in here. I thought you said—"

"Administrative fee," Murphy said. He slowly nodded up and down.

Angelo slowly nodded up and down.

Jimmy slowly nodded up and down. "So, what's next?" Jimmy asked.

"Thank you very much, Mr. McCarthy. We'll take it from here," Angelo said as he stood. "Sergeant Doherty will show you out."

They all shook hands and Jimmy shoved the envelope into his breast pocket. He was glad he'd been truthful. *The nuns were wrong.* He'd told the truth and it had been a good day. Doherty, entered the room. He was an expressionless cop in a uniform, potbelly, close to retirement age. He held the door for Jimmy and showed him to the exit.

Jimmy drove back to South Seventh Street and when he got to his row house, he found a spot right in front. *More good luck.* He looked at his watch. He was having dinner with April in a few hours and decided he'd take her to the track for a little dinner and a little betting. Then it would be back to Fishtown for a little April. *A good day all around.*

He held his trench coat under his arm and started walking toward his house when he heard a car door open. He turned to see a black Cadillac Coupe de Ville, vaguely similar to his car, double-parked in the street. A man stood next to the car, holding open the back door. It was his friend Sean O'Brien. He waved Jimmy toward the car with a short hand motion, just two fingers. Jimmy took a deep breath and approached.

"Yo, Jimmy," Sean said.

"Sean. I guess you got home early from North Carolina?"

"Something like that."

Jimmy noticed Sean was wearing a gold cross around his neck, April's gold cross. As Jimmy got closer, he had a hard time meeting his friend's eyes. They nodded to each other. Jimmy extended his hand toward Sean, but Sean glanced at it, then let it hang.

He looked behind the wheel and saw his old friend, Shamy Duffy. Duffy's right arm extended along the seat, his left hand on the wheel. He didn't smile, just nodded one tight nod.

"Been a few years, Shamy," Jimmy said.

"But not forgotten, it appears," Duffy replied.

"You know, the cops. I didn't tell them anything."

"Whatever." Shamy paused, then said, "Did you know that Callum Doherty is my cousin? Mother's side."

Jimmy shook his head, lifted his hands, and shrugged like he didn't know what Duffy meant.

"He's a sergeant in the Kensington precinct. I think you met him earlier today."

Jimmy blinked, but didn't reply. Sean tapped him on the shoulder and pointed to the back seat. "Get in."

Jimmy leaned into the back seat and saw a man he didn't recognize. "I assume this is Pat Donaldson," he said to Sean.

"You assumed right, friend-o," Sean said.

Jimmy continued standing, frozen, next to the open door.

"Have a seat, Jimmy. We want to take you for a little ride."

Jimmy swallowed hard. "I have to go inside the house. I have some stuff to take care of."

Duffy tilted his head so he could see out the door. "I wouldn't be worrying about that if I was you. Get in."

"Can I just check one thing?" Jimmy asked. He didn't wait for an answer, but strolled to the back of the Caddy.

He took a quick look at the rear of the car.

No plate.

Sean glared at Jimmy and pointed to the open door. Jimmy got in and was gone.

A former Philadelphian, Joel has published two environmental legal thrillers, *Drink to Every Beast* (2019) and *Amid Rage* (2021), as well as several short stories. He took Second Place in the 2020 PennWriters Novel Beginnings competition; was a quarterfinalist in 2019 for the ScreenCraft Cinematic Book Competition; received honorable mentions at the NY Festival of Books; Best General Fiction; and Readers' Favorite for Fiction-Legal Thriller. Joel was selected as the 2019 Lawyer of the Year in Environmental Litigation (for Central PA) by *Best Lawyers in America*. Burcat lives in Harrisburg, PA.

A Murder in Rabbit Town

Steve Carr

It was one of those nights. It was a night when every lowlife and desperate bunny in Rabbit Town hopped up from the bowels of the warrens and crowded the rain-soaked streets. Thugs, mugs, dolls, dames, and pickpockets huddled in the darkened storefront doorways, waiting for a break in the downpour before hightailing it to the nearest sleazy nightclub, gin joint, or dive. I didn't have time to spare to try to avoid getting my new gray wool fedora and tan trench coat wet. Anyway, as my mother always said when she used to lick my ears, unusually long even for a bunny, I wasn't made of sugar so a little water wouldn't melt me.

I'm a copper, a flatfoot, a detective, a Lepus chaser. My name is Harry Rabbit and I was looking for a bunny with an unsavory reputation who had suddenly disappeared.

The eyes of every bunny in every doorway were on me as I passed by them, splashing through the puddles with every leap. They all either knew me or knew of me. I was well-known in Rabbit Town, but loathed. Being a snitch is part of my job, but I couldn't shake that label when I was off duty. In the warrens, other rabbits didn't like sharing their burrows with a bunny who had caused their son or uncle to be sent to the slammer. I was always a private rabbit, so keeping to myself suited me just fine.

In the glare of the flashing neon signs and under the yellow orbs of light cast by streetlamps on Clover Street, I dashed into Lucky Rabbit's Tobacco Emporium, shook the rain from my trench coat, and stepped up to the counter. The heady aromas of a dozen flavors of pipe and cigar tobaccos hung in the air. Lucky was behind the counter putting freshly rolled turnip-leaf cigars in the glass case under the counter. Lucky was a scrawny rabbit with one bent ear and drooping gray whiskers. When he was younger, he spent several years in the big house for robbing a carrot store and shooting its owner, fortunately only injuring him. Murdering another rabbit was usually punishable by being fried, and no rabbit wanted to end their life in a big skillet. The time in the hoosegow had hardened him, but educated him. That was before I was even a kit. He kept his shop open late on Saturday nights to cater to the swells and gangsters who bar-hopped, had pockets loaded with moola, and liked to show off by buying expensive cigars.

"What can I do for ya, Harry?" he asked, his upper lip curled into a sneer, exposing his brown, tobacco-stained buck teeth.

"A beet-leaf cigar," I said. I reached into my coat pocket and pulled out a slice of parsnip and tossed it on the counter. "And I need some information about your pal, Whitey Rabbit. He's missing."

Lucky grabbed a cigar from a box on the shelf behind him and placed it on the counter. "What gives you the idea I'd tell you anything about Whitey?"

I picked up the cigar and rolled it between my fingers. "Because you wouldn't want to see him go to the joint and into the skillet on a bad rap for the murder of Snowy Rabbit," I said.

Lucky picked up the parsnip and put it in the cash register. He eyed me suspiciously. "What do you want to know?"

"Where was Whitey last Friday night?" I asked.

"Playin' poker in the back of Alice's Tavern," he said. "I know that 'cause I was there, too. I lost a basketful of parsnips."

I put the cigar to my nose and inhaled the sweet fragrance of dried beets. "If you're lyin' Lucky, I'll make sure you end up back in the slammer."

Lucky glared at me, locking his eyes with mine. "If you're lookin' for Whitey, go to Alice's and quit comin' to me every time you need information. I ain't a stoolie."

"Why Alice's?" I asked.

"If you don't know it already, it was where Snowy hung out. He wasn't liked by some of the rabbits who swill their carrot juice there," he explained. "Snowy had a habit of rubbing other rabbits the wrong way. He and Whitey didn't get along, but I'd bet a wheelbarrow of parsnips that Whitey didn't kill Snowy."

"I may hold you to that bet," I said.

I put the cigar in my coat pocket, turned, and hopped out of the shop. Rain fell in sheets. A fast-flowing stream ran down the street gutter carrying pieces of celery and rabbit pellets with it. I pulled the collar of my trench coat up around my neck and hopped toward the sounds of croaking toads. Alice's Tavern sat on the edge of the algae-covered pond located on the outskirts of the city. In the two years I had been a detective, I had only been to Alice's once. Its clientele was mainly the bucks on the verge of being outright down-and-outers and the does who followed them. It had little to offer the upper-class partiers in search of slum-life thrills, or the mobsters and their molls who wanted to rub elbows with the rich.

I hopped down the street as fast as I could, stopping at times only to shake the water from my tail. At first, I thought the sound of footfalls I heard behind me was coincidental, but then it became clear, they stopped when I did, and started again when I began to hop. Before leaving the last light provided by streetlamps, I stopped in front of a bookshop and pretended to peruse the used books shown in the window. After several minutes the rabbit came up to me.

"I'm sorry I was followin' ya, but you're Harry Rabbit, ain't you?" she asked.

The bunny was a pretty, albeit trashy doe. She looked as if she was wearing her maiden aunt's ratty hand-me-downs. Between her petite ears, she wore a small, red hat with a black veil, festooned with dead sparrows and berries. Rain dripped onto her rain-soaked and motheaten faux fox stole. A small red purse hung from her arm. Her lips were covered in thick fire-engine-red lipstick. She cracked her chewing gum.

"Yes, I am," I said. "Who are you?"

"I'm Beatrice Rabbit," she answered. Her voice was high-pitched and squeaky, as if she had inhaled helium. "I used to be Snowy Rabbit's girlfriend. That was before that floozy got her furry paws on him."

"What floozy?"

She looked around nervously, up the street from where we had just come, and at the stretch of dark street leading to Alice's. "I never found out her name but when I heard that Snowy had been murdered, I knew she had to have been involved one way or another." She raised the netting and stared at me with lovesick eyes. "Snowy was so good to me. Whatever I wanted, Snowy gave it to me. I had more carrots than any bunny in the burrows. That was before *she* came along." Her paw shook as she adjusted her hat. "Snowy didn't deserve ending up in the pond with his body riddled with bullets."

This dame was itchin' to get back at the doll who took her buck and she'd say anything to do it. I'd seen it a hundred times before. In almost every crime the doe who's been done wronged has been involved in some way. "Do you have any proof?"

"Proof?" she asked, gazing at me innocently. "She stole Snowy from me. Isn't that enough proof?" She wiped raindrops from her nose.

"You're just another dizzy doe," I said.

I expected tears to come next. That was the way it was with these types of does. Instead, she smacked me, right in the kisser. The surprise of it stunned me for a moment. I thought about punching her, to teach her that no bunny lays a paw on Harry Rabbit and gets away with it. But just then we heard thudding footsteps behind us. Beatrice stared at the large hare walking through the shadows cast by the streetlamps and coming toward us. She bit into her rouged lower lip, let out a small squeal, and then hopped across the street, and rushed up the sidewalk toward the heart of the city.

As the hare came closer, I recognized him as Jack Hare, a surly, short-eared Lepus with a scar across his cheek from a knife fight fought out in the cattail swamps on the far side of Rabbit Town. I knew him, but not well. Hares were a mean lot who mostly stuck to themselves, but Jack was a bit different. He was always looking for a fight with a rabbit. His black homburg hat was slanted over his forehead, hiding his black, seedy eyes.

His nose twitched. "What are ya doin' down in this neck of the woods, Harry?" he asked.

"Lookin' into the murder of Snowy Rabbit," I answered. "You know anything about it?"

In the shadow of the hat, I could see the cold glint of hatred in his eyes.

"I'm just glad someone had the good sense to knock him off," he spat. "I woulda shot him myself if he had provoked me even just a little. Jack always packed heat, and though nothing had ever been pinned on him, rumor had it that he wasn't afraid to use his gun. That doe you were just talkin' to owes a gamblin' debt to the Lepus mob over on the East End. When Snowy left her, she kept gamblin' but had no way to pay her debts."

"Why are you tellin' me this?" I asked.

"Even if she's not a Lepus, I hate seeing a doe like her get mixed up with the mob," he said. "It never ends well."

He was right. The Lepus mob meant business when it came to being owed anything, especially parsnips. I suspected that Jack was a member of the mob, but I couldn't prove it.

"Do you know the whereabouts of Whitey Rabbit?" I asked.

"Nah, but someone in Alice's might be able to tell you. He was a fixture there until Snowy was murdered."

"That's what I heard," I said. "Where ya headed?"

"I was goin' down to Alice's for a bit of juice," he replied.

"That's where I'm headin'," I said. "I'll hop along with you."

His lips curled into a sardonic smile. "No, thanks. Bein' seen goin' into Alice's with you would be like bein' asked to take poison. No decent Lepus keeps any kind of company with a flatfoot. You go first and I'll come along later."

He leaned against the building and took a cigar from his black trench coat pocket. I turned and hopped to the tavern. The red neon sign above the door winked on and off. I could hear music from the jukebox and the din of voices coming from the tavern. As I opened the door my nostrils were assaulted with the smell of fermented carrot juice. I had tried to kick the habit a few times, but even the slightest whiff of the juice immediately hooked me all over again. Some rabbits shot it into their veins. They ended up as down-and-outers begging for quick fixes in the back alleys of the city. I never got that bad. I stepped inside and every rabbit in the joint turned and glared at me. Only the two rabbits doing a tango on the small dance floor seemed unaware that a copper had walked in. The tavern was dimly lit, which hid the peeling paint and ramshackle décor.

The dozen-or-so customers sitting at the round tables quickly returned to swilling their juice. They was a motley group of petty criminals, floozies, and deadbeats. I scanned the room looking for Whitey. That's when I saw the dame sitting alone at the bar. She had legs that stretched from here to the other side of the pond and they were covered in expensive silk stockings. She wore a silver lamé dress that clung to her curvaceous body like a second skin. A long string of black pearls hung around her neck. She toyed with them as she sipped a glass of juice. Her silver purse sat on the bar.

I walked to the bar and sat on a stool two down from hers. I shook the rain from my hat and put it back on and laid my trench coat on the stool to the right of me, between us.

"I don't appreciate you comin' in here and depressin' my clientele," Bugsy Rabbit, the bartender, said.

"Knock it off and get me a juice on the rocks," I said.

After Bugsy put the glass of juice on the bar in front of me, I swirled the juice with a celery stick, making the ice tinkle. I took a sip and turned and looked at the dame.

Her eyes were on me like prison yard searchlights. She was a bunny that, from the looks of her, was born to plenty of parsnips. I'd seen plenty of dames just like her — dolls and molls that hung out in dives just to be noticed.

"Finally, I meet face-to-face with the famous Harry Rabbit," she said. You could have poured her voice over a stack of pancakes.

"I didn't catch your name," I said, and then gulped down the rest of the juice. My attraction to this doll was dangerous, and toxic. This dame could have easily turned me into a carrot juice junkie.

"Pufftail Bunny," she said. She sipped from her glass, adding glossy pink lipstick to what already ringed it. "What brings you here tonight, Harry?" she asked.

"I'm lookin' for a guy named Whitey Rabbit," I said. "You heard of him?"

She nibbled on the celery stick. "Yeah, I've met him here once or twice. What has he done?"

"He's been missing since Snowy White's murder was discovered."

The door to the tavern opened and Jack hopped in. His entrance caused a wave of hushed whispers among the rabbit patrons. He hopped across the tavern and sat down on the stool to the left of me. He placed a paw full of parsnip slices on the bar and said, "Give me a double juice with a mint chaser and keep 'em comin', barkeep."

Bugsy scooped up the slices and a moment later put a glass with juice in it and a second glass of green fermented mint next to it. The aroma of the mint wafted in my direction. I never liked the stuff; it was too strong for my tastes, but was a popular drink among the Lepus.

I turned my attention back to the dame. She was running her paw up and down her pearls like she was playing some kind of musical instrument. Dames like her displayed their jewelry the same way rabbits who were combat veterans displayed their medals. Dolls with jewels rarely spent time roosted on a bar stool in Alice's.

"Where were we?" I asked.

"You said something about Snowy Rabbit's murder," she said.

"Did you know him?" I asked.

She straightened the seam in her left stocking. She coulda had her gams insured for a million parsnips. "Yeah, I knew him. He was one helluva great rabbit. He didn't deserve to die that way."

The tone in her voice was a mixture of fire and ice. My thoughts of making kits with this dame had blinded me to who she was. There was no doubt in my mind that this was the dame Beatrice told me about.

"You were Snowy's squeeze, weren't you!" I said accusatorily.

Her eyes turned cold, as if they had been replaced with ice cubes. "It wasn't like that with Snowy. I loved the guy and that weasel Whitey murdered him 'cause he wanted me himself. I would shoot him and throw his body in the pond, just like he did with Snowy, all over again if I could."

The sudden surprised expression on her face revealed her awareness that she had accidentally confessed to the murder of Whitey Rabbit.

I flashed my badge. "You're under arrest for the murder of Whitey Rabbit," I said.

"No copper is going to take me to the stony lonesome to be fried in a skillet," she snarled.

As I bent over to get my gun from my trench coat, she opened her purse and took out a Smith and Wesson and aimed it at me. I lurched at her just as she fired the gun. The bullet missed me but hit Jack in the throat. He fell from his stool onto the dirty floor where he died, his legs twitching until his final breath. I wrestled the gun from her paw and turned it on her.

"Put me out of my misery and shoot me," she begged.

I took the cigar from my trench coat and put it in my mouth. "Sorry, sister," I said. "I'm not a judge or jury. I'm just a rabbit who's a cop doin' his job."

Steve Carr, from Richmond, Virginia, has had over 430 short stories published internationally in print and online magazines, literary journals, reviews, and anthologies since June 2016. He has had seven collections of his short stories, *Sand, Rain, Heat, The Tales of Talker Knock, 50 Short Stories: The Very Best of Steve Carr, LGBTQ: 33 Stories,* and *The Theory of Existence: 50 Short Stories,* published. His paranormal/horror novel *Redbird* was released in November 2019. His plays have been produced in several states in the U.S. He has been nominated for a Pushcart Prize twice. His Twitter is @carrsteven960.

https://www.stevecarr960.com/

https://www.facebook.com/steven.carr.35977.

"A Murder in Rabbit Town" previously appeared in *The World of Myth.*

Eerie Justice

Joe Giordano

Had Sammy already crushed the car, we might've never known.

"The economy's in the crapper and scrap metal prices aren't paying the rent."

That was Sammy's lament as we trudged around his junkyard just past dawn on Monday. We'd been best friends since kids in East New York, and I was contemplating some face-saving way I could stuff cash into his pocket. My name's Bragg, and I'm a gold-shield homicide detective. I'd stopped by Sammy's before heading to Brooklyn South.

"Is that a new arrival?" I pointed to a 1959 faded-red Impala with a grimy white vinyl top.

"Left outside my gate last night," he said. "According to the VIN, the car hasn't been registered for decades. It's dirty but in decent shape. This baby sat under cover, maybe in a garage for quite some time. If I had the money, I'd invest in restoration."

"What will you do with it?"

"Probably crush and sell it for scrap. Why? You interested?"

"I wouldn't pay you more than a thousand."

Sammy smirked. "Since when did you become stupid with your money?"

I reddened. He'd seen through my clumsy attempt to overpay. I tried to recover. "Once she's fixed up, I'll make my investment ten times over."

"Bullshit. What's up?"

We neared the Impala, and I was saved from answering Sammy's question by an all-too-familiar odor.

Sammy's nose crinkled, and he took a half-step back. "What the hell is that?"

"Pop the trunk," I said.

Sammy pried the lid open with a crowbar, and the stench of death hit me like a liver punch.

"Shit." Sammy's eyes grew wide as hub caps.

I lifted the black Burberry trench coat partially covering the body. "Late-twenties male, as best as I can tell." I called my lieutenant.

My caseload overflowed, but I wanted to protect Sammy from possible blowback, so I kept myself apprised when Lieutenant Dixon assigned the murder to other detectives. The double gunshot victim's name was Gabriel Turner. The detectives arrived at Turner's apartment before noon and found Richard Grant lying on a sofa, needing to shake him awake from a deep sleep. He claimed he'd never met Turner, had been drugged, and had no memory of the previous twenty-four hours.

A glass with roofie traces sat on an end table. The .38 revolver murder weapon lay on the sofa next to him. He tested positive for gunshot residue on his hand and was arrested. The coroner's report said the victim carried the AIDS virus.

The Trench Coat Chronicles

The prosecutor argued Grant killed Turner to avoid a date-rape and the jury convicted him of manslaughter. At the trial, a couple of former girlfriends testified he wasn't gay, which raised my doubts about motive. A month after his conviction, he hung himself in his cell.

When I approached one of the arresting detectives, a grizzled thirty-year veteran, he gave me the standard line. "If murderers were Rhodes Scholars, we wouldn't catch them."

"Why would Grant hook up with Turner if he wasn't gay?"

The detective wheezed with impatience. "The case is closed, and I have other murders to solve."

The Impala had been wiped clean of fingerprints. After considerable digging, I discovered the last registered owner had a grandson, Simon Fester. But the owner hadn't written a will to tell me who inherited the Impala. I found Fester in the Iron Rabbit bar. He was blond, sinewy, and in his forties. I flashed my shield and asked if he knew Richard Grant.

"Shame about his suicide," he said casually.

"Tell me about him."

"Always cheerful." Fester's lips curled into a sneer. "I found naïve his refusal to see the putrefaction of human nature. I suppose prison cured him of that."

"How close were you two?"

"We'd been intimate once as teenage boys. He never showed interest in a repeat performance."

"You felt rejected?"

"I admit to jealously observing his bevy of bimbettes."

"But you remained friends?"

"Richard insisted on nicknaming me 'buddy-boy.' Infuriating. My name's Simon, never Sy, and certainly not buddy-boy. Although I frowned at his greeting, Richard persisted."

Fester's clothes seemed a size too large for him. His forehead glistened, and he had a persistent cough.

I said, "You look feverish. Are you well?"

"I won't lie to the police. One unprotected liaison doomed me. I should've suspected that cherub-looking innocence masked poison under the skin. When the doctor diagnosed me with AIDS, I stopped listening and came here. I drink, but don't enjoy, Glenfiddich thirty-year-old single malt Scotch. I resolved to empty my bank account before I left this life as a drooling skeleton, ignored by an indifferent hospice staff."

That sounded like motive. "Were you infected by a cherub named Gabriel Turner?"

Fester didn't hesitate. "Who?"

"Did you consider taking revenge on the man who gave you AIDS?"

"Don't be melodramatic. Have a Scotch, on me."

I waved off the tattooed barmaid and left.

The snub-nosed .38 used in Turner's killing had no registered owner. I suspected gang origins and tracked down likely sellers. Without admitting the sale, one remembered "a White dude." He shrugged at photographs of Richard Grant, Gabriel Turner, and Simon Fester.

The next time I approached Fester at the Iron Rabbit, he appeared upbeat.

"My doctor proscribed a cocktail of three antiretroviral drugs. The disease hasn't worsened, and the chance I'll pass AIDS onto my partners has been minimized. I've stepped into the sunlight."

I grunted, then confronted him. "I'm investigating the revolver used in Turner's murder. Will you be identified as the purchaser?"

"Gang bangers are such unreliable witnesses," he said in a vague tone.

"Did I say the gun was purchased from a drug dealer?"

"Where else would one find an untraceable pistol?"

Every word he spoke supported my suspicion of him. "You've thought about this."

"I'm being logical."

"What happened to your grandfather's red Impala?"

Fester smirked. "Granddad died twenty years ago."

"Turner was found in the trunk of your grandfather's car."

Fester displayed mock surprise. "What an amazing coincidence."

Prick. My face got hot, and my tone turned edgy. "You think you're clever."

Fester responded coolly. "Richard Grant was convicted of Turner's murder. Why are you harassing me about a closed case? Don't you have other murders to solve?"

I huffed in frustration. "I'm keeping my eye on you."

Fester called the barmaid for another shot of Glenfiddich. "Are you sure you won't have a drink?"

I walked away.

That afternoon, Lieutenant Dixon called me into his office. An African American with closely cropped gray hair. Bosses are never wonderful, but he was better than most.

"Simon Fester launched an official harassment complaint against you," he said.

"I'm sure he killed Gabriel Turner and framed Richard Grant for the murder."

His eyebrows rose. "You have concrete evidence?"

I blew out an exasperated breath.

"Stay away from him," he said, waving me out of his office.

I poured over the Turner file searching for a basis to reopen the case. Too often I'd worked homicides where I never discovered the murderer. Here, two men had been victims and I couldn't touch the perp. I wanted to punch walls.

I disobeyed Dixon and saw Fester at the Iron Rabbit.

He looked surprised to see me. "Must I report you again?"

I smiled benignly. "I'm here to congratulate you for pulling off the perfect murder."

"You're a stuck record."

"Seriously, you've stumped me, and that doesn't happen often. Perhaps you're in a good enough mood to tell me how you did it?"

"Whatever do you mean?"

"You killed Turner and framed Grant. Doing something amazing is more fun when you share. And, the opportunity to admit what you did to a homicide detective who can't do a thing with the information would be sweet irony."

Fester smirked. "Would you like me to speak into the microphone?"

I unbuttoned my blue dress shirt. "Check. I'm not wearing a wire. Anyway, Grant was convicted of Turner's murder. The case is closed, and thanks to you, my boss is on my ass."

Fester mused. "I might be willing to conjecture, hypothetically."

"Everything's off the record."

He chuckled. "You're right. I'm dying to tell somebody."

"I'll take that Scotch now."

Fester waved to the barmaid, and she poured me a double. He began his story.

"New York's gun laws are draconian, so of course, I had no problem obtaining a revolver in the neighborhood where drugs are plentiful. Crack cocaine and guns go together like rice and beans. I arranged another tryst with Gabriel, this time inside his seedy apartment next to an El. I'd stepped inside, and he was on me, but I held him off until I heard the roar of a passing train. At the sight of the pistol, Gabriel blanched. I relished his fear. I had to fire just a single shot. I was proud of that."

I did my best to keep my face impassive, silently willing him to keep talking, which he did.

"I'd arranged for Richard to meet me in my condo. A welcoming Scotch and soda with a 'roofie' kicker quickly put him into a pliable condition. I thought to rape him, but my nervous excitement left me unable to perform, so I half carried him to my grandfather's Impala. I'd kept the car in a barn on property I own upstate. I drove across town, then helped him into Gabriel's apartment. I pressed the murder weapon into his hand, had him trigger a second shot, then left him in a slumbering state. I managed to drag Gabriel into the trunk of the Impala and left the car at a junkyard."

Fester had admitted to murder, but I had no witnesses and didn't record his admission. I continued to listen, wondering how I could bring this bastard to justice.

Fester sipped his Scotch before continuing. "Richard's incarceration went badly. The time I visited him, he'd been sodomized. When he said I was his one true friend, I revealed what I'd done to him. He aged twenty years before my eyes. Sad, the choice he made. He could've loved me and thrived."

Fester's arrogance and the double Scotch raised the heat on my neck and face.

Over my shoulder, I heard, "Cheerio, buddy-boy."

Grant's greeting of Fester.

I snapped my head around but saw only the crowd of revelers, talking and laughing. My imagination?

Someone playing a bad joke? Fester appeared not to have heard.

Later, patrons told detectives I was standing, facing Fester, when the retort of a single pistol shot shocked the crowd silent. Fester doubled over like he'd been gut-punched, then crumpled to the floor as his life bled away.

Gray smoke had billowed and stung my nostrils. I finished my Scotch before calling an ambulance.

Although the .38 revolver used to murder Gabriel Turner was missing from the evidence room, the bullet that killed Simon Fester had been mangled beyond the ability for ballistics to identify the weapon. Everyone at the Iron Rabbit heard the gunshot, some witnessed Fester collapsing, but no one saw the murderer fire the pistol. The detectives assigned to the case interviewed me without conclusion.

When Lieutenant Dixon heard I was with Fester when he was murdered, he waved me into his office and closed the door.

"I gave you an order to avoid Fester."

"Before he died, he confessed to killing Turner and framing Grant."

"What were his motives?"

"Turner gave him AIDS. Grant was an unrequited love."

Dixon nodded. "You have a witness to the conversation?"

"Only me."

"You recorded everything?"

I shrugged. "If I wore a wire, he wouldn't have spilled."

"The .38 that killed Turner is missing. Know anything about that?"

I produced the revolver from my jacket pocket and clunked the gun onto his desk. "I forgot to sign the weapon out of evidence. Sorry."

Dixon stared at me before he picked up the pistol and smelled the barrel.

"Hasn't been fired recently," I said.

"You intended to shoot Fester?" he asked.

"If I had, someone else saved me the trouble."

"Who do you think killed him?"

"Moments before he was shot, someone over my shoulder called out, 'Buddy-boy,' a nickname Grant had for Fester that he hated."

"Grant's dead."

"Maybe you want to exhume the body to be sure."

Dixon grimaced. "Besides him, any other ideas for suspects?"

I shook my head.

He blew out a long breath. "Of course, if you did shoot Fester, you wouldn't have used the .38 you lifted from evidence."

"I'd be happy to submit to a gunshot residue test."

"Too late for that. You've washed up."

"Anything else?" I asked.

He slowly shook his head.

As I rose to leave, he said, "Bragg, I'm placing a disciplinary note in your file. This isn't baseball; one more strike and you're out."

I slept fine that night.

Joe Giordano's stories have appeared in more than one hundred magazines. His novels, *Birds of Passage, An Italian Immigrant Coming of Age Story*, (2015) and *Appointment with ISIL*, (2017) were published by Harvard Square Editions. Rogue Phoenix Press published his third novel, *Drone Strike* (2019). Read the first chapter at http://joe-giordano.com.

Miss Pinafore versus the Creeper

Tony Conaway

Waving her knives in the air, the girl was dancing around the corpse of the man she'd killed. Naked.

No, let me start again. I'll have to write up an official report in a few hours, so I'd better describe the scene in a way that will hold up in court. And I have to stop calling her a *girl*. Her rap sheet says she's 24 years old. She just *pretends* to be an innocent young girl. It puts people off their guard, before she kills them. It's helped her skate several convictions. She sits there in court, lower lip trembling, looking innocent as can be. Juries find her not guilty. So, she goes free to kill again.

She's not a girl. She's a homicidal maniac. An assassin-for-hire.

This is how my report will read, thus far:

Subsequent to the rumor that Francis Angelo Ottomanelli had fallen out of favor with his mob bosses, we decided to surveil him in the hope of getting him to turn state's evidence. I took the evening shift, alone, on June 3, 1943, at his residence on 35221 Mulholland. Reports indicated that Ottomanelli had sent his wife and children away.

(Presumably for their own safety, although I don't put speculation in a police report.)

At 9:10 p.m., I witnessed Ottomanelli driving away in a late-model black Packard sedan. I followed in my vehicle. He parked in a downscale neighborhood on Sunset Boulevard near Gardner Street and entered the adjacent hotel. (Check street address.) *I parked down the block and waited several minutes so as not to be seen, then followed, trying to stay out of sight.*

The structure is known as the Greylock Hotel, although most of its neon signage is burned out. Currently, its only working neon reads "at popular prices." The name of the hotel and the word "rooms" are burned out.

The time was 10:04 p.m. when I entered the hotel.

(I won't report that I started breathing hard just going up the six steps into the entrance of the hotel. I should've retired months ago. But there's a war on, and half the young guys on the force have enlisted. The chief asked old guys like me to keep working as long as we can.)

The only occupant of the small, rundown lobby was a man approximately 60 years old, behind the front desk. I showed him my badge and asked about the man who had just entered. He was cooperative, stating that Ottomanelli had rented Room 34. After searching through a drawer for a few minutes he found a master key and handed it to me. He also said that Ottomanelli had met a short blonde girl who had been waiting for him in the lobby. The man had never seen the girl before, but said she appeared to be underage. That gave me probable cause to enter Room 34 without knocking.

Several prostitutes and their johns started coming down the narrow steps; there was no elevator at this hotel. I had to wait for them to clear the stairway before I could venture up to Ottomanelli's room. Neither Ottomanelli nor anyone fitting the description of the underage prostitute came down the steps. Which brings me up to date: I opened the door to find

Ottomanelli dead and the woman dancing around his corpse, nude.

I drew my gun as she turned around. I'm a foot-and-a-half taller and have over a hundred pounds on her, but I'm not as agile as I used to be. Or as fast. She looked like the sort who could outrun me with ease. Plus, she had a knife in each hand.

I identified myself and ordered her to drop her knives.

She cursed, but complied, dropping the knives at her feet.

For a long moment, we stood there in silence, eyeballing each other. I'm used to stares. It's not just my height. I'm the ugliest guy on the force.

Even though I was old enough to be her father (or her grandfather), it was hard not to stare at her naked form. Dressed, she looked like just a cute kid. Naked … well, most male police would stare. And make some lewd comment. Probably some line about the carpet not matching the drapes.

Me, I try to keep things professional.

I moved closer to her and kicked the knives away.

"A big man like you," she said. "And you're scared of little ol' me?"

"I'm sure a lot of men have underestimated you. Including him." I nodded toward the corpse. "You know who that is? Was?"

"Sure. Ottomanelli. 'The Little Turk,' his name means. Which is an odd name for an Italian mobster, don't cha think?"

"You always dance naked around your victims?"

She shrugged. "I'm just trying to dry off. He bled like a stuck pig. I had to wash the blood off my clothes. And my body." She caressed herself to emphasize the point.

"You're a piece of work all right," I said. I stepped back and took in the small room. There was a sink but no toilet or bathtub—no doubt there was a shared bath down the hall. There was one small hand towel provided by the hotel, now dripping wet. Her wet clothes, no doubt washed in the sink, were spread around the sparse furniture in the room.

"Well. If we're not going to have any fun, do you mind if I get dressed? Or are you planning to march me down to the precinct in the altogether?"

Slowly, I took off my trench coat. I was careful to keep my gun aimed at her, first in my right hand, then in my left. I emptied my coat pockets onto a wobbly end table, then tossed the coat at her feet.

"Your clothes are evidence. I'm sure there's some blood still on them. Besides, they're wet. They'll loan you some clothes at the precinct. For now, put on my trench coat."

She smiled. "But it's SOOO big," she said. When I didn't respond, she turned around, making sure I got a good look at her backside as she bent from the waist to pick it up.

When I wore it, the coat only came down to my knee. The hem dragged on the floor when she put it on, but at least she was dressed now. She gathered up the loose fabric and belted it tight.

I picked up my handcuffs from the end table. "Hands out in front of you."

"You're no fun," she pouted. Her wrists were so slender that the cuffs barely locked on them.

"That's right, Miss Pinafore." She had lots of aliases, but that's what we called her, after the little-girl romper she usually wore. There was one drying on top of the radiator right now. "No fun at all. Let's go."

I locked the door behind us. Ottomanelli wasn't going anywhere. Aside from being with the mob, he must have gone up to that room with Miss Pinafore thinking she was just another underage prostitute. I'd shed no tears for him.

We walked down the stairs, three flights. The steps creaked under my weight. Barefoot, her footsteps made no sound at all.

Angry that she couldn't seduce me, she tried to insult me instead. "Look at you. You're a monster. You have no appreciation of beauty at all."

I should've saved my breath for the stairs, but I responded anyway. "Believe it or not, I was good looking once. I was damn handsome when I got sent to France to fight in the Big One. But I got gassed by the Krauts. The docs say the mustard gas triggered my acromegaly, but who knows? None of the other guys who were gassed got it."

"Acro-what?"

"Acromegaly. I was fully grown, but after the war, I started growing again. Another six inches in height. My forehead, my jaw, my nose … they all got huge. Distorted."

"Boohoo. The war made you into a monster. So what?"

"I'm just saying, I know what it's like to be pretty. In high school, I was voted 'Most Handsome.'"

I was breathing hard now. I covered it with a cough. "Looks don't make you a good person, or bad." Soon I'd be gasping for air, but we were almost down to the lobby. "And lady, you are as bad as they come."

"Just wait and see. It's your word against mine. I'll talk in my little-girl voice and deny everything you say. No one ever convicts me."

"That's the job of the D.A. Not me." But her fingerprints on the knives, and Ottomanelli's blood on her clothes — that should go a long way with the jury.

She must have been thinking the same thing. As we reached the lobby, I saw her glancing around, looking for an escape route. To make sure she didn't bolt, I marched her over to a radiator. I undid one of her handcuffs and cuffed her to the radiator. It was a warm June night, and the radiators had been shut off — she wouldn't get burned.

The desk clerk was staring, goggle-eyed. I called the local precinct from his desk phone — there had been no phone in the hotel room. This neighborhood was under the jurisdiction of the Hollywood Division. As a detective, I work out of the Central Division, but a collar was supposed to go to the precinct in which the perp was arrested. I also phoned Central and informed them about Ottomanelli. I reminded them to call off the stakeout in front of Ottomanelli's home. You'd think they could figure that out for themselves, but you never know.

Then we waited for the local cops to arrive. She kept silent, staring daggers at me.

I used the time to interrogate the clerk. Yes, she was the girl who went up with Ottomanelli to Room 34. Ottomanelli had signed the register as "Bob Smith." He had been here several times, with several young prostitutes. No, he'd never seen this girl before. She'd arrived just before Ottomanelli did. As far as he knew, there were no other witnesses. Since he was sitting at a desk with pen and paper, I had him write it all out.

Then I sat and listened to the lobby clock tick its way toward midnight. Idly, I ran my tongue over my teeth. Since my jaw had grown so large, there are spaces between most of my lower teeth. And, as if the constant pain in my joints weren't enough, I felt one of my headaches coming on.

Surprisingly, the coroner and the police photographer arrived before the cops. I handed them the master key and told them where to find Ottomanelli's body. A radio car with two uniforms pulled up shortly after.

I introduced myself, which was probably unnecessary. There's no one else on the Los Angeles Police Department who looks remotely like me. Even if they haven't met me, they've heard of me.

The older of the two did the talking. "Sorry it took so long, Detective Hatton. It's a busy night."

The coroner's van arrived with two men to take the body to the morgue. They propped open the hotel's front door to make it easier to carry the body out.

I was feeling lousy and would've been happy to have the local police take Miss Pinafore off my hands. But through the open front door we heard a call come in over the police radio. The younger cop ran outside to answer. The older one followed.

He returned shortly. "Sorry, Detective. There's a riot on Main Street. Them Mexican Zoot Suit punks. The ones what call themselves *pachucos*. They're fighting with some sailors. We gotta go."

"Can't you drop the perp off at your precinct before you head over there?"

"No can do. Me and my partner, we're with the Vengeance Squad. On duty or off, when they call, we go bust heads. You'll have to take her in yourself." He exited the hotel, and I heard their radio car roar away.

Vengeance Squad. It was strictly an informal designation, of course. Whenever Mexicans, or Blacks, or Filipinos got out of line, the Vengeance Squad put them in their place. That's the way we do things in the City of Angels.

I let the coroner and the photographer know I was leaving, and uncuffed my collar from the radiator.

"Taking me home to introduce me to Mother, Detective?"

"Shut up. I'm taking you to the local precinct, and then you won't see me again until your trial. Although I may come to witness your execution."

That made her laugh. "They won't even convict me, let alone execute me!"

I thought about cuffing her to my wrist but decided to put both cuffs on her instead. I'd need both hands free to drive her to the precinct. Instead, I held the chain between her handcuffs.

My head pounded with each step down the stairs in front of the hotel. At the bottom, it took me a moment to recall where I'd parked my car. I finally remembered that I parked in front of a half-demolished brick building. Earthquakes are tough on masonry structures — they don't sway like wood houses or steel skyscrapers. They just crumble.

Despite the hour, the sidewalks were filled with people. Was it because of the riot? The sooner I could get us into my car, the better.

"This way," I said.

She'd been cooperative since I'd cuffed her, but now she resisted with every step. "NO!" she screamed in her little-girl voice. "Let me go! Somebody, please help. He's kidnapping me!"

Passersby all turned to look at us. This wasn't good.

"Help, please. He's a monster!"

"Hey," said a man. "Let the little girl go."

I pulled out my badge. "I'm a police officer. Don't interfere."

But my looks spoke louder than my badge. For that matter, my badge looked like a toy in my gigantic hand.

"He's too ugly to be a cop!"

"What's that creep doing?"

A woman moaned, "Someone help that poor girl."

There were a half-dozen sailors ahead, right near my car. If I had any hope that they might assist me, that was soon dashed.

"Oh, help me, help me, please," my prisoner sobbed. The sailors surrounded us.

One of them punched me from behind. Another tried to pull my prisoner away.

"Back off! I'm a—"

I never finished that sentence. Some of the sailors picked up bricks from the demolition site and thew them. One hit another sailor, who fell. But one hit me square in the mouth. I felt at least one tooth come loose. But I held onto my prisoner. With my free arm, I covered my face to shield it from bricks.

My prisoner pressed up against me. For protection from bricks, I assumed.

I was wrong. She took my gun out of its belt holster and gut-shot me, point blank. I fell.

"Back off," said Miss Pinafore. She punctuated that by firing a few rounds into the air.

I heard, rather than saw, the sidewalk empty of pedestrians. I spat out blood and at least one tooth.

Then I felt her searching my pockets. She found my wallet. "Good," she said. "I need cab fare."

While she took the cash out of my wallet, I managed to extract my handcuff key from the small watch pocket where I kept it. "Looking for this?" I wheezed.

Then I tossed the key down an adjacent sewer grate.

"Bastard," she said. Then she shot me again. I passed out.

I must have been out for only a minute or two. I looked around. The sidewalk, alive just moments ago, was deserted. It was after midnight, and the only place that seemed open nearby was the hotel we'd just left. It was less than a block away.

I couldn't seem to stand, so I dragged myself on my backside toward the hotel. It was agony, but I'd become used to pain in the past few years.

A few people walked by, studiously ignoring me. I didn't have the extra breath to cry out for help.

I managed to stand upright at the stairs to the hotel. My legs weren't working right, so I hoisted myself from step to step by pulling myself along the railing.

My strength gave out before I could ascend the top step. I sat heavily and looked out from my new vantage point. A smear of blood and other fluids marked my progress from a block away. More blood trickled from my body down the stairs. I'd survived the Great War and dozens of bad situations as a cop. But I realized that this time I wasn't going to make it out alive.

From my perch, I could see a few blocks down the road. Someone in a trench coat had just hailed a cab. I had no idea if it was my prisoner or not.

"Former prisoner," I corrected myself. My head seemed too heavy to keep upright. I lay back, looking up at the half-lit neon sign. I couldn't recall what the burnt-out portion said.

"At popular prices," I whispered. "Death at popular prices.

Author's Note:

The protagonist of this story is inspired by Rondo Hatton, a bit player in Hollywood in the 1930s and 1940s. He was billed as "The Creeper" and "The Ugliest Man Alive" due to his acromegaly-distorted features. Although the movie studios blamed his condition on his being gassed in World War I, today we know that the condition is usually caused by a tumor on the pituitary gland.

The Zoot-Suit Riots and the L.A.P.D.'s "Vengeance Squad" are also based in fact.

Tony Conaway has cowritten nonfiction books for such publishers as Macmillan, Prentice Hall and McGraw-Hill. His fiction has been published in many magazines and anthologies. His odder work includes cowriting the script for a planetarium production and selling jokes to Jay Leno that were performed on *The Tonight Show*. Connect with him on Facebook, Too.Hip.For.The.Room.

The Trunk

Frank Kozusko

The telegram was in my mailbox when I returned from the country club.

> *January 6, 1960*
> *Jake,*
> *Need help. Son arrested for murder.*
> *Please call 415-Klondike 5-1019.*
> *Patti*

Patti had been my secretary when I was a private eye in San Francisco until I retired in 1955. Since then we had only communicated by Christmas cards.

My business, Jake Malloy Investigating, had been small but enough to keep me and Patti out of the poor house, she, a woman alone with a son to raise. I did a lot of divorce work, getting the goods on wayward spouses. I'd track down a "missing" person, maybe a guy hiding from alimony payments. The best money came if I were lucky enough to get a wealthy client in a murder case. Those were few but kept bread on the table between the snooping jobs.

I got really lucky when I snagged a case working for a rich old dame accused of making herself a widow, with the help of a little poison. She knew her husband was having an affair but wouldn't spill to the cops and give them a motive. Money couldn't be used as a reason; all the dough was hers. The widow's attorney, Lloyd Bentner, knew my rep and asked me to look into things. It didn't take long to find that her husband's side-squeeze had a jealous ex-boyfriend who had purchased the same poison that had done the job. The widow got off and the ex-boyfriend got 25 to life in Folsom.

Whaddya know, the grateful widow, having no living relatives, changed her will and left me her entire fortune. I gave Patti a good-sized pile of money and retired to Palm Springs for the California sun. Now I give tennis lessons and provide other services to wealthy divorcees and widows.

When Patti answered, her voice was so weak that I didn't recognize it.

"Patti, this is Jake. What happened with Tommy?"

"Oh, Jake, thanks so much for calling," she replied, her voice quivering. "It's awful. They found his girlfriend's body in a trunk that had washed up on Alcatraz Island. The police know about the big fight Tommy and Laura had the night before. They charged him with murder. He's in the San Francisco County prison. I couldn't afford the bail."

"OK, Patti. I'll take care of this. Just be patient. I'll make a few phone calls then I'll get up there."

"Thanks, Jake. Please hurry," replied Patti before hanging up.

Tommy needed a good lawyer. I decided to call Bentner since he had been smart enough to hire me. He agreed to take Tommy's case and work on busting him out on bail.

I made a few other calls to cancel my upcoming appointments. The ladies would just have to do without me for a while. I'd miss them, too.

It was a nine-hour drive from the warm desert sunshine of Palms Springs in January to the bone-chilling dampness of Frisco. I'd have to ditch my golf shirts and Bermuda shorts.

I found some old suits hanging in the spare bedroom closet. They'd do. More importantly, stored there in a sealed bag, was *de rigueur* for a private dick: my double-breasted khaki trench coat with button-down epaulets. I tried it on, tightening the belt. My fedora, which had been hibernating in a hatbox on the top shelf, completed the look. Admiring myself in the long mirror on the back of the door, I put my hand to the tip of my hat and gave my reflection a salute. I was back in business.

Patti had used most of her windfall to purchase a new cookie cutter bungalow in the Sunset District. By the time I arrived, Tommy was there, out on bail. Patti gave me a big, tearful hug. It was a handshake for 19-year-old Tommy. Patti made coffee and we sat down for a parley.

Tommy explained how he had met Laura, an older woman of thirty-four, in North Beach. North Beach was the notorious center of gangster activity in Frisco. Recently, it had been drawing members of the Beat Generation to the new poetry/coffeehouses that had sprung up. Tommy, sporting a scraggly beard and long hair, worked the docks by day and spent his evenings as a beatnik at the Bitter Beat Cafe. He and Laura had been living together for a couple of months before they had the big argument in the coffeehouse. Laura told him to get his stuff out of her apartment before her shift was over. Tommy said he went back to Laura's place, gathered his things and spent the night at his mother's. The next morning, they found Laura's body in a trunk on the rocks of Alcatraz. Tommy had no idea who would want to harm Laura.

I assured them that I would get on the case immediately and advised Tommy not to talk with anyone but his lawyer.

I checked into the Mark Hopkins Hotel atop Nob Hill — great views of the city and the bay. I had lived in some dumps when I was last in Frisco. Now I had the bucks to live high on the hog.

$$\text{\Large ✗ ✗ ✗ ✗ ✗}$$

I still had connections at the San Francisco PD and found that my old friend Mike Farrell was handling Tommy's case. He was a straight-up guy, only interested in getting at the truth, and let me in on what he had, including photos of the trunk with the fully clothed corpse.

Farrell pointed to her Bitter Beat necklace adding, "That's how we ID'd her so fast."

The coroner's preliminary report concluded that the cause of death was manual strangulation, no signs of sexual assault. Farrell claimed the trunk belonged to Tommy. Farrell's theory was that Tommy was waiting for Laura at her apartment when she got home from work. Their argument continued and got violent. Tommy strangled her, then put her body in the trunk. According to Farrell, Tommy dumped the trunk off the Embarcadero pier where he worked.

"Doesn't sound like you have any evidence against Tommy," I challenged Farrell.

"His fingerprints are all over the trunk," replied Farrell.

"Well, if it's his trunk," I shrugged. "Say, what about his car? Did you check it? Find anything?"

"Yeah, we checked it. Nothing."

The way I saw it, the cops had a flimsy, circumstantial case. But I wasn't about to argue with Farrell; the lawyer could handle that. I needed to keep friendly faced with Farrell.

Well, even the most inexperienced gumshoe would know: You gotta go to the scene of the crime. Farrell agreed to take me to Laura's apartment.

✸ ✸ ✸ ✸ ✸

Laura had a one-bedroom apartment in an upscale building a few blocks from the Bitter Beat. Farrell opened the door and we did the limbo under the crime scene tape. The place was a mess, as if there had been a knock-down-drag-out fight. Sure, but I had a different take; it also looked like someone had been searching for something. I kept that thought to myself. My job was to find evidence to clear Tommy. If I solved the case that was OK, too.

When we got back to the stationhouse, I asked Farrell if he could get me to Alcatraz. Farrell grinned and nodded. "Sure. Anything for you, Jake."

The Trench Coat Chronicles

Alcatraz Island, one mile out into the San Francisco Bay, was occupied by the federal penitentiary: The Rock, The Big House. I got a chilly ride on a supply boat, buttoning up the collar on my trench coat. The guards were ready for me and escorted me down to the water's edge, and the spot marked with yellow paint on the rocks. That gave me just the info I needed. I spent the war in the Coast Guard, sailing in and out of the bay. I knew the tides well.

After another cold boat ride, I was back in my car with the heat on, racking my noggin to come up with a theory. Judging from the wet rocks, the trunk had washed up about an hour after high tide hit, which, according to the newspaper, was 6:24 a.m. No doubt, the real culprit (I was still assuming Tommy was innocent) would have deep-sixed the trunk on the outgoing tide and in the dark. I figured the trunk had been in the water less than an hour traveling with the currents at an average speed of about two miles per hour. That speed and distance, and my knowledge of the direction of the tidal flow led me to one place: the piers at North Beach, not Tommy's Embarcadero pier the cops liked for the launch of the trunk.

I called Bentner and asked him to find an oceanographer to work up the actual numbers. We anticipated the evidence would point to the trunk entering the water when Tommy was back at Patti's. Since an alibi provided by mama is always suspect, I needed to keep investigating and follow the North Beach lead.

I decided to approach the North Beach inquiry slowly. First, I took a cab ride through the area to get the vibes and eyeball the Bitter Beat Cafe. It became clear that my suit and trench coat would make me stand out like a pig in a hen house. I needed some new old clothes. I asked the cabbie to take me to a thrift store where I purchased some faded slacks, a turtleneck sweater, and a coat of dried and cracked leather.

Next, it was back to Patti's place to talk to Tommy about the trunk and get the skinny on the Bitter Beat. Patti stayed in the living room while I questioned Tommy in the kitchen.

"Tommy, the police think you owned the trunk."

Tommy gave a little nervous laugh before answering. "The trunk was Laura's. I complained one time that I had no place to put my stuff in her apartment. She emptied that trunk and said, 'You can have this all to yourself.' Later, she painted my initials on it with her red nail polish."

"Your initials, hah, so that's why the cops think it's yours."

"When we had the fight at the Bitter Beat and she told me to get my stuff out, I emptied the trunk, it was there when I left," said Tommy.

"What time did you leave the Bitter Beat?"

"About midnight."

"And what time did you get home?"

"Just after two."

"Did your mother see you come in?"

"Yeah, she had to let me in 'cuz the chain lock was on the door."

That was all I needed on the time frame and trunk. Later, I verified the two o'clock story with Patti. I squeezed Tommy for all he could remember about the goings-on at the café. Laura had a best friend, Viv, who worked the same shifts. Their boss was a lug named Benny. No one had any idea who the owner was, maybe a mob guy. Tommy didn't know anything about Laura's history before she started at the café, only that she was from Detroit.

I arrived at the Bitter Beat about 10:00 p.m. Viv got off work at midnight, while the café might be open till sunrise. I figured I'd have time to talk to her and case the place.

A guy dressed in black greeted me at the door. "Welcome to the Bitter Beat. First time here?"

"You got it," I replied.

"Thought so. Empty table over there," he said, pointing.

"Thanks," I replied, and headed for the table.

The café wasn't much more than a big dimly lit room lacking a good cleaning. On a small stage, a poet with a beret was reciting, accompanied by a bongo player. There was a menu scrawled directly on the wall: coffees and soft drinks, no booze. The women wore baggie sweaters over tight skirts or capri pants, the men sweatshirts and jeans, scraggly beards or goatees. Scattered among the twentysomethings were a few middle-agers, helping my 45-year-old mug blend in.

166

I was staring at the menu when a waitress with a tight-fitting outfit over a dynamite body knocked on my table. "I'm Viv. See anything you like?" she said in a seductive voice.

I wasn't going to touch that one. "Yeah, double espresso. Is Laura Morgan around?"

Viv gave me a startled look. "What do you want Laura for?"

"I'm her Uncle Bill Morgan from Detroit. I was driving through on my way to L.A. when I remembered my brother said Laura worked here."

Viv sat, put her hand on mine and sadly related the story of Laura's demise. She included the fight with Tommy, which she had witnessed herself. I gave what I thought was an Oscar-winning performance as the grieving uncle before I tried to get any more info from her.

"The boyfriend, heh! Did she have trouble with anyone else?"

"Nothing more than the usual. Some guys try to get grabby, but the regulars protect the girls."

"Anything else you can think of?" I asked.

"No ... no," she said slowly, shaking her head. "Do you still want your coffee?"

"Sure," I replied.

I listened to more poetry and a little jazz combo for a while. As I headed to the door, Viv cut me off.

"I just remembered. A little while after the fight, I overheard a guy talking to Benny. He said he was from Detroit and he showed Benny a picture. 'That's Laura. She's around here somewhere,' Benny said. I caught Laura in the ladies' room. When I told her about the Detroit guy, she got excited, grabbed her coat and purse, and snuck out the back door."

"What did this guy look like?" I asked.

"Big guy … heavy black wool coat." Laura shrugged. "That's about it."

"Did you tell the cops any of this?"

"No, this is my first day back. Benny, he's the boss, called me off vacation because of Laura."

"I should talk with Benny."

"He already left. That was him you were talking to when you came in."

I thanked Viv and caught a cab. Back at the hotel, I continued to mull over the appearance of the mystery man and study the crime photos. I got a hunch. I needed to inspect the trunk.

I got to Farrell's office early the next morning carrying a box of doughnuts.

"Doughnuts!" remarked Farrell. "You must want another favor. Do you think I can be bribed with a few doughnuts?"

"No, no way," I answered. "Just something for you and the boys."

"But you do want something, right? What is it?" asked Farrell.

"I want to see the trunk. Not pictures, the trunk itself."

"What for?"

"You'll have to trust me."

"All right, all right." Farrell grabbed a doughnut. "Let's go."

✗ ✗ ✗ ✗ ✗

The Evidence Property Room was in the dungeon-like bowels of the building. We followed the clerk through a labyrinth of shelves until we reached the trunk.

The trunk was an ornate copper-scrolled vintage steamer. The lock was intact. The leather straps that held the lid tight to the bottom were dried and cracked. There were Tommy's initials in red. I opened the trunk. It was dry inside.

"Satisfied?" asked Farrell.

"Not yet, just let me check a few more things."

I carefully felt around the inside, looking for any anomalies in the surfaces.

"What are you looking for?" asked Farrell, irritation evident in his voice.

"A hidden compartment," I answered.

"Sure," responded Farrell sarcastically.

I checked the outside for anything that felt loose. On the right side, I found a decorative scroll that I could twist in a counterclockwise direction, uncovering a finger hole. I soon discovered that the finger hole allowed me to raise a secret slide panel that revealed a hidden drawer in the false bottom of the trunk. The drawer was full of cash, wet cash, loose cash, bills in wrappers.

I gave Farrell a smile, an open-handed point to the money, and a triumphant "Voila."

"How'd yah guess at that?" asked Farrell.

"Remember, I was in the Coast Guard during the war. Sometimes we had to search luggage for people trying to smuggle American money out of the country. I was studying the photos of the trunk last night when it popped into my head that this trunk looked like the one we had busted."

Farrell called the Property Clerk to inventory and take possession of the money. The count was a little over $200,000. All the wrappers were stamped: Brinks Co. Detroit, Michigan.

"Must be some of the money from the Brinks heist last year," surmised Farrell.

We went back to Farrell's office where he found the notice on the Brinks job; a clerk had managed to get away with over $214,000.

"We'll contact Detroit and work with them on the robbery, but none of this changes my mind about your boy," said Farrell. "I consider the case closed. I'll recommend the District Attorney take him to trial."

I had a different opinion and things were starting to gel. Laura was from Detroit. She had most of the loot from a Detroit robbery, which explained how she could afford that nice apartment while working at the café. I had thought someone had searched her apartment. Then there was the guy from Detroit who asked about Laura.

I figured whoever killed Laura was looking for the money. She fought with him and he tried to shut her up and ended up choking her to death. He decided to make the body disappear as if Laura had skipped town after she found someone had searched her place. But he needed to get her out of the apartment before sunrise. He didn't have time to complete the search. He kept her keys, tossed her purse, and planned on coming back later. That plan went south when the body was found so soon, and the police closed off Laura's apartment.

It was time to let Farrell in. I told him about my conversation with Viv and my version of the crime.

"The murderer obviously didn't know the money was in the trunk. He probably thinks it's still in the apartment," I told Farrell. "Can you keep quiet about the money for a while?"

"I can do that," replied Farrell.

"And tell the papers the investigation is over, and Laura's apartment is no longer a crime scene?"

"What will that do?" asked Farrell.

"I'm betting the killer will come back and finish searching the apartment once he thinks the coast is clear."

"OK," replied Farrell, with exasperation in his voice. "But we don't have the manpower to sit on the apartment waiting for your mythical killer."

"I'll do the sitting," I promised Farrell.

I spent the next two days quietly in Laura's apartment, lights out after dark. On the second night, I am embarrassed to say, I had dozed off in my chair when the door opened, knocking down my tin-can alarm. I woke with light from the hall pouring into the apartment, showing a silhouette in the doorway.

The intruder spotted me and pointed his gun. He had the drop on me. "Freeze," he yelled. Blinding me with his flashlight, he asked: "Who the hell are you?"

Before I could respond, a second figure burst through the doorway and knocked the intruder to the floor. Then he flipped on the lights.

"You OK, Malloy?" he asked.

"Yeah," I replied. With my eyes adjusting to the light, I could see he was carrying a gun, and wearing a heavy black wool coat. I looked down to see Benny, Laura's boss from the café, out cold on the floor.

"Name's Evers, Brinks Security," he said, leaning over to pick up Benny's gun. "Been following Benny here since they found the girl's body. Her real name is Lisa Millington. She kept the same initials."

"Can you clue me in?" I asked.

"Millington stole over $214,000 from our Detroit office where she worked, then disappeared. Since all the bills were new, we had serial numbers. The bills started showing up in San Francisco banks, many coming from the Bitter Beat. Someone at the bank must have tipped off Benny about the money. He got real nervous when I showed him a picture of Millington. Benny said she was there, but she gave me the slip. When I read about the murder and no money mentioned, I figured Benny for the job. I've been following him, hoping he would lead me to the money."

I told Evers how I found the money and called Farrell to retrieve Benny.

The cops found Benny's fingerprints on the trunk and booked him for murder. They dropped the charges against Tommy. Laura's, that is Lisa's, parents brought her back to Detroit for burial.

Before returning to Palm Springs, I said goodbye to a grateful Patti and Tommy. I called the country club and told them to start booking my tennis lessons again.

When I got home, my trench coat and fedora went back into storage, saved for another day.

Frank Kozusko is a retired U.S. Navy submarine officer and nuclear engineer. After the Navy, he spent 20 years as a university professor of mathematics. Third beat: writer. He's been published in *Bewildering Stories*, *Ariel Chart*, *Pilcrow & Dagger*, *Literally Stories*, *The Avalon Literary Review*, and *Over My Dead Body*, and anthologized in *Paradox: The Inner Circle Writers' Group Crime/Mystery/Thriller Anthology 2019*, *The Twofer Compendium*, and *Bubble Off-Plumb*. His retro-noir detective Jake Malloy appears in *Shotgun Honey* and in *The Trench Coat Chronicles* and future anthology *Jersey Pines Ink Whodunit Anthology*. His poem "The Vietnam Veteran" will be published in the anthology *Thank You for Your Service*. circadianrs@yahoo.com

174

Date with Destiny

Karen Keeley

The big Indian Chief flew around the corner and Malloy took a swan dive for the ditch, shoulders bunched, head tucked in low. For a fleeting second or two he thought he must've looked like a turtle. He rolled and came up standing, a move that surprised him, never believing he still had it in him to have accomplished such a feat. Maybe it was his trench coat that saved him. He'd laid down a pretty penny for that coat, an important symbol to his stock-in-trade. That and the hat.

The hat too, had gone flying. He found it in the ditch, brushed leaves and dirt from the brim; glad he hadn't lost it in the dark.

The big Indian Chief made a hard brake. The back end of the bike whipped back to front so the motorcycle now faced toward the direction it had come. Malloy felt certain there'd be a skid mark on the asphalt but in the dark, it was hard to tell. The Indian's single headlamp held Malloy in its beam, the bright light blinding him. He put up a hand, blocked the light, and listened to the soft idling of the engine.

"Golly, mister! I didn't see you there, I'm really sorry!"

"Obviously," said Malloy. He swiped dirt and leaves from his beloved trench coat, a tad miffed he'd have to spend yet more dollars on dry cleaning but what the hell, the coat had been christened with blood spatter two days earlier when wrapping up the Rawlins case. And he still hadn't gotten 'round to the dry cleaners, another something on the to-do list.

He walked toward the Indian, moved a bit off of centre to get out of the glare of the motorcycle's cycloptic eyeball. Whoever was driving cut the gas; the bike grumbled and went silent. The eyeball too, went dead.

"Are you OK?" The kid asking the question was maybe nineteen, ginger-haired and freckle-faced, and not much bigger than the motorcycle, a luminous machine of cogs and gears gleaming under a starry nighttime sky. Away from the city lights, Malloy easily spotted the Big Dipper and with it, the Great Bear and the Bull constellations. The kid was having trouble keeping the bike upright, the weight of it tipping him sideways. He leaned hard to the left, fighting the play of gravity.

Malloy told the kid he was just jim-dandy, and then asked, "This baby yours?" He plunked his well-worn fedora on his head while brushing more leaves and dirt from the knees of his trousers as he stood near the bike.

The kid nodded. "Just got 'er today. She's a real beauty, eh?"

"I'll say." Malloy ran his hand over the teardrop-shaped gas tank, thinking about the couple of Indians he'd seen earlier that afternoon. He fished out a pack of Camels from one pocket of his trench coat and lit up a smoke, tossed the spent match to the side of the road. "Why now? Why out here in the middle of nowhere in the dark?"

"I could ask the same of you," said the kid.

Malloy smiled. "I'm working."

"Walking down the middle of the North Shore Highway at midnight is working?"

"It is this night," said Malloy. "I'm a private investigator—I'm investigating. Name's Syd Malloy." He held out his hand.

The kid gave it good hard shake. "Mark Redcliffe." He gave the kickstand a hard kick and leaned the bike over on a slant. The big Indian, metallic green, thick fenders front and back, stayed put, propped upright on the asphalt like a giant insect. "Whatcha investigating?"

Malloy studied his Camel; the tip glowed red in the dark. "Some doofus took a header off the highway last weekend, drove his car over the side of the cliff. The police are ruling it a suicide but the wife thinks it was murder. She asked me to investigate."

"That was days ago. What could you possibly find now?"

"Won't know till I look," said Malloy.

"In the dark? That's crazy," said the kid. "You can't see anything at night."

"Exactly," said Malloy, and he smiled.

Oliver Pratt's death had been ruled a suicide by the cops, the coroner, and forensics. The cops felt certain there'd been no sign of foul play, no skid marks to indicate the guy had hit the brakes before plunging his '47 Buick with its automatic choke and wood-grained instrument panel off the highway and down the side of the cliff. The coroner said no lumps, bumps, bruises, or broken bones that couldn't be accounted for after the fact, Oliver Pratt having taken a header through the windshield. Alcohol levels in Pratt's bloodstream showed him to be thoroughly tanked, so yeah—the guy was probably a doofus driving impaired, especially on the North Shore Highway around midnight, a two-lane highway well known for its S-curves as it snaked its way through West Vancouver and out toward Horseshoe Bay. Somewhere out there in the dark were residential homes built into the side of the cliffs along with acreages home to beef cattle, chickens, and quarter horses, and nobody heard anything. Forensics said the vehicle hadn't been tampered with, brakes in good working order, nothing wrong with the steering mechanism. And after the vehicle had been towed to the cop shop chop shop, the mechanics validated the state of the vehicle as nadda, zip, zilch, no use trying to bang out the dents, the Buick was toast, but, hey! Helluva a nice car before it crashed!

Amanda Pratt didn't believe it was suicide. She knew her husband, knew his faults, his idiosyncrasies, and understood his lapses in judgement, but even for all of that, he would not have ended his own life. She knew that as well as she knew the schematics for tearing down the Happyland Giant Dipper to make way for a 5½-furlong racetrack coming in at a cost of $200,000 to be built at Hastings Park because that was where she'd invested a chunk of her inheritance, money from her rich philanthropic father, he too, now deceased. She prattled on about that enterprise while taking Malloy's trench coat and hanging it in a hall closet and then waving him into her living room. She also told Malloy that McGill Street would have to be re-routed and the new racetrack dug down two feet, packed with Lulu Island peat and top-dressed with dirt and silt from the Fraser River, making it one of the best and safest racetracks in North America. Malloy was having difficulty wrapping his head around the narrative when the grieving widow's husband lay dead in the city morgue, but grief had a funny way of showing itself, including a comment made about the blood spattered on Malloy's beloved trench coat. "A souvenir from the last job I was on. The blood's not mine," he'd told her while accepting her offer of a highball. He also added, "Far be it from me to turn down a job, God knows I can always use the money, but the cops, the coroner, and forensics are all saying suicide."

"Rubbish," stated the grieving widow as she handed him his drink, whiskey and soda—light on the soda. "Someone deliberately forced Oliver off the road, which resulted in his death."

"And you say this why?" Malloy had asked.

"Because of Clara Brooks," Amanda Pratt told him.

"And who's Clara Brooks when she's home?"

The grieving widow drank a healthy portion from her own generous highball and set the glass on the coffee table. "Clara Brooks was Oliver's little piece on the side."

Malloy butted his cigarette into a crystal ashtray—he'd been smoking the cigarette when he'd first arrived. He'd done his homework on the Pratts. He knew the grieving widow was the one with money. He also knew Amanda Pratt was fifteen years older than her husband,

Oliver Pratt, now deceased. And with a ruling of suicide there would be no payout on his $35,000 life insurance policy, ten times as much as what most people earned in a year, and no doubt the premiums paid for by the grieving widow.

"I know what you're thinking, Mr. Malloy. Why am I not berating my husband's cheating heart?" She wore a cashmere cardigan over a silk blouse, a light woolen calf-length skirt, a single strand of pearls at her throat and sensible walking shoes. Malloy noted his drink contained good old Canadian rye whiskey, probably Canadian Club as he admired her trim ankles thinking she seemed a no-nonsense kind of woman with her cap of dark curls, perfectly coiffed, and expressive brown eyes. He took her for somewhere in her thirties but the society pages put her closer to fifty. She had certainly aged well, but then having money did have its perks. He also wondered if Amanda Pratt was playing him for a chump, acting like the grieving widow when all along she'd come to hate the man she'd married, and that meant hiring a professional, get them to do the dirty work, make it look like an accident. Then the damn fool cops, coroner, and forensics rendered a verdict of suicide which threw a monkey wrench into her plans. Hire Malloy, get him to find evidence pointing at murder and kill three birds with one stone, get revenge on Clara Brooks, get rid of a philandering husband, and get double indemnity on the life insurance payout.

"I loved my husband," she said. "I admit I wasn't happy about his bit on the side but he always came home to me."

He would, thought Malloy. You're the dollface with the dough.

"I told the police about Clara Brooks. A Detective Simms, but he didn't seem interested."

Malloy knew the detective well; they'd been partnered years ago when Malloy too, had been a proud member of the Vancouver police force, and Malloy still considered Simms a good friend. It was unlike Simms to drop the ball on Clara Brooks. "Did the detective say why he wasn't interested?"

"He followed up with Clara and supposedly she has an iron-clad alibi. She also denied having any kind of a relationship with Oliver other than knowing him through the Point Grey Country Club. But she would've said that, especially if she was involved with his death, an attempt to deflect suspicion from herself. I'm certain they were having it off and she was pressuring Oliver for a divorce. She wanted him to marry her."

"Most women do," said Malloy. "They like to think commitment comes with the territory."

"What can also come with the territory is a child," said Amanda Pratt. "Clara told Oliver she was with child — I think that's the delicate way of putting it. Knocked up, if one wanted to be crude about the whole affair."

"Not to be crude, Mrs. Pratt — but did your husband believe her? Was the child his?"

"He did not. He referred to her as a gold-digger, a little trollop who flaunted her charms amongst the men at the country club. She was now using the pregnancy as a way to try and trap him into marriage." She drank the remainder of her highball, ice cubes tinkling. "If it is true, her family's most upset, their darling Clara pregnant."

Malloy was thinking Oliver Pratt had truly been a doofus if he'd been canoodling with this Clara Brooks dame. Why chase after rotgut when champagne was offered for free at home? But he kept those thoughts to himself. Instead, he told Amanda Pratt he'd look into it, see what he could find. Just as he was leaving, he asked the grieving widow why her husband was driving the North Shore Highway at midnight.

"Oliver enjoyed driving, especially at night," said the widow. "He was a chronic insomniac and found driving relaxing. He'd listen to Jack Cullen's radio broadcast, *Owl Prowl*, music from the hit parade. He called it his Friday night date with destiny, something we laughed about."

Sadly, there'd be no more laughing—not for Amanda Pratt, not until she got some answers regarding her husband's death. After he took his leave, Malloy stood at the curb under the leaves of a giant maple and lit up another smoke. He tossed the spent match into the street, plunked his well-worn fedora on his head and figured his next stop would be at the precinct to call on his old pal, Detective Al Simms.

"She's humiliated," said Simms. "Doesn't want to admit her much younger husband decided to kick the bucket rather than stay married to her."

"If the guy was so unhappy, why go for a permanent solution to a temporary problem?"

The Trench Coat Chronicles

"How should I know?" Simms growled. "We ruled it a suicide, as did the coroner and forensics. The guy had a screw loose, some nut job. Maybe the wife browbeat him, turned him into a milquetoast crybaby and that's why he gravitated to the booze. Maybe she cut off his monthly allowance. Maybe he owed a wad of lettuce to his bookie and couldn't pay. The wife did say they were frequent flyers at the racetrack, her investing in that upgrade they got underway. Jesus! The traffic jams around McGill Street, all of it playing havoc with my ulcer. I've got robberies, vandalism, bank fraud, and murders to solve. I don't need you wasting my valuable time. Like they say in the movies, Malloy — scram!"

Malloy decided trying to reason with Simms when he was in a foul mood was like trying to reason with an enraged bull on the attack. He didn't stay to argue. He returned to his office at the corner of Broadway and Alma where he looked up contact information on Clara Brooks, letting his fingers do the walking through the white pages.

The Brooks family too, lived in Point Grey just as Amanda had said — another six-bedroom mansion with hydrangea bushes and a couple of Japanese maples in the front yard. Around back there was a large three-car garage, wooden doors pulled open, a couple of nice-looking Buicks and two motorcycles, both Indians. A tall, lanky fellow somewhere in his mid- to late-twenties, a grease-stained cap on his head and wearing grease-stained overalls was working on one of the bikes, the crankshaft by the look of it. Malloy walked over, introduced himself, showed the fellow his credentials.

"Whaddya want me for?" the grease jockey asked.

"I don't. I was just interested in the bikes. I used to drive something similar when I was stationed in Europe during the war, dispatch service. Not all of the memories are bad."

"This one's a holdover from the war," said the grease jockey. "I got it cheap from a guy newly married with a kid on the way and the wife doesn't want him ridin' anymore, said it's too dangerous."

Malloy nodded, looked thoughtful. "I'm here to see Clara Brooks."

"She's my sister." The grease jockey's congenial mood now morphed into something suspicious, the protective older brother. "Whaddya want her for?"

"Just a few questions about the death of Oliver Pratt."

"That guy? They say it was suicide. Clara's pretty cut up, she knew him from the country club."

"So I've been told," said Malloy.

"Whaddya mean by that?"

"Just thinking out loud," said Malloy.

Clara's big brother approached Malloy, tapped his chest hard with a finger. "Don't you be thinkin' too hard and upsetting her. She's had a rough couple of days."

Malloy looked down at the grease smeared on the lapel of his coat, tipped his hat, and walked away. He was beginning to understand why his old pal Detective Al Simms was as grumpy as an old bull, never mind the ulcer. He found Clara Brooks and asked his questions, thinking the drive to Point Grey had been a lost cause, like trying to get blood from a stone. He didn't think Clara looked pregnant, she was as slim as a pussy willow, but then it could be early days. Or maybe she'd made up the whole thing to try to coerce Oliver Pratt into divorcing his wife. Or maybe she, too, was a simple nut job, a rich brat who thought she could have whatever she wanted, consequences be damned, canoodling with the men in the old boys' club at the country club, and she'd grieve for about half a heartbeat then move on. Malloy felt certain he was looking at crocodile tears, nothing genuine about them or the girl. He couldn't get a read on her and wasn't sure he wanted to. What he did get was her iron clad alibi. She'd been at the Point Grey Country Club with a host of family and friends, some all-night dance marathon as part of a charitable fundraiser, and yeah—her brother had been there, too.

Malloy was out of ideas.

Six hours later, there he was checking out the scene where Pratt had been killed when Mark Redcliffe rounded the corner on the big Indian and sent Malloy diving for the ditch. Given the lateness of the hour, Malloy and Mark Redcliffe were alone on the North Shore Highway, no other vehicles in sight. Malloy had just finished telling Mark about Oliver Pratt when they heard a rustling in the bushes. They turned and saw a big Brahman bull—close to two thousand pounds of Prime Grade-A beef come charging out of the bush and onto the road, a look of meanness in its eye.

Malloy thought about making a run for his vehicle parked a quarter-mile back down the highway, a cream-coloured LaSalle convertible. Mark Redcliffe, now straddling his big Indian Chief, yelled, "Use your coat — get its attention!"

"I do that, I'm toast!" shouted Malloy.

Mark hollered back, "It's you or me and I'm the one with the bike!"

Malloy shrugged out of his beloved coat and began flapping it for all he was worth. There wasn't a hope he'd make it to the LaSalle. The big bull turned its attention from the kid to him and began to paw the ground. Malloy heard Mark Redcliffe crank up the big Indian, rev the motor and then pop the clutch. The bike reared up like Gene Autry's wonder horse Champion in a Saturday matinee serial. The kid pulled a wheelie followed by the front tire hitting the asphalt and then both tires gripped the road, the bike racing straight for Malloy. Malloy, backlit by the light of the big Indian's headlamp, feinted right; the bull took the bait and Malloy threw his trench coat at the bull as it swept past him, two thousand pounds of muscle and sinew, the coat caught on the bull's horns, blinding the big beast. Enraged, the bull twirled, shook its head, stamped its front feet, tried to dislodge Malloy's beloved trench coat which it eventually did, pawed at the coat, snot and steam snorting from the bull's ringed nose.

During the huffing and puffing, Malloy had hopped on the back of the big Indian as Mark Redcliffe tore by in the dark, a maneuver Malloy didn't think he had in him — he knew deep down he was no match for Gene Autry no matter how many Westerns he'd seen. He and Mark were both dumbstruck as Mark tore off down the highway. The kid eventually shouted back at Malloy, "Where did that thing come from?"

Malloy shouted in return, "Haven't got a clue! But I'm beginning to understand why Oliver Pratt drove his Buick off the highway." Pratt, the unfortunate schmuck, driving his car with its shiny chrome rims and whitewall tires, the vehicle hugging the S-curves of the highway, him be-boppin' to the music, hadn't seen the big Brahman until it was too late. Instinct would've had him reef the steering wheel to the left and that would've been his fatal flaw, his final date with destiny. The Buick careened off the side of the road and down the steep embankment where it ended up with its grill kissing an old-growth cedar, Pratt torpedoed through the windshield.

Mark Redcliffe slowed the big Indian, pulled over to the shoulder. They looked back the way they'd come, the big bull disappearing into the underbrush.

"When I tell my buddy what we just saw he's gonna burst a blood vessel," said Malloy.

"Want to go back for your trench coat?" asked Mark.

Malloy shook his head. Damn! He'd lost his hat too, it lying somewhere back there in the weeds, in the ditch, in the dirt. "Head for the nearest telephone booth," he said. "I'm not coming back for my vehicle until the cops or the SPCA or the goddamn army comes and collects that big brute from the brambles."

"Copy that, Chief." Mark Redcliffe revved the big bike, again popped a wheelie and sped off into the night.

Karen Keeley has published short fiction in a number of anthologies; the most recent, *Mid-Century Murder* (Darkhouse Books), first featured her PI, Syd Malloy. Yukon in Canada's north was home for many years where Karen worked as a Communications Analyst. Now retired, she makes her home in Calgary, Alberta.

Fire Brigade

Karen Keeley

Malloy met up with his old pal and former partner, Detective Al Simms, at the lunch counter at Woodward's downtown. They hadn't seen each other in a couple of months and Malloy was wondering why the big guy wanted the meet. He shrugged out of his trench coat, set it on the stool beside the one he'd grabbed, slid onto the vinyl, and tossed his hat on the counter.

Simms grunted an acknowledgement as he looked at the plate the waitress had plunked down in front of him, scrambled eggs and two slices of dry white toast.

"Jesus—Simms! You on a diet, or what?" asked Malloy.

"My damn ulcer; it's acting up again. Doc says I have to stick to a bland diet, baby food for Chrissakes, and scrambled eggs, no caffeine, no booze. I might as well be dead."

Syd Malloy, private investigator, didn't have a retort for that so he ignored his long-time pal and ordered the special—corned beef on rye. When his order came, Detective Al Simms shoved his own plate away in disgust, popped a toothpick in his mouth, waggled it side to side and continued to look glum.

"Why the face?" asked Malloy, digging into the sandwich.

"Remember that big Brahman bull that destroyed your beloved trench coat?"

Malloy nodded, his mouth full.

"Seems the bull and its owner went and got themselves killed," said Simms.

Malloy swallowed, swivelled on his stool, and faced his old-time pal. "What happened?"

"Arson," said the detective. "Someone set the barn on fire. Old man Ronald Webster who owned Samson, that's the bull's name, the two of them died from smoke inhalation before the flames got 'em. Looks like Webster was trying to save the bull."

Malloy let out a slow whistle.

Simms continued with the narrative, telling Malloy that Samson had been a Grade-A champion according to neighbours, with the papers to prove it, lots of blue ribbons and a bunch of loving cups won at county fairs across the country. "We got the call the day after the fire," he said. "Fire brigade was suspicious and now that they've finished up, they're sayin' arson. Someone tossed a kerosene lantern into a bale of hay."

Malloy chewed on that, almost feeling sorry for the big Brahman bull that had scared the bejesus out of him the night he'd been walking the North Shore Highway — the night he'd met Mark Redcliffe .If not for the kid and his big Indian Chief motorcycle, Malloy too, might have been ground beef, run over by the big bull when it charged out of the bushes and took a stand on the highway.

Simms removed the toothpick he was sucking on, gave it a twirl, watched it spin. "Interested in finding out who did it?" he asked.

"Of course," said Malloy. "That bull destroyed my favourite coat and I lost my hat. You're now telling me the bull's dead, and its owner, well—hell, my appetite just went up in smoke." He too, shoved his plate aside.

"I'm headed to the scene after this," said Simms. "This was supposed to be lunch—but this slop," he indicated the congealed scrambled eggs, "I'm done. You wanna ride with me?"

Malloy nodded, paid for both meals, neither one much eaten, took up his hat and trench coat bought with the proceeds from the case that had involved the kid with the big Indian, and followed Simms out of the downtown cafeteria.

The drive into the hills in West Vancouver took close to twenty minutes, traffic not too busy over the Lion's Gate Bridge, cars, vans and trucks all moving along at a good clip. Simms had been to the Webster farm the day before, so he had no trouble finding the place in daylight. Webster had lived alone, his wife having passed a few years earlier, his grown daughters married and living somewhere back East.

Simms parked in the muddy rutted driveway. The stench of burnt lumber, what remained of the torched barn, hit Malloy when he exited the detective's four-door sedan, his nose wrinkling at the campfire charcoal stink left behind after the fire brigade extinguished the flames. A German shepherd came from the side of the house, the dog wagging its tail. Malloy was thinking about approaching the mutt, figuring it must've belonged to Webster, when another vehicle pulled into the driveway. The driver of that vehicle, a '47 Dodge pickup with its V-shaped front grill and free-standing headlamps, introduced himself as Hans Schmidt who lived next door, owner of the adjacent property on the west side. He'd come to feed the dog, gather eggs, and check on the two quarter-horses in the back pasture. The three men conversed about the sad state of affairs, and the deaths of Ronald Webster and his beloved Samson.

Schmidt then told the detective he should be talking to Gabe O'Brien, the director of the Brahman registry. "He's got an office downtown but he lives just over there." He pointed through the trees to the east, another twenty acres of farmland. "Him and Webster locked horns over who had the better bull. O'Brien thinks his Midnight is head and shoulders above Samson, no pun intended. What you got to understand, a prize bull can sire calves worth their weight in gold. Whoever owns the number one bull in the province can demand big bucks for stud fees."

Malloy and Simms thanked Schmidt and headed across the pasture to the O'Brien spread. The German shepherd started to follow, then hung back when Hans Schmidt gave a sharp whistle. The dog turned, loped back to the Webster front porch. Malloy was feeling sorry for the mutt—not a good thing to do when working a case. He needed to stay sharp, help his old pal Detective Simms gather the facts.

It being a work day smack dab in the middle of the week, neither Malloy nor Simms thought they'd find Gabe O'Brien at home, but the weathered old geezer was there.

Plenty of laugh lines crinkled his face but Malloy didn't think they had come from a natural capacity to find any humour in the world. The guy was too intense, wound up tighter than a watch spring. He was up above in the hayloft, forking hay into a couple of stalls below. O'Brien tipped his tweed cap back off his forehead, squinted into the bright sunlight backlighting Malloy and Simms, and asked why they were sneaking onto his property.

"Lookin' for you," said the detective. He told O'Brien who he was, as did Malloy, then both men flashed their credentials.

Gabe O'Brien stabbed his pitchfork into a bale of hay and climbed down the ladder. "I take it you're here about Ronald Webster."

Simms answered in the affirmative.

Barn swallows flitted above in the rafters, a shaft of sunlight coming in from an opening in the hay loft. There were a dozen bales of hay stacked against one wall, along with another pitchfork. Malloy and Simms hadn't been in the barn five minutes when the missus arrived. A black Labrador retriever accompanied her, an older dog with a silver muzzle, showing its age. It walked with a limp and stayed close to the missus. She was a short stout woman with shrewd grey eyes. Malloy took her for somewhere in her fifties, a tad younger than her husband. She wore a faded cotton housedress overlaid with a ratty old cardigan and a pair of gumboots. She kept looking between Malloy and Simms while fondling the dog, giving its ears a rub.

O'Brien was explaining how the registry worked, what it meant to the cattle owners to have a bull worth its weight in stud fees. He then told Simms and Malloy that sure, he and Webster had argued. "What cattlemen don't? I thought my Midnight was better than his Samson, and him the reverse. It was a harmless rivalry. I don't know what that damn fool Schmidt's been saying. He's just as competitive as the rest of us who own top-grade bulls."

"Whaddya mean by that?" asked Simms.

"Schmidt was trying to purchase Samson off of Webster, but Webster wouldn't sell, told Schmidt to take a powder, to leave him be. You should be hassling him, not me."

"We're not here to hassle anybody," said Simms. "No need to get your knickers in a knot."

"My knickers are just fine," snorted O'Brien. "I'm upset. Somebody settin' Ronald Webster's barn on fire. Jesus — what if it happens to us? I been sleeping out here the last couple of nights, policing my own property. Maybe it was kids playing with matches, maybe it was vagrants, maybe it was somebody who's got it in for us cattle growers. There are those lookin' to buy our land, wanting to convert our farms into more residential. You must've seen how West Vancouver's growing. Houses poppin' up like mushrooms on the hillsides. My family has owned this land since the turn of the century, emigrated from Ireland. I'm not about to be selling or getting rid of Midnight. That bull's brought me and the missus some good coin the last few years. Ain't that right, Ida?" Ida, the wife, said nothing.

Malloy watched her eyes, those shrewd grey eyes telling him the missus didn't agree with her husband. She'd turned her attention to something outside the barn, looking through the wide doorway toward the thick brush at the back of their property, a kind of longing in her eyes, as though life held something better away from the barn, the farm and the few heads of cattle they owned.

Detective Simms thanked the O'Briens for their time and turned to leave.

Malloy asked, "Where's Midnight?"

Cynicism clouded O'Brien's face. "Not here," he said. "After what happened, I moved him out to Abbotsford to my brother's place. Didn't want to take a chance on his safety, not until you lot figure out what happened."

"We're working on it," said Simms.

"Well—work harder," growled O'Brien. "I got a business to run," and with that, he went back to forking hay.

The next day, Malloy hit the downtown library and read what he could on cattle breeding. It wasn't much but following that bit of research he visited Simms at his precinct.

"Did your lot find any insurance documents on the big bull?" he asked after tossing his trench coat and hat onto an adjoining desk.

Simms growled and grumbled, rubbed his belly, waggled another toothpick in his mouth, something he'd done for as long as Malloy had known him. Malloy lit up one of his preferred Camels and tossed the spent match in the ashtray on Simms's desk.

"Yeah—there was insurance on Samson," said Simms. "A cool thirty-five thousand smackeroos. You thinkin' the bull didn't have the juice to sire those Grade-A calves Schmidt referred to?"

"Just thinking out loud," said Malloy. "If Samson couldn't deliver then he wouldn't have been worth much. Maybe killing the bull was a way to save face and reap the benefits of the insurance."

"Meaning Webster set fire to his own barn and his plan backfired, killing him, too."

"Just a thought," said Malloy.

Simms grunted again. "Webster's daughters will divvy up the insurance payout. They're pretty cut up about what happened. I'm told two of the gals are driving out from Ontario with their husbands, supposed to arrive later this week. They're gonna work with Webster's lawyer and settle up the accounts, sell off the property, and get rid of the remaining livestock Webster owned."

"Probably to some construction outfit looking to build more residential housing," stated Malloy. "You think that could've been a motive? Webster didn't do it to himself, somebody else got to him first. Get the farmers off their land, builders looking to buy up the properties for dirt cheap and then make a killing with the housing."

"Anything's possible," said Simms. "I hadn't thought of that angle."

"That O'Brien fellow, he as much as hinted at that, him sleeping in his barn. His wife didn't seem too pleased by what was taking place."

"Whaddya mean by that?"

"Her look," said Malloy. "Right pissed off we were there, not saying a word, just listening like a kid with their ear pressed up against a key-hole."

"Jesus, Malloy — don't be so goddamn suspicious."

196

"It's my nature," said Malloy, now looking glum.

He leaned back in his chair while wondering if Samson had been the intended target, and if so, who would've wanted him gone? Was it O'Brien because it would've given Midnight a better standing in the registry? Schmidt had mentioned earlier Webster and O'Brien's ongoing rivalry, who had the better bull. Or maybe it was Schmidt himself because Webster wouldn't sell. If Schmidt couldn't have the bull then no one could.

Malloy contemplated the length of the growing ash on the end of his cigarette, thinking greed as a motive was right up there with revenge. The answer then hit him. He grabbed his coat and hat and hollered at Simms, "Follow me! This time I'm driving."

Simms legged it, hat and coat in hand, and followed his old pal and former partner to Malloy's LaSalle convertible, the first time he'd been in the vehicle. "What's got you on fire?" he finally managed to grumble once he'd gotten himself settled.

"Neither Samson nor Webster were the initial target," said Malloy, weaving the convertible in and out of traffic, pushing the dial on the speedometer up over fifty while crossing the Lion's Gate Bridge. "They were a means to an end. Avarice was the motive."

"Avi-what?" snapped Simms.

"Greed, desire, a longing for something different. It's the wife, she did it."

"You're nuts," hollered Simms. "Why torch Webster's barn?"

"Because she wants out, she's tired of being a farmer's wife. She's the one that wants the properties sold, take the money and move into the city, a nice quiet neighbourhood with a green grocer on every corner, somewhere that's easy living instead of being stuck on a farm on a hillside gathering eggs, slopping out that pigsty, wearing ratty tattered cardigans and gumboots."

"I still say you're nuts," said Simms but held his tongue, keeping further comments to himself.

Malloy turned in at the O'Brien homestead and they saw flames licking up and around the barn door. No sign of Gabe O'Brien but the missus was sitting on her front veranda with a glass of lemonade, looking as cool as a cucumber as she rocked back and forth in a wicker rattan rocking chair, the old black lab curled at her feet. She didn't acknowledge Malloy or Simms when they jumped from the LaSalle after Malloy pulled on the parking brake.

"Where's your husband?" shouted Malloy.

The missus turned her haggard face toward the barn and Malloy took off running. Inside, the flames had taken hold of the bales of hay stacked against the far wall. No sign of any animals. He saw Gabe O'Brien lying face down, a bad gash on the back of his head, blood matted in his hair. The missus must've hit him with a pitchfork before lighting the fire.

Malloy shook off his trench coat thinking, not again! Not another trench coat lost, this time to burning flames in a burning barn! He helped a groggy O'Brien to his feet, the smoke getting thicker by the minute, making it almost impossible to breathe. He threw the trench coat over himself and O'Brien, used it as a kind of blanket and duck-walked O'Brien to the doorway. They were coughing and hacking up black tar as they stumbled into the light. Detective Al Simms was there; he grabbed Malloy, pulled him clear of the burning barn.

Malloy and O'Brien both went down in the mud. Malloy landed on one knee. He felt as though he was coughing up a lung, it hurt with every breath, but at least he was breathing. O'Brien too, was horking up snot and spitting up more black tar. Malloy then heard the sound of the fire brigade getting closer. Simms must've called them from the house. He looked over and the missus hadn't moved. She was fondling the black lab, rubbing the dog's ears, a kind of faraway look in her shrewd grey eyes as she rocked back 'n forth, lost in another world.

Later, Malloy would realize he'd scorched his trench coat in a couple of places, a badge of honour, a kind of branding that he'd done a good deed. At the precinct, he and Simms sat in their chairs, leaning back, feet propped on Simms cluttered desk, the missus O'Brien in custody, where one of Simms's colleagues was filling out the arrest report while waiting for legal counsel to arrive. Gabe O'Brien was at the hospital getting his head stitched up, his neighbour Hans Schmidt with him, the two of them joined at the hip like a couple of old war buddies who'd somehow survived the latest skirmish, any previous animosity between them gone up in smoke. Gabe O'Brien had been mystified as to why his missus had killed Ronald Webster and then tried to kill him — the woman had to be batshit crazy! He'd hollered that colourful phrase while being led to the ambulance, which eventually delivered him to the hospital. The missus said nothing during her arrest, other than would someone please take care of the dog. She'd had the black Labrador retriever for close on fifteen years, her only companion. Maybe Hans Schmidt would look after Lucy — that was the dog's name. He was, after all, feeding the Webster shepherd, wasn't he? Malloy had told her he'd make sure the dog was cared for.

A week later, most of the loose ends tied up, Simms met Malloy at the lunch counter in Woodward's downtown. This time the detective ordered a good-sized helping of the steak and kidney pie. Malloy surmised his old pal's stomach was open for business.

"You were right," said Simms. "Her husband spent more time and money on the damn bull than he did on her. Midnight was his pride and joy. The missus said she was fed up having to listen to her husband's rivalry with Webster over who had the better bull, the endless arguments, her thinking it was all bull, nothing but bull. Big dumb-ass animals on four legs taking priority over her own measly lot in life."

"Nothing like a woman scorned," said Malloy, but he was thinking it was usually another woman who brought out the fangs and the claws, and not a goddamn hunk of Grade-A beef.

"She figured if both men lost their bulls, lost their barns, they'd sell up. That would leave Schmidt with his land, and possibly he'd sell, too. She figured there was no stopping progress — the builders coming in and buying up land all throughout West Vancouver, residential houses springing up like mushrooms just like her husband said."

"And how did she expect to get away with it?" asked Malloy.

"Just what we were thinking," said Simms. "Webster torched his own barn for insurance purposes, and we'd figure the same for her husband. It came as a complete surprise Midnight wasn't in the barn. O'Brien neglected to give her that bit of news, the bull moved to his brother's farm out in Abbotsford for safekeeping. That's what tipped her over the edge, her husband putting more importance on the damn bull than her. What if it had been kids playing with matches, or vandals, or what if her home had been set on fire — knowing Gabe O'Brien, he'd have gone running for Midnight and taken care of the damn Brahman bull before thinking of his wife."

"Think she'll get off?" asked Malloy.

"It's with the Crown now," said Simms. "She'll go to trial, no doubt about that. But as to her mental capacity, who knows? Maybe she'll get off on diminished capacity. It's out of our hands now. Let the courts do their due process."

Malloy dug into his own slice of steak and kidney pie, wondering if it was Grade-A beef. He figured it had to be, after all, raising beef cattle was big business throughout the province.

"How's your coat?" asked Simms. "I keep meaning to ask."

"Got me a couple of scorch marks on it," said Malloy, "but other than that, it's OK. At least the hat was saved. It's taken me a month of Sundays to break in that fedora."

"Jesus, Malloy—you were like the goddamn fire brigade." Simms was smiling but he also gave Malloy a sharp cuff upside the head. "You ever do something stupid like that again and I'll kick your sorry ass from here to Timbuktu."

Malloy sopped up gravy with the last of his toast, knowing his old pal and former partner wasn't stringing him along with a bunch of bull—the big galoot actually cared.

Karen Keeley has published short fiction in a number of anthologies; the most recent, *Mid-Century Murder* (Darkhouse Books), first featured her PI, Syd Malloy. Yukon in Canada's north was home for many years where Karen worked as a Communications Analyst. Now retired, she makes her home in Calgary, Alberta.

Saving Time

Gary Zenker

"Too stupid to come in from the rain."

If my neighbors were looking out their windows and could see me, lit from the lightning flashes, that's what they'd say. They'd probably add "pathetic loner loser, responsible for his own situation." But I'm out here in my front yard precisely because it *is* storming. That's the only way this thing works.

By *this thing*, I mean the time travel. I haven't figured out exactly how it works from a technical aspect. Only that if I am out here in a lightning storm, and the rain is heavy, and I'm wearing the damn trench coat, I can go to the past. My past. And I need to do that before I can't anymore. I need to fix things.

This time, I am better prepared. Earlier, I went to the bank, walked up to the teller station and slid my card through the reader as ID.

"Good morning, Mr. Jackson," the bright-eyed teller greeted me after my name popped up on her screen. I avoided her eyes and looked down, partially covering my face with my hand.

"I saved the old bills for you, since you collect them."

She counted them off and pushed the stack toward me. Old bills, the ones with the old look and dated before 1996 without the fancy security threads running through them. Bills I can use in the past without calling undue attention.

"Thanks." I took a step back from the counter.

"You know, we offer a senior account that has no minimum balance." The teller looked to be in her mid-thirties, my actual number of years on earth. But to her I look like I'm in my 70s ... so I just smiled and paused, pretending to consider her suggestion.

That's the curse behind my time travel. Each trip ages me six years. Three round trips there and back is 36 years, give or take. I look old enough to be my own father. But of course, I can't be him, since my parents died in the accident 15 years ago. So, grandfather is a better mask to wear.

"Sharing the account with my grandson has worked well so far. But thank you." I left the bank with my cash. My seventh withdrawal in as many weeks. I imagined that they'd talk about me after I left the branch, rehashing the accident. In communities like mine, people love to talk. Nobody forgets anything, including a person responsible for the death of his own parents. I'd do anything to change it. And I will.

So here I am standing in the rain, again. Waiting. "OK jacket, do your thing," I yell to the sky, then reach in the pocket to feel for my keys, the cash, and a lucky rabbit's foot. The original note from Uncle Jake is always there as well. I've discovered that anything in my hands, the jacket's pockets or that I'm wearing, travels with me. Everything else is left behind, in the future. The note always stays with the jacket.

"Wilmington, Delaware. June first, 1995. Ten p.m.," exactly two weeks before the date that changed my whole life. I say the words out loud, not certain whether it helps but thinking that it can't hurt. The old fedora's brim keeps most of the water out of my eyes. But given the downpour, it's impossible to know visually that I've arrived. It's a feeling that I get, a combination of nausea and vertigo. I turn back to the house and can barely make out my old Jeep parked in the driveway.

OK, I'm here. 1995. And feeling older still. Because I am. I puke a little less than I did last time, experienced enough to avoid my shoes, and start my walk across the sodden lawn to the front door. It always needs to be in a lightning storm when I leave, but I can't ever seem to catch a break on the arrival day.

This jacket and worn fedora were what Uncle Jake was wearing the first time I saw him. That was a dark time: depression, booze and thievery, just after Mom and Dad died. If it hadn't been for Jake, God knows I could have ended up with a toe tag before I was 22. His tough love, as brief as it was, pulled me out of a tailspin. He wasn't with me long; he died … or did he just leave? When? I'm not sure. I have the damn memory capacity of an old man, as well. Full of holes. I can't even remember what he looked like.

The Trench Coat Chronicles

Last year, I rediscovered the trench coat he left behind and realized its time-travel ability. The first trip was an accident.

On my second trip, I came back here purposefully to save my parents from the accident I caused. But I arrived too late to warn them against taking the fatal drive.

The third time, I concentrated on arriving two days early but arrived too late … again. I have no idea how time travel works. Was I distracted? Do the leap years mess me up? What the hell am I missing? My memories of the trips, like all of my memories, are imperfect. For obvious reasons, it's hard to keep them straight chronologically. I'm tired. So very tired.

This trip, I'm planning a different approach. I pick my arrival date two weeks earlier. That should be plenty of time even if the cosmos drops me in a bit later. I can correct my mistake, the one that put my life in a shit can.

And I'm bringing money … everything left of the settlement that I didn't squander on booze and drugs. Used the right way early on, it's enough to change the course of a life. Three lives. Mom's, my Dad's and hopefully, mine. This time, I'll get it right.

Drenched top and bottom from the walk to the door, I ring the bell. Then I ring it again. A young face appears at the side window and then I hear the door latch open. The door swings one quarter open. From the angle, I see mounds of trash in the hall and the stench of stale beer hits me in the face. Oh God. I'm too late. Again.

"What?" One word, full of anger and attitude. It's me. Younger. Isn't there some rule about not coming in contact with your earlier self, or physical contact breaks the cosmos? I'm frozen in place, trying to figure what to do next. He won't give me the time to think. "Who are you, old man?"

"A relative," I fumble for an answer, anything. "On your father's side."

"He never talked about relatives on his side," younger me sneers.

"Half-relative of your father." I make it up and leave it vague. I don't ask me for details. "I'm here to help."

"How can a relative I have never heard of help me?" I remember the anger, the frustration. Here I was at my rawest. Honestly, I was lucky to have lived through those years. I can't remember how I managed it.

"I heard about your mom and dad," I choked back real tears. "I loved them, too."

"So? I'm supposed to care?"

"I'm here to help," I repeat with far more confidence than I should have.

"Can you bring them back, old man?" If he had only known how I have tried. What I have tried. What I sacrificed.

"No. I'm here to help *you*. I'd like to come in."

He opens the door, a shocking sign of wanting help beneath it all. I walk in and step over the trash. The water runs off the coat and creates a puddle on the floor. We both look down at it, then back to each other. My goal has changed. Now I need to stay long enough to start the healing process, redirect my younger self's efforts, and talk with Uncle Jake when he arrives. I can't tell him the truth, but I can seed the needed cash and give a push on direction.

"How do I know you are who you say you are?"

I pull out my wallet and show him some faded photos of him, which is me with the parents. He grunts and I pull them from my wallet. "You can keep them if you like."

He takes them and grunts at me again. "Thanks."

"I have some business in town. I'd like to stay here, if you don't mind too much. It would save me the cost of a hotel. I could give you that money toward electric and groceries."

The money from the settlement won't come for months, after the insurance company affirms it was an accident of badly installed brakes by an auto repair student and not purposeful sabotage of a vengeful child. That report will be the event that pushes me even deeper down the bottomless pit of my life.

He pauses and then answers without looking me in the eyes, "Do whatever you like. Just stay out of my way. Old man."

Over the following weeks, I become a surrogate parent to myself. Younger me resents it, but I can also see moments where he secretly appreciates the company. I ask whether any other relatives have turned up. I'm hoping to speak to Uncle Jake when he arrives but don't want to tip things in the wrong direction by staying too long.

"Nope," he answers. "I'm alone and that's the way I like it."

"Except for me. I'm here now."

"We'll see how long you stay. Old man."

But I do stay and the environment shifts. We talk. About the tragedy, about the past, and about the future. About guilt and blame. About possibilities. And surprisingly, he listens. Just a little at first and more over the coming days. It's not perfect, but it's a start. There's less drinking, no more arrests, and the trash disappears. But I'm always the "old man" to him.

My memory is fuzzy, but I believe that Uncle Jake is due to make his appearance soon. He is destined to be the real stabilizing element in all this. But the longer we go, the longer I know that I may not be able to wait for his arrival. I don't understand time travel theory, except a feeling that I shouldn't be here for too long. Two weeks becomes four, and despite reaching something of an accord with younger me, I know that I can't stay much longer. So the weather forecast becomes one of the constants in our conversations. I have to plan my exit.

"What's the weather for tomorrow?" I could look it up myself, but it generally leads to conversations and bonding.

"Why are you always so focused on the weather? You should be a TV weatherman."

"Preparation," I tell myself. He looks at me puzzled and I chuckle, knowing that one day he will understand the irony of the conversation.

And then, finally, thunderstorms are forecast. Late in the evening, I crawl out of bed, grab my trench coat off the coat rack, and wander outside.

I stand there, rain pouring down, waiting to return home to the future. But I don't. I am rooted in the spot and in the time. "Take me home," I beg the trench coat. Take me home so I can make the trip one more time, so I can come back to the first stormy night *before* the accident. But nothing happens, except I get soaked. I stand there in the front yard, the rain pelting at me, running down my hair and face for half an hour before I give up. Younger me watches me through the window.

Shivering, I re-enter the house, take off the trench coat and shuffle toward the fireplace to warm myself. Why didn't it work? Everything is all the same. Am I too old? What am I forgetting? I look over to the chair and spot the fedora, dry and resting against the sofa cushions. I look away and then back at it again.

A clarity I haven't had in weeks comes over me. The overlapping pieces of my past and future settle into place. I can see what I couldn't before.

I grab a scrap of paper from the end table and begin to write. "It's not the coat" is all I manage before the room starts to spin and the pencil slips from my grasp. It lands on the floor, breaking the point.

"What are you doing?" young me walks in the room.

"Nothing, just writing myself a note." I push the scrap into the righthand pocket of the coat. I can always finish it later. I watch as young me takes the coat and fedora to hang in the closet.

"That's mine. I don't want you touching it."

"Shut up, old man, I'm just putting them away." I don't want him touching them. They cost me my entire life. Thrown away for nothing. My parents still die. My younger self is still lost in his anger. Uncle Jake could be months or years from arriving. He places the coat in the closet but returns with the bag of cash I brought with me.

"What the hell is this?"

"It's money. For you." Since he found it, I can't delay giving it to him. And another thunderstorm is scheduled for tomorrow night. It needs to be now.

He opens the bag and pulls out a stack of bills. "What'd you do, rob a bank? There's probably fifty grand here." There's a pause before he asks the real question. "Why?" Younger me squints at me and I squint back, like a mirror image in time.

"Your parents would have wanted you to have this. To help you make everything easier. They loved you very much. They believed in you." I could see him holding back the tears and a softening of stance. "We'll deposit it in the bank tomorrow. You can use it to start a business. Invest part of it. Pay off the house and bills. Make things better and honor your parents' hopes for you."

There's silence as he thinks through it all. He exhales deeply through his nose and looks at me again.

"I know you're still angry at life, that you may not like me. But *you're* jake with me," I tell my younger self.

"What the hell does that mean?"

"It's an old phrase, meaning you're OK."

"Old phrase for an old man. Jake … fine. …" Young me bites his lip and repeats as if in deep thought.

"Tell me some stories about your mother and father."

So younger me does. Familiar stories I had long forgotten, and they make my heart happy until I'm too sleepy to keep my eyes open. His tone gets softer. Cold and achy, I just need a short nap. Something to recharge my batteries after the day I have had. Then I can get back to everything. Maybe I have one more trip in me, after all. Now that I know the *real* secret to time travel. This next time, I'll get it right. …

That day, four weeks after I first met Uncle "Jake," he never woke up from his nap. I was too afraid to call the cops or 9-1-1 so I buried him in the backyard. The stories I told him of my mom and dad were probably the last things he heard. But something about having him there, to listen to my stories, and being really concerned about me, started a change in me. I deposited the money in my bank account. Paid off the house and the bills. But I never touched auto repair again.

I forgot about that dirty trench coat for years, when I found it shoved in a box at the back of a closet with the fedora, buried under more than twenty years of crap, in the same house I have always lived. I don't even know why I would have kept them. But I did.

It was raining outside so I thought I could wear it. I grabbed the fedora as an afterthought and looked in the mirror. Humphrey Bogart stared back, or maybe a younger version of Uncle Jake. The jacket is grimy and needs to be cleaned.

I put my hands in the pockets and find a scrap of paper. "Not the coat," was shakily scrawled on the paper. It's like a half message. What the hell would that mean?

Uncle Jake was a very odd guy, but he was all right. I raise the collar and make my way to the car.

Lightning lit the sky as the rain created rivers in the street. I stepped left and my foot sank inches deep, soaking the bottom of my pant leg. I pushed the fedora onto my head, to avoid getting soaked. I cursed and thought how I wished I could go back in time, just two weeks, to before my girlfriend leaves me for that gym rat trainer.

If only I could go back in time, maybe I could change my whole life.

By day, Gary Zenker is a marketing professional, banging out plans and copy for B2B and B2C clients. By night, he takes the lessons of human behavior and crafts them into flash fiction stories. He also runs two writers' groups, which help local authors better their craft and reach their publishing goals. His party game, WritersBloxx, helps others bring their stories to new audiences. www.GaryZenkerStoryteller.com.

214

The Halston Butcher

Elaine Marie Carnegie-Padgett

"What in nine kinds of holy hell do you think you're doing?" Harold half-stood and shouted at Terra McClintock as she grabbed her old coat from the rack. "You can't cover this one, sister … too dangerous. He's killing gals. I'll send Manny."

"I'm goin' to the library," she grinned, shimmied into her coat and pulled the press badge over her head. She stowed her purse in the desk drawer.

He shook his head, biting on the cigar he never smoked. He'd quit three years ago but continued to chew them to pieces just the same. He grinned as he watched her move toward the elevator in that old trench coat. It was her lucky charm and, weather permitting, she always wore it. She was hands down his best investigative reporter out of the roughly thirty he kept employed in this city. He shook his head and grabbed his phone. "Jimmy. Catch Terra at the elevator on the bottom floor and go with her." Harold slammed the receiver home without saying goodbye.

Jimmy was used to that. He slapped the SD card into his camera and ran. He was waiting when Terra stepped off the elevator.

She threw back her head and laughed. "I knew you'd be waiting for me. After six years, you'd think he would have learned his lesson by now," she chuckled.

"Don't let him fool ya, Terra. He loves your work; he doesn't understand you ... but he loves you anyway," Jimmy said as they reached the white Impala with *Halston Herald* artfully wrapped around it.

"I'm driving today. I need to get a feel for the neighborhood and the people gathered at the scene," Terra told him.

Jimmy got in without protest as she slid into the driver's seat and started the car. "Three murders in five weeks is a big deal in Halston."

"So ... what have you got?" he asked.

"A prostitute and a female high school student. ... No common ground or connection except for gender and the way they were killed. They didn't know each other. Race, hair color, different. They did have the same color eyes, but I think that is possibly random. It's the scariest version of a serial killer ... *random.* ... The trouble is, this guy is *not* random. Nothing for forensics. Not a hair or fiber, not a partial print, nothing on or in the bodies; still, there must be something. He's leaving a calling card we haven't found yet."

"Have you studied the crime scene photos?"

"Only last week's. You're right, Jimmy. I'll need all three today. Perhaps the calling card is a visual one. Thanks for letting me bounce ideas off you. We make a good team," Terra told him.

"So ... Evan will be working the scene. Is that still a problem?"

"No. That's what my time off was about. He told me I'd have to choose, right there and right then."

"What'd you do?" Jimmy asked, incredulous.

"I chose my job. He understood then how much it means to me. We worked at it, reached a compromise we can both live with, and from now on we work together." She grinned at Jimmy as the bright yellow crime scene tape came into view.

"Get the usual," she told him as she got out, slammed her door, locked the vehicle, and stood for a moment taking in the visual information. She walked toward the sidewalk in front of the Choice Resale Store where the sidewalk ended in crime scene tape at the mouth of the alley. Jimmy was already strolling toward the gathered crowd, taking pictures.

The store was closed, and a rundown boarding house bordered the other side of the alley. Terra watched the crowd for a moment, feeling the air, the sorrow, and fear of the people. She spoke into her recorder, then tucked the recorder into the breast pocket of her trench coat, saving her impressions for later review. Doug Parker, a bookkeeper at the *Herald* where she worked, stood on the sidewalk watching the crowd.

"Hey Doug," she greeted him, her recorder still in her pocket.

"Hey, Terra. Fancy meeting you here," he said, and half-smiled at the cliché.

"You look terrible," she quipped.

"It's the same guy, I guess." He ignored her comment. "The murderer is the one who called the police to tell them where he left the body." She noticed his hands were trembling.

"Damn," she looked down.

"There was a lot of blood." He pointed at the street gutter where the congealing blood looked almost like tar mixed with gravel and candy wrappers.

"I wonder if it was another woman?" Terra queried.

"I don't know for sure. I was one of the first here. The body wasn't covered yet. …"

"You saw the body and don't know the gender?" Terra interrupted him, eyes wide.

He shivered. "You couldn't tell by ... you just couldn't tell."

She swallowed hard as she moved off the sidewalk. "Take care, Doug. I'm going to walk around. You better get some rest."

Terra left the recorder in her pocket as she walked among the people, listening to their stories.

"I hear it's only prostitutes. Serves them right," a shabby middle-aged woman said to a woman standing next to her.

"The *first* one was a prostitute. The second was a female student from Andover. Not even out of high school yet, butchered like an animal while she was still alive. Do you think that served *her* right as well, madam?" the second woman asked and then walked away.

The first woman screwed up her face and wiggled her head from side to side at the woman's back and whispered, "Uppity bitch."

Terra continued to walk through the onlookers, listening, being careful not to meet anyone's eye. "I was the first one here," a man next to her whispered to another, crying softly. She moved closer to him as she pretended to tiptoe to try to catch a glimpse of the scene.

"It was awful," his voice broke.

"Come on, let's get you home," his friend said and guided him away.

Terra moved into the space they vacated. She watched faces and body language, listening. You could learn a lot from the casual conversation in a crowd like this.

That's when she saw him. That guy in the orange shirt across the street on the east side of the crime scene, exactly where he had been at the last one. She looked around for Jimmy and waved at him. They met near the end of the tape where it cut off the sidewalk on the western edge.

"Don't look, but across the street, there is a guy smoking, wearing an orange shirt. I need a picture. Please don't be obvious."

"I think I got him, but I'll make sure." They parted, going in separate directions as Terra caught sight of Evan waving at her.

He met her at the tape. "There's a closed press conference at one o'clock at City Hall."

"Press only?" she asked. "Is it the same guy?"

"Yeah. They've called in the FBI and they have a couple of profilers working on it. No blatant forensics on this one either. It's bad. He's butchering them alive."

Terra shook her head. "Are you all right?"

"We've got to catch this son of a bitch," he mumbled. "I'm beginning to think the way he kills them is what they have in *common*. He's got a screw loose. looking for a name."

"Hey, Evan," someone called from the middle of the suits. He looked at Terra and shrugged.

"I'm going to drive through the neighborhood and then go back to the office. I'll see you at City Hall," she told him.

"Be careful and lock your doors." He looked down. "Let's have dinner."

"Great idea, my house. Seven-ish?"

"It's a date," he said.

"Evannnn!"

"No orange shirt, sorry," Jimmy told her when he got back in the car.

"Did you cover the first scene when I was away?"

"Sure did."

"Good, we'll look at the pictures when we get back. It's funny that the guy was standing almost in the same place in correlation to the last murder scene and wearing the same shirt or almost the same shirt. It might have been red when I saw him at the second scene, but you know how people come and go. There didn't seem to be anything special about him until I saw him again today."

Terra drove slowly through the adjoining neighborhoods. "Look, it's Orange Shirt, coming out of that store on the right. Don't let him see you," she cautioned as she slowed the car.

The man stopped and opened a car door. "Got it," Jimmy said. They kept moving and Jimmy kept taking pictures.

"I don't think it's him," Terra said. "I don't get the vibe."

"What do you mean?"

"He's not observant. He like ... doesn't have a care in the world." She laughed as he tripped taking his shopping cart back. "I'll be surprised if it's him."

"I was hoping it *would* be him," Jimmy said. "I think he's escalating."

"Three weeks after the prostitute, the schoolgirl was killed. Two weeks to the day, the third kill. *He is escalating*," she said.

"Yeah, and the murderer made the call to police this morning. That's also a sign of escalation."

"How'd you know that?"

"Doug," he mumbled. Jimmy continued to snap pictures of the neighborhoods and the people. Sometimes, they got lucky.

✗ ✗ ✗ ✗ ✗

As soon as they arrived at the *Herald* offices, Jimmy copied the crime scene photos from all three scenes onto a sim card for her. "Thanks, I'm going to look at them. I'll call you if I need anything enhanced."

Terra marched off to her cubby and searched the photos scene by scene. She jotted questions she would ask at the press conference.

Question. *Name. Age. Gender. Death by …*

"There was so much blood," she whispered.

Question: *Was the blood at today's crime scene from one victim?* She scribbled, then tapped her cheek with her pen.

There was that guy at Scene 1, wearing a yellow shirt. Scene 2 wearing a red shirt, and today in the orange shirt, standing in precisely the same mid-scene location on the east side of the body each time. Evan will at least want to talk to him.

"The pic of the car?" she asked herself. "Yes, you can read the license plate." She printed those four pictures, let them dry and slid them into an envelope for Evan.

She printed three more pictures, sat back and stared at three covered bodies; she studied the way the sheet lay across them, how their legs were positioned and their surroundings. Each of their heads faced the dead end of the alleyway; then she noticed a wheel rim in every photo. They were different rims, but each was positioned at the end of the alley sitting against the fence, and in the latest case, against the curb. She wondered if the police had gathered them for evidence. She tapped the pen against her full lips.

Her desk phone rang. "Hey," she answered.

"Time to go," Jimmy said.

"Be right there." Terra slid the additional photos into the brown envelope for Evan, pulled her trench coat off the chair and wiggled into it, then tucked the brown envelope into her coat pocket. She slipped her recorder and pad into her purse and slung it over her shoulder, trying to hurry. She caught the elevator just before it closed and beat Jimmy to the parking lot.

"Did you find anything?" he asked.

"I don't know yet. Are we late?"

"Naw, right on time."

He pulled the car against the curb and they joined the press inside.

At exactly one o'clock, detectives walked out from the direction of the Mayor's office. Liaison officer, Burt Jennings, stepped up to the microphone. "Quiet, please," he motioned with his hands. "We will not be taking questions today. This morning Mr. Antione Tolar was found murdered. We believe it is the same perpetrator, and at this time we have called in the FBI to assist with the investigation. Profilers say the killer is White, male, small in stature, with a median income. Possibly a store clerk or salesman, and no family. Probably a loner, no pets. The kind of guy you wouldn't notice. His victims had no connection to each other; they all lived alone and had not been reported missing. That's all we've got for now. We will be updating you as soon as we know more. Thank you."

"How did he kill them?" someone shouted from the back. The detective ignored him and kept walking.

Terra hung around after the conference waiting for Evan. He gave her that "eye." Their agreement included *professional space.*

"I'm not asking. I'm offering." She grinned at him, holding out the brown envelope. "Did you notice the same guy on the east side of the body at each crime scene? Also, did you evaluate the blood to see if it was from just one victim? Last, did you notice the wheel rims at all three scenes?" He looked at her with his mouth open and then cleared his throat.

"OK, that's all I got."

He shook his head. "I guess you have pictures here," he asked, reaching for the envelope.

"Yes, and of the guy's car."

"My God, Terra. You have to be ..."

"Here." She pushed the envelope at him and tiptoed to kiss him lightly on the lips. "See you tonight."

A SWAT team descended on Robert Jensen's home two hours later. He was practicing soccer with his seven-year-old son in the backyard. His wife was at the kitchen table on her laptop. She screamed when the officers broke into the house.

"Why do you have to shout like that?" she shrieked right back at them with a haughty stare, then ignored them completely as she bent to the bassinet beside her. She picked up her infant daughter, who was also screaming by now.

Her husband and son stood wide-eyed in the kitchen staring at the officers as she scolded them. Robert answered their questions, then showed them his scanners and radios. He was a shortwave radio buff and listened to the police scanners as a hobby. Sometimes he went to the crime scenes. He worked as a data technician. Detectives took him to the station as a person of interest. His alibis were solid, and he was home two hours later. He still had a pissed-off wife to contend with.

Evan arrived at Terra's apartment at a quarter till, and he could smell the aroma of his favorite meal, shrimp scampi, before he knocked on the door.

"Here," she smiled, handing him a chilled glass of Chardonnay when she let him in.

"Aw," he kissed her. "You make me remember all the reasons why I love you. It's been a terrible day."

She kissed him again and said, "Have a seat. It'll still be a minute for the garlic bread. Did the info I gave you help?" she asked.

"The guy was a dead end, some kind of radio nut who visits crime scenes sometimes. He's writing a book. We gathered the wheel rims from two of the scenes; the one at the first scene was gone. You were right, they are connected to the murders. Both rims were covered by fingerprints of the victim. Of course, that's off the record."

"Off the record," she promised. "What about the blood?"

"No results yet, but it looks like only one victim."

"Wow ... he must have let them bleed out there. I wonder why no one heard anything. I mean the boarding house was right there ... if the victim was screaming?"

"Off the record?"

"Off the record," she promised again.

"They were all sedated. Probably during the entire thing. The amount and type of drugs they found in their systems, they probably never even realized they'd been taken."

"Well, that's something," she said. "The garlic bread is ready. Let's eat in the dining room."

She carried a dinner plate filled with a fragrant buttery toast to the table. They began with salad. Terra grabbed a piece of hot toast and talked with her mouth full. "What did the killer say when he called this morning?"

Evan stopped, his first bite in mid-air, and put his fork down, leaning forward. "Who told you the killer had called?"

"Doug. Why?"

"Nobody knew except me, because ... well, I took the call, my supervisor, the FBI supervisor, and the killer."

Her eyes were wide, "Jimmy knew too. *Doug* told him, also." A knock at the door interrupted their conversation. Jimmy just opened the door and walked in as Terra moved across the living room.

That's unusual, she thought until she saw Doug behind him with a gun in his back.

"I'm worried because I didn't plan this," Doug told Terra, his voice small and confused. "I always plan so carefully. I knew you'd put it together. Slip of the tongue," he clicked his tongue against the roof of his mouth. "If only I hadn't said anything." Doug rambled. "I can't help myself, you know. It just happens. They're going to call me the 'Halston Butcher.'"

"Wha ... what are you talking about, Doug?" Her voice rose as she asked the question.

"That's why I butcher them." He smirked. "That's what I'm talking about ... The Halston Butcher ... get it?"

"I can help you, Doug," she ignored his question. "You don't want to do this," Terra said quietly, trying to distract him.

"Shut up!" he shouted. "I can't wait. You're always snooping! I knew you'd figure it out and ruin everything. Sit down on the couch," he patted the back of her overstuffed leather sofa. "It won't hurt. I don't want to hurt anybody," Doug told her, trying to smile. He had produced a large syringe filled with amber liquid.

Terra stood where she was. If she moved, Doug would see Evan in the dining room. "No. I won't sit down and if you fire that gun the neighbors will hear. You have a *flawed* plan. They'll see you leave," she said. "Ruin everything ..."

"Sit," he growled, interrupting her. Doug swung his arm up and aimed the gun at Terra, his face a pasty mask. "It doesn't *have* to be painless ..." he almost whispered.

Jimmy saw his chance and when Doug swung the gun up, he turned and hit Doug's arm, forcing the gun down. They struggled, and as he tried to take the gun, it went off. Terra hit the floor, screaming. Evan shot Doug.

✗ ✗ ✗ ✗ ✗

"It happened so fast," Jimmy said, holding his bleeding shoulder as police stormed the apartment. "For a minute I thought we shot you, Terra. I was terrified," he said.

He looked at Evan. "I saw you moving toward us, and I knew he'd shoot her if *he* saw you."

"You did good, Jimmy," Evan said as the ambulance carted him off.

Terra went to the hospital to check on Jimmy after she had given her statement. Evan picked her up when he was finished.

He helped her with her coat and shook his head. "How old *is* this trench coat, Terra? You've had it forever."

"Yes, I have, and I love it."

"I'll buy you a new one."

"Don't bother. It won't be the same. I'll just wear this one," she said, grinning.

"My house?" he asked.

"Yes, we can't go back to mine tonight."

"I've been meaning to talk to you about that ... well, ask ... how would you feel about moving in with me?"

When Terra turned to look at him, he was holding a small white box with matching gold bands inside. She smiled and put her arms around his neck, her lips close to his.

"I think that's a hell of an idea," she whispered.

Elaine Marie Carnegie-Padgett is a published journalist, poet and short story author. Her first novel, *The Gaia Factor Trilogy*, is in the works. Her background is in law and journalism. Today she makes her home in the East Texas Piney Woods ... writing and living her best life!

Trouble in Jades

Larry Lefkowitz

She sat down without waiting for an invitation, immediately crossing her legs—not out of modesty, I sensed, but to display them to their advantage. Her legs were on the plump side, but because I had seen too many perfect legs in my profession as a private detective, I found her less-than-perfect gams somehow worthy of my scrutiny—in the same way that I was attracted to gapped front teeth on the rare actress who hadn't been perfectly smiled by a cosmetic dentist.

Miss Bankcroft—she had stressed ever so slightly the "Miss"—caught my scrutiny of her legs. She did not seem overly disturbed by it, though she quickly adopted a mildly reproving expression, as if catching me in the act made her superior. Or maybe it was the fact, which she wasted no time in making clear, that she worked in a museum—though she used the word "represented," a word I usually associated with a lawyer referring to his client, and in my business, invariably referred to a client accused of a crime.

But she wasn't the problem, the chrysanthemums were. Her museum's jade chrysanthemums (she had called them "chrysanthemi"). I assumed the moment she began describing the jade chrysanthemums, that they went missing. "No, Mr. Grant, they are not," she told me. I then assumed that one chrysanthemum had been taken. "Wrong again, Mr. Grant." She let me hang there for a moment, and then clarified. "A second, identical chrysanthemum has appeared, found sitting in the display case next to the original, the original which is the centerpiece of our Chinese jades and porcelains museum."

"So, what's the problem?" I said, recovering quickly. "Somebody made you a gift of a chrysanthemum, and now you have a set."

Miss Bankcroft put on the kind of longsuffering smile a bevy of grade-school teachers had bestowed on me when I tried to come up with an answer to a question in their area of erudition. "The problem is one of uniqueness, Mr. Grant. *Uniqueness.*" I expected her to spell the word on my behalf, but she apparently understood that I was a quick learner. Or maybe not, for she added, "The Louvre wouldn't display two Mona Lisas. Don't you see?"

I saw. I didn't like even one Mona Lisa. That smile is overrated. Clients with the same smile invariably come to me to find proof of their husband's infidelity. I didn't think it advisable to tell Miss Bankcroft my opinion of Mona. "So, display one chrysanthemum and keep the other in storage — in case the first gets broken. Or jaded."

She smiled dismissively at my humor. I was sure she would've appreciated it more if she weren't caught up in her problem. Still, I was disappointed.

"The word will get out. We're endeavoring to keep it quiet, but the word will get out. Unless …"

"Unless I work fast."

"Pre-cis-ely, Mr. Grant."

"Pete," I corrected, hitting her with my Bogart smile.

"We have closed the museum temporarily—for 'repairs.' As soon as you make your measurements, et cetera, Mr. Grant, and find out what's behind the 'gift,' we will handle the situation discretely. The jade chrysanthemum is the prize of our collection."

Since business was slow, working fast wasn't a problem. I ruffled through my appointment book for effect, then beamed at Miss Bankcroft. "You caught me on my golf day," I lied. "I can come with you to the museum now. Let me put on my trench coat. Just to let you know you are dealing with a real detective."

She smiled. Her dimpled knees seemed to smile. I smiled to make it a totally smiling moment. I was rewarded by her leaning forward to stand up, and I noticed she didn't wear a bra. That surprised me. The image of perceived virginity vanished. I felt a certain disappointment.

There were no prints on the chrysanthemums—I checked them both. Maybe the donor had used Chinese silk gloves. "Which is the original?" I asked Miss Bankcroft. She turned to Walter Freeman, who stood next to her.

"We're not certain," said the museum's director. "Our initial survey indicates both."

"Any idea why the gift chrysanthemum appeared?" I asked him.

Freeman shrugged. "Perhaps to make us look ridiculous. There's a lot of competition in the small museum field these days."

I nodded. I pictured myself having to make the rounds of a number of small, intimate, Far East specialty museums, done up like this one, except in funereal black. Miss Bankcroft would probably christen the decor "chiaroscuro" and they would be filled like this one with knickknacks. Miss Bankcroft would probably call them "items," or worse, "pieces." In short, they would be the kinds of museums that if you took out the junk, could be trendy singles bars — or upbeat funeral parlors. I refrained from giving Miss Bankcroft the benefit of my interior design savvy. I wouldn't put it past her to have had a long-fingered hand in the place's layout.

I would sleep on it since moving fast wasn't my style. While I was sleeping on it, Miss Bankcroft was sleeping also. Unlike me, she never got up. Freeman's call caught me, feet on my desk, following Jordan's baseball misfortunes in the sports column. I hadn't expected murder. Why murder somebody to cover up a donation?

On my way to the scene of the crime, or crimes, depending on how you looked at it, I was angry at myself. Not that there was anything I could have done to avoid the murder. It had come out of the blue, or out of the green since, as I soon discovered, the murder weapon was a jade knife.

As Freeman confirmed, "Yes, from our collection. Ming dynasty."

"Two in the Han is worth one in the Ming," quipped Grossman, the museum guard.

I shot him a sharp look.

"I thought it might help," Freeman said.

I wasn't sure how it could. "You think Ming came back and did it?"

Freeman smiled depreciatively. "I was thinking that whoever murdered Miss Bankcroft might have been a specialist in that era."

I frowned. "But the knife came from *your* collection." I didn't have to emphasize the "*your*," but I did.

"The murderer was obviously someone who had come to steal the knife and was caught *in flagrante delicto*, I believe is the term, by Miss Bankcroft. Possibly a Ming dynasty collector. Some collectors specialize in specific dynasties."

The only one who had collected anything was Miss Bankcroft. A jagged cut in her neck put her dimpled knees to shame. I felt as if her perceived virginity had been more violated than her existence. She still gave off that faint odor of powder. It took all my willpower not to look to see if she wore a bra.

I refrained from pointing out to Freeman that his "collector" had failed to collect anything, Ming or Shming. On the other hand, if he was connected with the two chrysanthemums, he at least hadn't complicated matters by supplying a third chrysanthemum. I was tired of sparring with Freeman. "Call the boys in blue," I ordered.

"I had hoped to keep the police out of this."

"Yeah, nothing like bulls in a China shop."

Freeman ignored my wit.

The police didn't take long to arrive, which was just as well as far as my research was going, since they didn't interrupt anything. Fortunately, my relations with the badge boys topped that of most private eyes — particularly with respect to their boss, Lieutenant Phil Forester.

Forester didn't have to call on his deductive skills to assume that I was present in connection with the murder. I didn't add to his troubles by bringing up the chrysanthemums. He asked me what I knew about the victim, so I filled him in with what little I knew about her. In turn I received his promise that he would "share information" with me. This was all a kind of a game which meant that each of us would keep out of the other's hair. Forester questioned Freeman and Grossman.

After Forester and his cohorts left, I re-questioned Grossman, leaving my second time around with Freeman for later.

I tried to come up with something more about Miss Bankcroft.

"How about boyfriends?"

After a few moments of silence, Grossman answered. "I wouldn't have said anything on the subject in other circumstances — everyone to their own private lives being my motto — but murder. . . . Something was going on between her and Mr. Freeman."

"How long did that go on?" I was bothered by the fact. I couldn't picture the two of them as a couple. He seemed too old for her. She was between twenty-five and thirty; he looked about fifty, maybe even fifty plus. But then, who knows? Maybe she liked older men, and she was reaching the age where you compromised. I had long since passed it. My problem was that I hadn't compromised enough. Besides, he was her boss. Bosses can put on a lot of pressure.

"Until about two weeks ago," volunteered Grossman. "Then things suddenly got chilly between them."

"Chilly enough for him to make her a gift of a jade knife to the neck?" I shot back.

"I'm not sure. I had the feeling that Mr. Freeman could get very angry. He was usually in control, but once in a while ..."

If Freeman had killed her, was there a connection with the chrysanthemum twins?

"There's another thing." Grossman hesitated. "Normally, I wouldn't mention it, but under the circumstances ..."

"The smallest bit of information can sometimes be of help, Al," I prompted.

"I heard them arguing once in his office. I'm not an eavesdropper, but the place was empty and the jades and porcelains don't make much noise." He paused in his narrative for me to acknowledge the humor.

I granted him a nod. "Go on."

"They were arguing about somebody, a woman. I gathered that Miss Bankcroft had discovered someone else in his life. There was this woman who visited Mr. Freeman every two months or so from Australia. He said that she was very interested in jade. I think she was interested in him."

"And Freeman was interested in her?"

"Yes," Grossman said. "But less so when Vivian Bankcroft was around."

"OK, so the Australian lady—does she have a name?"

"Cindy, I think it was," volunteered Grossman. "I called her 'Wally' as a kind of code name."

"Wally?" I asked.

"Short for wallaby," explained Grossman. "Australian—'wallaby.' You get it?"

"Uh-huh. So, either Cindy killed Miss Bankcroft, or Freeman did it." I, of course, had left Grossman off the suspect list.

"I never thought somebody connected with the museum did it. Neither Wally nor Mr. Freeman seem like the murdering type."

I threw out another hypothesis. "You said that Freeman sometimes had a violent temper. Maybe the two of them did it. Maybe Miss Bankcroft threatened them that if they didn't break off their relationship, there would be trouble. Or she could've threatened her boss with something if he didn't break off their relationship." Against my will, I could imagine her using the words, "dire consequences."

"What could she threaten him with?" Grossman asked.

"How about something connected to the superfluous chrysanthemum?" I suggested.

Grossman was silent, but I could see by the look on his face that the hypothesis was not entirely out of the ballpark.

I had gotten enough information for the present from Grossman. I needed to talk to Freeman.

Freeman was haughtier than the day before, and I wondered if it was because I wasn't making progress on the case. I decided to take the wind out of his sails. "How's your Aussie bird?" I opened.

"I beg your pardon?" he said, but I saw by the tensing of the lines that led from his nose to the sides of his mouth that he knew I wasn't referring to the kookaburra. I let him know I was aware that Miss "Down Under" dropped by now and then. A matter of business, he parried. *Not the way I hear it*, I pushed. He accused Grossman of having violated his loyalty to the museum, by which he meant he had talked too much. I decided to protect Grossman; I owed him it to him. So, I lied that Miss Bankcroft had told me. I figured she wouldn't mind and, after all, I was trying to ferret out her murderer.

Freeman blanched. "How much did she tell you?" he blurted out, no longer the cool, crisp, museum head.

"Enough," I said.

Freeman was one of those types that once you penetrated his defenses, he was finished. He slumped in his seat. His words flowed like scotch at a wake, the gist of which was that Cindy was a buyer for an Australian-based Japanese company that sought out unusual art for well-heeled Japanese businessmen, and that Freeman had sold off an occasional museum piece. I surmised that some of the money went into his pocket, and that his relationship with Cindy had been more than commercial. Whether Cindy was romantically interested in him or played him along to get a better commercial deal, he didn't reveal. I bet on the latter and something more – somehow, she must be connected to the chrysanthemums.

Since I had Freeman groggy on the ropes, I would hit him with the right hook. "So you murdered Miss Bankcroft!" I shouted at him. I figured he didn't like to be shouted at.

Freeman stammered the *de rigueur*, "What?!" Yet he seemed generally surprised — or he feigned it well.

"You killed her to keep her quiet — about the chrysanthemum twins. She threatened to tell all about them if you didn't break off with Wal – Cindy. You were two-timing her — and not just with chrysanthemums."

To my amazement, Freeman came clean faster than a one-hour dry cleaning service. I expected him to blame Grossman or even Cindy, but he didn't. Maybe he wasn't a complete prig.

"You've got it all right," he said with a mixture of begrudging admiration. "Vi and I were a cozy pair until I met Cindy. There developed the conventional *menage-a-trois* – that is to say – "

"I know what it means. I saw *The French Connection*."

"To make a long story short, Vi got possessive and said it was her or Cindy."

Succinct, I thought, trying to keep a lid on my anger. "And it was Cindy."

"Well, yes. Vi was all well and good, but Cindy had more to offer."

"It's called money."

"In a word," admitted Freeman.

"And so you killed Vivian, or you and Cindy did, in two words. I hope you aren't going to tell me that Cindy did it alone. I don't relish a trip to Australia."

"No, Cindy had no part in it. I acted alone. I tried to reason with Vi, but she had a will. Talk about 'Ligeia' — but maybe you don't read Poe."

"I prefer Leonard."

"If Vi's problem was her will, mine was a hot temperament. Why, but for it, I could have been director of … " Here, Freeman made an expansive gesture which took in some famous museum. "In any event, I lost control completely. Unfortunately, a jade dagger was close by. You can put two and two together."

"Except for the chrysanthemums. That two I can't put together."

"If the existence of the two chrysanthemums were known, the museum could be ruined. The original chrysanthemum was unique because of its workmanship. Its many leaves demanded exactitude in carving. The ancient artists employed bronze or iron hand tools. A second chrysanthemum, obviously of modern workmanship and a product of our present un-venerable dynasty, was a threat to the uniqueness — and considerable monetary value — of the original. Museums, as the art they house, are built on uniqueness, Mr. Grant. Vi knew that was my Achilles' heel."

"I'm afraid it will all have to come out now," I said.

"But must it, Mr. Grant? It will devastate the museum, perhaps even necessitate its closing."

I began to boil. His museum's continued existence was more important than Vivian's demise. "I can't exactly keep your murdering her under my hat," I said.

"I'm aware of that. It's the two chrysanthemums that I want you … to keep under your hat, as you put it."

Despite being a murderer, he had a point, and Grossman worked there. I hesitated.

"Miss Bankcroft was dedicated to the museum," he said.

How did that bastard know I had a soft spot for her? Maybe my anger hadn't been so controlled.

"I won't be here," he added. "Somebody else will. And it's a lovely museum."

"Maybe it will stay that way—if you clear up the mystery of the second chrysanthemum."

"Oh, *that*. Wang, a Chinese craftsman who worked with the museum repairing jades, made the second. With the chrysanthemum, he wasn't quite good enough to fool an expert of my caliber, but most others wouldn't be able to differentiate between the two."

"But why did you have him make it? I mean, what about the uniqueness you prize so much?"

"Oh, I didn't have him make it."

I looked blank. It's not good for a detective to look blank, but I was stymied. This case had more twists and turns than the Great Wall of China.

"Miss Bankcroft arranged that."

"Miss Bankcroft!" I blurted out, violating the second rule of detective-ology, that of displaying surprise. The first rule is not to look blank. "But why? Like yourself, she claimed to prize uniqueness."

"As much as she prized uniqueness, she prized passion more. And as I stated previously, she was on to Cindy and me."

"Blackmail? It doesn't—didn't—seem to fit Miss Bankcroft," I snarled.

Freeman presented a most supercilious smile. "I see you didn't know Vi well."

He had me there. "I wonder why she came to me in the first place," I mumbled.

"Why, to blow the cover on the chrysanthemums after she planted the second one with the first in order to get her revenge on me. Incidentally, she said that you were putty in her hands. That's a quote. I don't myself employ manual metaphors."

It fit. She used me to get back at Freeman. Seems *he* wasn't putty in her hands, but despite learning this, it was hard to get her out of my mind.

"Why did Wang cooperate with her?" I finally asked.

"She used her not-inconsiderable charm on him – not physically. He admired her and she flattered his jade workmanship. And he may have been angry at me for dumping her, though I cannot be certain if she told him."

I asked him if I could have the second chrysanthemum "as a souvenir of the case."

He went out, under my watchful eye, and came back with the two chrysanthemums and a lecture, maybe his swan song. "In Chinese tradition, jade was esteemed as a mirror of virtues. Its hardness suggested intellect, its polish, purity, its visible flaws, sincerity."

Maybe when it was formed into chrysanthemums it had the opposite effect, I mused, but I refrained from laying this on Freeman.

He handed me the two chrysanthemums and asked, "Which is the copy?"

I looked at both, but I couldn't tell the difference. They looked like two peas in a pod. So much for the parameters of art.

"The one in your right hand," he revealed after a long moment. "I told you when you first came that they were both the originals. At that point it served my purpose.

"Of course, I recognized it as a copy after careful examination. That's where Vi erred. She underestimated me. She knew that because of the nature of jade, dating is difficult. But Wang is a good worker. He cleverly constructed the chrysanthemum out of the bottom of a jade jar that he 'borrowed' from the storeroom for this purpose. Unlike the original chrysanthemum, it was made from nephrite, the less prized of the two jade minerals, jadeite and nephrite, from which jades are carved. He even used traditional tools of workmanship, but made the mistake of using power tools to shorten the time. Apparently, Vi was in a hurry. Somebody less astute than myself might not have spotted that it wasn't Ming."

Freeman's astuteness hadn't helped him in the end. Untypically, I refrained from pointing this out to him. Maybe being surrounded with so much culture was having a bad effect on me.

"I guess the only player that came out of this affair intact is Cindy," Freeman said soberly.

Yeah, I thought, bouncing the two chrysanthemums in my hands. She was fancy-free in Australia, which at least gave me something to spring on Grossman. Two in the hand were not always worth one in the bush — the Australian bush.

Larry Lefkowitz has had more than 150 stories and poems published, as well as an anthology of humor. His literary novel, *The Critic, the Assistant Critic, and Victoria* is available as an ebook and in print from Amazon. Lefkowitz's humorous fantasy and science fiction collection, *Laughing into the Fourth Dimension*, is available from Amazon books. His story collection, *Enigmatic Tales*, published by Fomite Press, is available from Amazon and Barnes & Noble.

The Haunted Detective

James Pyles

The rain assaulting the corrugated door behind me sounded like gunfire. A yellowing streetlamp outside threw macabre shadows across the murky interior of Alvin's Garage.

Reaching a hand across my trench coat, I felt the reassuring hardness of the .38 in my purse, though I always packed a spare. Weasel said what I'd find in the office safe upstairs would send Boss Gus Ramsey away for life. I couldn't wait.

Flat leather soles slapped on metal steps, making me thankful I don't wear heels like most dames.

At the top of the landing, I played my flashlight beam across the floor below at the empty car racks, toolboxes, and wheel blocks below.

I used a gloved finger to nudge the office door open. Beat-up desk, swivel chair with a broken wheel, five-year-old cheesecake calendar on peeling wallpaper, puke-inducing orange upholstered sofa. I swung left.

"Awfully careless of you, Ramsey, leaving this rusting hulk around." I shrugged off my purse strap, the large bag landing with a dusty plop. I slowly turned the dial, listening to ticking tumblers. "Miles'll be sore, but for all I know, Rizzitello's playing me for a sap."

I turned the cold handle and heard the heartwarming thud of the bolt releasing. "You've still got it, Marguerite." I ran with a rough crowd as a kid, picking pockets by age six, shoplifting by seven. This cracker box was a lead-pipe cinch.

Clenched the flashlight in my mouth, smearing ruby lipstick. Lifted a stained manila envelope out of the safe, but what I saw inside made me almost hurl.

"Come on, baby." A man's muffled voice. Crap. Must have come in the front door. *Who's he talking to?* I killed the light, stuffing it and my prize in my purse.

"Not a chance." I couldn't see her face through the smeared office window, but she sounded like a teenager; another of Ramsey's street girls.

"Hey!" His clammy meat hook yanked her hard enough to make her squeal.

"You'll do what I say, or I'll tell your lousy pimp you've been skimming, capisce?"

"Sure, Eddie. You don't gotta get rough, even if you are one of Ramsey's ..."

"Shut up about that." He towed her onto the metal staircase heading up to this cheesy office, to the broken-down sofa, and toward me.

"Let's get this over with. Guido wants me back by two."

"You don't want me to go slow, baby?" I could've heard his leer from across the Bay. Then two pairs of shoes clunked onto the landing.

I'm a big girl in a few ways—one of them's being tall—but I managed to squat behind the safe. Once they got started, I heard wet, smacking lips and Lorraine pretending she liked him. Unfortunately, the dish opened her eyes and turned toward me as I was tiptoeing out.

"What the … Eddie!"

I danced down the steps two at a time, trench coat fluttering like Superman's cape.

"Stop, damn it!" He was bellowing and I was running. Some folks have good luck, some have bad. Mine's always stupid. I heard the shot as I tripped over a lead wheel block.

Hitting the cement floor, my shoulder popped, then I felt familiar agony lancing down my arm.

The room echoed with the thump of Eddie landing on concrete. Scrambling up, I sprinted for the exit, Jesse Owens with 36C cups.

That's me flying outside into the hard rain and dark of the streets of San Francisco, my flesh ripping, and blood spraying as Eddie's bullet connects. The name's Marguerite Potter, I'm a Private Investigator, and you're probably wondering how I got into this mess.

Dressed like a two-bit tramp, my legs stretched across my desk, giving Police Inspector Miles Cowen a gander up to the garter straps. The Inspector never tumbled. My body was shamelessly flirting, but my brain was all business, phone receiver pressed at my ear. "Yes, Mr. Patterson, I'm glad we got little Effie out of that mess, too. Terrible thing her running away, then falling in with …"

I listened to his burbling, caustic emotional mixture. "Docs'll have her fixed up in no time. Then you can take her home." Miles scowled, knowing seventeen-year-old Effie Patterson would still have to testify at the trial.

"Tomorrow's fine. Settle up with Moshe Katz. He'll give me my cut. You're welcome. Goodbye." Setting the receiver in its cradle, I plopped my feet down.

"All jake with your first client?" Miles was sitting forward on the sofa.

"Yeah. Launch of the Potter Detective Agency went off swell … almost." I fingered the fat lip the murderer gave me before I pulled my roscoe on him.

Miles looked around my office, lit by a single bulb dangling from the ceiling and my second-hand desk lamp. The boxes I hadn't gotten around to unpacking made my newly rented office look like a tornado-decorated warehouse. "You ought to straighten this up if you're going to get more business. Costumes and makeup lying around makes it look like backstage at an old vaudeville act."

"That's my trade. I've played everything from nuns to notaries."

"Plenty of evening girls, too."

"Earned me my keep while I was learning from Katz."

"What did Moshe say when you told him this was your last case together?"

"Cried like a baby."

"Katz wouldn't cry at his own mother's funeral."

"Scram, Miles." I smirked, then winced. Lip still ached from the beating I took. The killer worked over Effie, and iced a half dozen other streetwalkers. The coppers Katz flagged kicked down the door to that deserted tenement where he'd been murdering women, but I got the drop on him first. "Need some shuteye. You heading home?"

"You kidding? I've got hours of paperwork to do. Worth it though, taking that killer off the streets." He stood, garish light above his head highlighting his age. "Good work, Margie."

"Dumb luck. Katz and me were hired to find a runaway, except she'd fallen in with Ramsey's pimps. Ended up square in the killer's sights."

"We still can't pin any of this on Ramsey."

"We will someday."

"Wish we had you on the force, Margie. You've got the best instincts in the business."

"Too bad you don't hire dames. Besides, I'd never get used to the rules. Grew up in an orphanage getting my knuckles rapped by Sister Mary Capital Punishment."

I saw I'd hurt him. Good Catholic boy like Miles was as straight as they came. Cop for thirty-five years, married for thirty, four kids.

I got up, took the hat out of his hands, and settled it over his brow. "Blow. It's not good for you to be seen in a woman's boudoir." He was the Dad I always wanted but didn't deserve.

"You sleeping here?"

"Yeah. Got a room in the back with a kitchenette. I can't afford rent on an office and an apartment."

He glanced around again. Varnish on the floor planks worn bare in places, plaster cracked on the wall to the outer office, my crud spread all over the joint.

"Come by the station tomorrow to make your statement." He winked. "Try to dress like a lady."

"I will, but I'm no lady."

"Sweet dreams."

He let himself out and I doused the lights, listening to his heavy feet tromp down the stairs. Retrieved a bottle of cheap bourbon out of a box by my desk. First swig went down like acid as I stared out the window. Second-floor view of Grant Street, Sutter crossing it, just north. My beat-up '39 Ford coupe at the curb below.

Capping the bottle, I tumbled onto the sofa like a broken doll, using my trench coat for a pillow.

A shrill scream snapped my eyes open. It was my office, but it wasn't. Still nighttime, but more light, two standing lamps on either side of the door. Sofa, chairs, desk all brand new. Door from the outer office banged open. A burly son of a gun dragged a woman by her forearm. Threw her to the floor at my feet. It was pretty little Preta, all of twenty-one again, thin, dancer's frame, green cotton dress, blazing red wildfire hair. She was the sweetest kid I'd ever known, the first friend I made when I blew into Frisco. The last time I saw her was a week after Pearl Harbor.

"I told your old man what I'd do if he didn't play ball." He was standing over her, a bestial Colossus in a pinstriped suit. It was Gus Ramsey, one of San Francisco's top crime bosses.

Preta was up on one elbow, tearing eyes filled with terror. "Please, Mr. Ramsey. I can get Pa to see reason."

"Too late for that. No one double-crosses Gus Ramsey." He grabbed her arm, yanking her halfway to her feet, and then punched her. I could hear her nose break through the shrieking.

"You piece of crap." He didn't even look at me as I swung a right cross at his jaw.

My hand passed through his face like it was made of fog, and a second later, so did I. Saw the calendar on the far wall near the door announce, "December 1941." My mouth went dry. Office was the one I'd just rented, but it was kept up, furniture brand new, light fixtures different, even Gus Ramsey, who I'd only seen in photos, looked younger. Not a gray hair on his head.

Preta wailed as he pounded on her, but all I could do was watch, like a ghost haunting a murder.

He belted her one last time, the back of her head smashing against the corner of his desk. I don't know how she stayed conscious with a shattered skull. The seconds passed like decades as I watched her die.

I woke up screaming, rolled off the sofa, banged my knees on the floor, and then sent the booze bottle spinning under my desk. My rumpled trench coat flowed off the couch.

Preta was standing over me, whole, unsullied, imploring. I knew what she wanted.

I was on my butt, sofa at my back, gaping. Her face was stone cold, like the grave. For the only time since we first met and roomed together, I was scared to death of Preta.

"I died here. My soul is chained and can't rise. You have to make him pay. I can't rest until you do." The room violently shivered. Thought it was a quake, but then realized it was her. The windows, the whole room, rattled with her rage. I saw what being brutally murdered does to a soul, even one as kind as Preta's.

Hoisted myself back onto the sofa. "I'll try. Heck, one reason I got into this game was because you vanished. It kept eating at my guts."

"I'm not the first, Marguerite. We're all waiting, eternally suffering through our murders. You're the only one who can save us."

Pristine face and ballerina body melted and shattered in gushes and shards of blood and bone, like in my dream last night. I'd swore I'd bring Boss Gus Ramsey to justice, or else drag him with me into hell.

Couldn't sleep, so I hit an all-night diner around the corner. Swallowed greasy slop, then swilled coffee until nine.

Back at the office, I dialed the public library. "Myra Cowen, please. Oh, it's you. Had enough java yet? You're going to need it."

I listened to her jokes. Unlike Miles, she had a sense of humor. "Here's the deal. I need some history on the office I've rented. 1941 and '42. That's right, the works, who owned it, renters, scandals, everything. Sure, I can call back. Don't tell your flatfoot husband. Heading downtown to give him a statement. What's that, hun? OK. Bye."

"Appreciate you coming down this early." Miles looked like he'd gotten about as much sleep as I had. He was Atlas in a threadbare, wrinkled suit, supporting the world on rounded shoulders.

I was sitting across from him in his closet-sized office, scanning the paperwork chaos on a desk as beat up as mine. "Could we chitchat off the record?" Suspicion crossed his face. He saw that I wanted a favor.

"The answer's probably no."

"I need to know who Gus Ramsey's known associates were back in '41, especially fall and winter."

"If it's an open police investigation …"

"It's not … yet."

"Who's your client?"

"You know better than that."

"I don't fetch."

"C'mon, Miles." I batted my massacred eyelashes at him, knowing he'd be immune. "I really need this one. You owe me. If the Pattersons hadn't hired Katz and me …"

"I don't owe Katz."

"I played punching bag so he'd take me back to his place. You'd never have collared him without me."

He sighed, signaling my victory. "Give me a few minutes." He stood up, leaning his fists on the desk's ink blotter. "But after this, we're square."

I held up three fingers. "Scout's honor."

"When were you ever a Girl Scout?"

I sweetly smiled.

"You're impossible." He lumbered out of his office, leaving me to check my .38 and the other asset. Twenty minutes later, I had a list of the Bay Area's biggest racketeers, including Victor "Big Vic" Assaro and Carmine "The Weasel" Rizzitello, who both worked for Pete DeLuca.

An hour after that, I wore a Cheshire cat grin as I hung up my office phone. Myra came through like a champ. From '39 to early '42, my address was a suspected bookie joint. Graft-ridden cops laid off, so no connection to Ramsey. But the name on the lease rang a loud bell. "Big Vic" was having company for lunch.

Just before one, I breezed into the cool, dark splendor of Little Sicily's near Washington Square. Thought about ordering the cannoli as I stopped at Big Vic's table, strutting like a Vegas showgirl. "Say Vic, you want to buy a lady some grub?"

He always ate lunch here with thugs. I recognized Weasel Rizzitello from my list, but the others were strangers to me.

"Who the hell are you, and ..." I could see the light bulb flicker over his head. "Marguerite Potter. Son of a ... you've got cojones."

"Sure don't, but I am hungry." Started to shed my trench coat, then I saw the look on his face.

He nodded, and a waiter put another chair at the table to Vic's left. It was a tight squeeze since Vic weighed 350 pounds. Sweat dripped down his neck as he checked out my top. He thought he could use what I wanted as the admission ticket to get his way.

Didn't make it past the appetizer. I casually mentioned the office on Grant, and two of Vic's thugs gave me the bum's rush onto the sidewalk. I flipped off the laughing hyenas and yelled, "You could of at least fed me first, you cheap crumbs."

I skipped lunch, cashed my check from Katz, and was drinking dinner from a bottle in my office. Sitting behind the desk, I watched storm clouds shrouding the sunset.

"Look hun, it's been one day. Give it a chance." Preta's eyes bored into my soul. I'd blown it with Assaro. He was the only connection between Ramsey and the murder scene. I didn't have to worry about him dropping a dime on me, but now what?

Phone rang, and I wasn't drunk enough yet to say, "screw it."

"Margie Potter," I barked.

"You got a big mouth. Someday someone's gonna flatten it."

"Too late. Happened last night. Who's this?"

"Want the skinny on Big Vic, Ramsey, and that dump on Grant?"

I sat up straighter than a nun's ruler. "What's the deal?"

"A few of us don't like Ramsey using kid streetwalkers."

I shoved the boozy haze aside, remembering Rizzitello had four younger sisters.

"So give." I pulled a steno pad from desk drawer and fumbled for a pencil.

"Vic and Ramsey ran numbers plus a hot car ring back then. Here's the address." I started scribbling. "What you want is in a safe in the upstairs office, and it's golden."

Now you know how I ended up with a cracked wing, a hole in my shoulder, and flying like a bat out of Texas into a cold, hard rain, but that wasn't the end of it.

I owed Joel Cohen more favors than I could count. He was Katz's uncle, and the only doctor I could trust. He agreed to meet me back at my office. An hour later, I was patched up. I'm lucky: Cohen, Katz, and the Cowens still give a damn if I live or die. My bill was showing him the evidence. He was gone thirty minutes when Ramsey crashed through my door, a Colt M1911 in his mitt.

I was flat on the sofa, right arm in a sling, trying to push myself up with my left. The light from my desk lamp shone upward, illuminating his murderous yellow-gray eyes.

"Who hired you?" He was shivering, his gun barrel weaving like a cobra.

My .38 was in my bag on the desk, next to my dripping, bloodstained coat. I had one last move, and it was lousy. "I called the cops. They're on their way. You've still got time to get out the back."

"Bull. Tell me or I'll kill you and bury the evidence so deep no one will find it again."

"Like I'll ever squeal for a pig like you."

"No one could know unless…that rat Assaro. Nah, there's no percentage."

"I hired Marguerite."

Preta loomed over the same side of the desk where she'd died.

"What kind of trick is this?" Gus's eyes were fixed like a mouse on a starving cat. Pointing the Colt at her, he was trying to decide if he'd gone off his rocker.

"Time to pay the piper, Gus." She spoke with demon's lips. Her eyes stared out from the bloody gates of hell.

Terrified, he fired three times, slugs passing through air and darkness. Two of them broke a window, and the third hit wall plaster.

When he turned on me, he was looking down the barrel of the Colt .32 I keep in a holster strapped on my right thigh.

"Drop it, Ramsey." The corny line came from Miles Cowen. He stomped in from the outer office with enough cops to start a convention. "You OK, Margie?" He flipped the wall switch, and the ceiling light came on. Miles' worry lines got longer when he saw the sling.

One of the uniforms took Ramsey's heater. Lifting the envelope, Miles dumped the contents on the desktop, everything I showed Cohen. Ramsey took big game hunter photos of Preta's corpse. My office was recognizable in the background. A map of Holy Cross Catholic Cemetery in Colma tumbled out.

"Cohen phoned me, and a passing patrol car saw Ramsey casing your joint."

A handcuffed Ramsey stared murder at me. I stared back, my .32 aimed at his face.

"Put it down, Margie."

"This one's for you, angel." A very real, very dead Preta was watching. Even if he got the chair, the appeals would take years.

Pulling the hammer back, the raw metal action was deafening. I felt my finger squeezing the trigger.

"Lower your gun right now." Miles had his .38 aimed at me. I couldn't care less.

"Stop or I'll fire."

"Sweetheart." She was whispering in my ear. "It's over. I can go home now. I love you too much to let you do this." Preta kissed my cheek. I could feel the warmth of her lips, the breeze of her hot breath.

Quaking with sobs, I released the hammer, dropping the revolver onto my lap. Miles lowered his arm, sighing. "Get that trash out of here," he snarled.

Miles waited like a stone as the officers took Ramsey out, and waited until the echoes of their footsteps died. Then he holstered his gun.

"Gonna lock me up?"

"We've all lost someone, Margie. There isn't a cop in the world who hasn't felt exactly like you did, but you didn't pull the trigger. That's what separates us from them."

"What now?" I shrunk like a deflating balloon.

He scooped the evidence back into the envelope. "Cohen told us the plot number circled on the map. San Mateo sheriffs went out. It's Ramsey's mother's grave. Died December 12, 1941. Doesn't take a genius to figure out he buried Miss Preta Stevens' body with her."

Miles turned off my desk lamp and pocketed the envelope. "Get some sleep. Cohen said he'd come by in the morning. You look like hell."

"Thanks." I couldn't even manage a smirk.

He shuffled toward the exit, then noticed my damp, beat-up trench coat. Picking it up, he shook out the dampness. I laid back while he tucked me in. I'd never felt so warm.

Miles stood, got to the outer office, and flipped off the lights. "When you're feeling better, drop by the house. We're having pot roast on Saturday."

By the time he'd closed the door, I was fast asleep. I dreamed Preta was happy.

James Pyles is a published science fiction and fantasy writer and freelance Information Technology author. Since 2019, his short stories have been featured in anthologies and periodicals. He has a passion for these genres and is currently working on more compelling projects. You can find him at https://poweredbyrobots.com.

Murder at the Museum

Steffi Siby

It was just another Saturday. Or so he had thought.

Tauren yawned widely. It was a spectacularly sunny day and he wanted to be outside. Instead, his mum had dragged him to a musty, old museum. He protested loudly about how boring it was, and his mother glared at him.

'It's about time you took some interest in intellectual matters,' she admonished him.

'But these are displays of jewellery; it's so boring, especially for a guy,' he wailed.

'Yes, but it's not just any jewellery. These are all of significant historic and tremendous monetary value,' his mother said in an excited tone.

'Fine,' Tauren conceded and rolled his eyes. *The quicker we look through the display, the quicker I can get outside.*

They had just entered a opulent looking room furnished with velvet curtains, oil paintings, and a chandelier. There were only a few displays in this room, but people were talking in reverent, hushed tones. His mum signalled him towards the displays, and he ambled forward unenthusiastically.

However, his eyes widened when he read the plaques that detailed how much some of the jewellery was worth. There was a particular set that was evidently the centrepiece: white, intricate pearls laced with sparkling diamonds on a thick gold chain. He heard his mother sigh in appreciation near him, and look at the necklace wistfully.

'You like it then, Mum. I guess I know what to get you for your next birthday, then,' Tauren joked.

His mum scowled but then laughed and said, 'I wish.'

They were still laughing when everything went black.

When he regained consciousness, Tauren looked around, startled. His head felt hazy and his faced itched. Thankfully, his mum was still right next to him.

'Are you OK baby?' she choked out, amidst coughs.

'Yeah, what on earth happened?'

As if conjured up to answer his question, a museum official appeared in front of them.

'Hello sir, madam. We are so sorry, but we have been the target of a crime. The criminal used teargas to incapacitate everyone. There are paramedics available if you need any assistance.'

They stared at him in shock, their mouths agape, their faces ashen.

'We're both fine. Wait, what did they do?' his mum asked.

'They stole the centrepiece, the necklace worth twenty-five-million pounds. And unfortunately, the teargas has killed an elderly gentleman.'

His mum looked at Tauren incredulously; she wasn't usually at a loss for words, but she was struggling now.

The Trench Coat Chronicles

Tauren thanked the museum official and they made their way out, his head reeling with questions.

The news was everywhere the following day. It still felt surreal to Tauren even though he had been at the scene. His mother still seemed to be in a state of shock. He did not want to disturb her further, so he held back from talking to her about the incident.

So many thoughts and questions whirled around in his head. Even though Tauren was a daydreamer, he also possessed extraordinary observational skills and an exceptionally good memory. He had noticed that he was always acutely aware of his surroundings. This was something he kept to himself, but now felt it could be used to catch the culprit.

Although he had been mainly pining to go outside, he had also absorbed the minutiae of the museum. Especially in the room with the expensive necklaces, he hadn't thoroughly scrutinised the jewellery itself as others were doing, but instead was more interested in the whole room. Ever since the incident, he had repeatedly recalled everything about the room.

There wasn't any one thing particularly interesting that jumped to mind. There were about a dozen people in the room when the lights went out. The velvet curtains were open, sunlight streaming in, and a window was also slightly ajar, a fact that irked him. He realised that the teargas could have been released through that window.

The ceiling was particularly ornate and did not seem to possess any obvious entryway into the room. The door through which they had come in was the only entrance/or exit. He hadn't seen any detectors or guards outside the room itself, which was puzzling, if there was a necklace worth £25 million inside.

But then he remembered something. When they had entered the museum, displayed on the screens was a message that there was to be a meeting for all museum staff for an hour that afternoon and therefore there would be no staff availability at that particular time. The criminal had obviously taken advantage of this fact, and Tauren thought that could mean it might be an inside job.

He knew he had to consider motive, and it seemed glaringly obvious: the monetary worth of the necklace. A murder had occurred too, but that seemed to be an unintended consequence. The newspaper claimed that the coroner had determined the cause of death: The elderly man had underlying respiratory conditions that caused the severe reaction to the teargas. Normally, it would only render the victims unconscious. Tauren almost felt sorry for the criminal who had inadvertently killed someone, but then realised he was being silly and if anyone deserved sympathy, it was the family of the deceased gentleman.

The days went by but Tauren's mind kept flitting back to the event again and again. He needed to get to the bottom of it, but the official investigations seemed to be progressing very slowly. He wanted to contribute but didn't think anyone would take him and his theories seriously. But he had to do what he could.

The Trench Coat Chronicles

He decided that going back to the scene of the crime would be the next best step. He knew it wouldn't be easy to get in there, but he formulated a plan and arrived at the museum brimming with determination. As expected, the museum was closed to visitors and there were police markings everywhere. Luckily, he could see the museum official who had spoken to him and his mum near the entrance.

Tauren approached him warily.

'Hi, I'm Tauren. I was in there with my mum when ... it happened.'

'Yeah, I remember you. How can I help?' the man asked in a friendly tone.

Tauren tried to keep his voice from quivering as it usually did when he lied.

'I ... erm ... need to get back in the room. You see, my mum lost something in there. When she fell. One of her earrings.'

The man's friendly demeanour disappeared.

'Well, it's a police zone now. There wasn't anything found but if they do find an earring, I'll make sure they let you know.'

'No, no, you don't understand,' Tauren said hastily. 'The earring is a family heirloom passed down from my grandmother. My mum's really upset. She would have come herself but she's been really shaken up after the incident. So am I. I think it would really help her get some closure.'

He knew this was a weak argument and the museum official looked unimpressed. A police officer nearby who had been listening to their conversation turned to them abruptly.

'It's fine, let him in. We already have all the evidence we need from in there. We aren't using the room now so he might as well.'

'Oh, thank you so much,' Tauren gushed.

'Yeah, it's fine, kid. But you said you were in there when it happened, right? Would you be able to help us out with the investigation then? Answer a few questions?'

Tauren agreed readily and arranged a time later on in the week to meet with the policeman.

Once inside the museum, he felt uneasy. He had not responded like his mum but he realised that he was still affected by the incident as he made his way to the room where it had happened. The room was sealed off and it smelled musty. The same velvet curtains, ornate ceiling, chandelier. He walked to the spot where he had fallen unconscious. It didn't trigger any particular memories or emotions.

The other cabinets in the room had been emptied as well; there wasn't much to see. He felt a wave of disappointment. The trip had been pointless. He went back to the spot where he had fallen. From that position, he could clearly see the cabinet that had held the centrepiece. Which meant that the perpetrator would have been directly in his vision — if he hadn't been unconscious, that is.

He decided to lie down where he had fallen before to assess his vantage point. Perhaps, just before losing consciousness, he had seen something? Nothing came to mind and he was about to stand up when something caught his eye. It was in the very corner of the carpet holding the cabinet. He reached out underneath the cabinet to grasp it. His arms strained; it wasn't easy to get to.

He stood up and stared at his finding. It was a piece of fabric with a crisscross pattern. It was difficult to say where it was from but he knew immediately that it was not supposed to be there on the floor underneath the cabinet. There was a high probability that it was linked to the criminal. But then again, he reasoned with himself, someone might have lost it a while ago.

The fabric looked to be torn at one end, which made Tauren speculate that it had ripped whilst handling the cabinet. He held it in his hand and wondered if he should tell the museum official and the policeman what he had discovered. Something inside held him back. He felt he needed more time to mull things over before giving up what could be an important piece of evidence.

Tauren was consumed by his thoughts over the next few days. The crime was gaining considerable media attention, so he also encountered it everywhere he looked. He kept taking out the piece of fabric to look at it, as though it contained the answers he was looking for. His head felt like it might burst from questions and he thought it would be useful to talk about it. However, he didn't feel like he could talk about it to any of his friends.

What he needed was someone who could empathise with his feelings. It would have to be his mum. After the initial shock had worn off, she seemed better. He knew she was avoiding all the media coverage and she had taken some time off work to recuperate. He hoped talking about it wouldn't be too difficult for her. It might even be what she needed right now, and so he approached her carefully.

'Hey Mum, I was wondering if I could talk to you about something.'

'Yeah, sure. What is it, Tauren?'

He detailed his trip back to the museum, the encounter with the museum official and policeman, and his search of the room.

His mum was aghast.

'Why would you do such a thing? Go back to that horrible room!' She visibly shuddered.

'I just wanted to find out what happened,' he said weakly.

'Well, that's not your job. There's the police for that,' she replied coldly.

'Yeah, I'm meeting that policeman tomorrow to answer questions. I think I might be able to help,' Tauren said, and showed her the piece of fabric.

A puzzled frown appeared on his mum's face.

'I recognise the pattern. I've seen it somewhere.'

'Really?' Tauren asked excitedly, hoping that her memory might help track down the owner.

'Not that you should even be getting involved, but yeah, I'll take a picture of the piece of fabric and send it to Sheena. She will definitely know which designer it is.'

Sheena was a friend of his mum's who worked in the fashion industry.

'Oh, that's great,' he said, and gave his mum an affectionate hug.

That evening, Sheena was able to tell them which designer the crisscross pattern belonged to, but she warned them it wouldn't be easy to trace it back to its owner.

'They're quite a new brand and they do shirts, jumpers, trousers, bags, and shoes. Basically, everything for both sexes. Their stuff is only sold in boutique shops and not the main high-end shops, so that narrows it down, but still, who knows where it's from?'

Tauren wasn't discouraged by this but instead looked forward to sharing his discoveries with the police officer the next day.

He woke up early the next morning, feeling a sense of anticipation at how things would unfold when he met the police officer. He was relieved to think that the whole case might be solved soon. He was about to leave the house when his mum called out.

'Don't forget your coat, Tauren!'

'Mum, it's so sunny outside. I don't need a coat,' he replied and rolled his eyes.

He started walking, his mind full of possibilities. He wasn't sure what questions the officer would ask. He wondered if his theories would be laughed at and ignored. The streets seemed crowded with people. Tauren noticed people eating ice cream and drinking iced coffee and became aware of how thirsty he was. He was bemused to notice two girls wearing long, thick coats. How did they bear the heat, he wondered fleetingly, and concluded that it must be some sort of trend.

Once he got there, the police officer greeted him warmly and led him through to another room. He asked several questions about what Tauren had noticed that day. The details of everyone present was needed alongside many other seemingly complex and miniscule things. It was quite tiring having to think so much, and Tauren interjected and brought up the fabric.

At first, the officer was bewildered. He kept saying he was absolutely certain there had been nothing in the room. It had been searched thoroughly. Tauren tried to explain how obscurely placed the fabric had been under the cabinet, then launched into what Sheena had said about its origins.

'Well, why are we assuming that the fabric has anything to do with this case? It might have been there for years, especially if it was so hard to find,' the officer countered.

'No, I'm sure it was from the day,' Tauren said with conviction.

'How can you be sure? Where's the evidence?'

'I was wondering, have you found anything on the CCTV?' he asked.

The officer looked at Tauren like he was stupid.

'There was no CCTV footage; it had been disabled,' he said, as if it were the most obvious thing in the world.

'OK, yeah. But I just have this feeling. ...'

'We don't work based on feelings here. We need witnesses and evidence. Thanks for your time anyway, Tauren.'

The Trench Coat Chronicles

Tauren was frustrated that the police officer didn't share his enthusiasm about the fabric and that he had been dismissed so quickly. But he knew that there wasn't much more he could say right now. On his walk back, he saw the girls with the long coats again. The sun was still ablaze and the air was starting to get humid. Tauren had the nagging feeling that he was forgetting something. He kept trying to remember what it was but it kept evading his grasp.

His mum was waiting for him to find out how the interview had gone. Tauren narrated the encounter and tried not to show his disappointment that the officer wasn't interested in the fabric.

'Oh, well, at least you tried. They're the professionals after all, so just leave it to them.'

'But mum, you don't understand. There's just something,' he said, deep in thought.

'It's so warm today Tauren, you were right, no need for a coat,' observed his mum.

Suddenly, a realisation hit Tauren full force. He knew what the nagging forgotten fact was. He stood up from the table abruptly.

'I've got it. I remember now!' he said excitedly.

His mum looked alarmed. Her brows knitted.

'What is it?'

'I'll explain later, I have to get back to the police station right away.'

Tauren hurriedly made his way back again.

He was panting and sweating by the time he got back but barely aware of it, he was so exhilarated. The officer looked surprised to see him again.

'Why are you back, Tauren?'

Tauren tried to steady his breathing.

'I ... I've ... I've remembered. I know who it was.'

'Remembered what?' the officer asked, frowning.

He collapsed onto a chair and gestured for Tauren to sit down, too.

'Officer. The fabric. I recognise where it is from. It's from a trench coat. The culprit was wearing a beige trench coat.'

'What?'

'Yeah. I wasn't really paying much attention to the necklaces as I told you. I just wanted to be out in the sun. But I definitely had a look at everyone else who was there at the time. And this woman, she was wearing a long trench coat. I remembered being a bit puzzled as to why she was wearing a massive coat when it was so sunny.'

The officer listened intently now, so he went on.

'But yeah, I just put it out of my mind because of becoming unconscious and all that followed. When I went back to check the room that day for, um, my mother's earring, I had another nagging feeling. The woman was very close to the cabinet just before the teargas overwhelmed us, you see. And then this morning, coats kept turning up around me ... my mum telling me to wear a coat, then I saw two girls wearing coats. So, I finally realised that the coat is the key to the case.'

The Trench Coat Chronicles

'I mean, it is something we could follow up, but I'm not sure,' the officer replied, dubiously.

'I'm definitely sure,' Tauren asserted. 'The trench coat comes with a removable insulated lining, and that is where the woman would have hidden the necklace. And it should be possible to trace back the coat with the pattern, as they're only available in boutique shops, and they'll have CCTV cameras there as well.'

'OK, we also need a full description of this woman, so we can get a sketch.'

Tauren nodded enthusiastically. He was glowing with pride.

Just a week later, the case was solved and the museum was set to reopen soon. Tauren's valuable observations and insights led the police to track down the owner of the trench coat. However, there were some surprises in store.

The trench coat belonged to a Mrs. Wickham, wife of Mr. Wickham, the museum official who Tauren had met. He had supposedly sought revenge on the museum. He claimed that they kept cutting his pay and treating him badly. So, he had concocted this plan alongside his wife. He knew the centrepiece was the finest asset and that the museum would be plunged into disgrace if it disappeared.

The Wickhams claimed that they were not interested in selling the necklace and making money, but the police did not find that statement very plausible. The Wickhams hadn't planned for anyone to get hurt, and the death of the gentleman had been a total accident. They confessed that their motives were to bring the museum under scrutiny, and to bring justice for the underappreciated workers. An investigation was to be launched to handle that but nevertheless, the couple would have to pay a hefty price for their actions.

As for Tauren, he was deeply impressed that his observational skills had led to solving the case. His mum was feeling much better now that things were resolved, and was back at work. The sunny weather continued and Tauren had to admit that museums were not as boring as he had initially thought.

Steffi Siby is a lifelong reading and writing enthusiast. She is currently devoted to volunteering with young carers and at her local library. She spends the rest of her time with her adorable puppy, Snickers. She posts weekly on her blog https://spreadyoursmile.home.blog.

Trench Coat Burial

Catherine Berry

Thank God for small town mortuaries, Floyd thought to himself, as he slunk into the dark building. It had been easy jimmying the lock. With a little luck, no one would ever know he was there. Following the thin beam of his penlight, Floyd made his way downstairs to where the bodies were kept. His niece, Casey's, funeral was tomorrow and this would be his last chance. Flicking on the light, he turned to the gleaming mortuary cabinet lining one wall.

"Where is she?" Floyd muttered, opening and closing drawers, looking for his niece's familiar face. Empty. Every single one was empty. "What the hell?" he hollered, slamming a fist against metal. *What happened to her body?*

"Something troubling you, Floyd?"

He froze, dread rising like bile in his throat. Slowly turning, his eyes landed on Detective Claire Wallace standing across the room. She was the person investigating Casey's murder.

"D-Detective! What are you doing here?"

"Y'know, I was just wondering the same thing about you," she replied, mouth curving in a humorless smile. "Would you like to explain what you're doing, Floyd? No, better yet, why don't we have this conversation at the police station. Officer Hogan. Officer Kennedy."

Two uniformed policemen slipped into the room. One droned on with his Miranda rights while the other pulled Floyd's arms behind his back. Floyd felt the cold press of cuffs bite into his wrists. *How did they know?*

"The evidence doesn't look good for you, Floyd," Detective Wallace clucked, setting down a file as she sat across from him in an interrogation room. "I caught you red-handed breaking into the funeral home looking for the body of your murdered niece. That's strange, Floyd. Don't you think?"

"I-I just wanted to see my niece one more time, in private," Floyd stammered, guts twisted as his mind scrambled. "Guess I wasn't really thinking."

"So, you broke into the funeral home in the middle of the night to say goodbye to your niece?" Detective Wallace questioned, skepticism clearly written on her face.

"Yeah. Yes. One last goodbye."

"You couldn't do that tomorrow at the funeral?"

"Like I said, I wasn't thinking."

"Huh. I didn't realize you and Casey were that close. I thought you two didn't really have much to do with each other."

"Uh, well, family is family, Detective," Floyd said with a helpless shrug, side-eyeing the door. "We had our differences, but Casey and I got along great."

"Well, I have to tell you, Floyd, your story doesn't make much sense. From everything I've heard in my investigation, Casey didn't like you, and you were pretty condescending, even misogynistic, toward her. What were

276

you really doing in the funeral home tonight?" Wallace questioned him.

Floyd tilted his head, tried to offer a boyish smile that was more of a leer. "Like I said, I wanted to see Casey."

"Why?"

"It was my last chance to say goodbye," he told her, straightening his spine. Floyd was a head taller than Wallace and far broader in the chest and shoulders. He was not going to be pushed around by a woman.

"You didn't know Casey was cremated earlier today, did you?"

Floyd paled as the room took a dizzying spin, the sound of blood rushing in his ears. Heat prickled under his skin. Numb fingers flexed and he cleared his throat twice before he finally rasped, "Cremated?"

"I think you were there looking for something. You only recently found out Casey had it, didn't you? She wouldn't tell you where it was and in a fit of rage you strangled her!" Wallace accused, slamming a hand down on the table.

Floyd flinched, turned away, irritated. "That's ridiculous. Casey was killed in a home invasion, and instead of looking for the guy responsible, you're trying to turn this into some TV drama," he scoffed. "The only thing you have on me is being in the funeral home."

"Unlawful entry, destruction of property, breaking and entering, intent to tamper with a corpse, intent to abuse a corpse," Wallace listed off, mouth twisted in a sharp smile, "and, oh yeah. The murder of your niece, Casey Barton."

"I didn't kill her," he insisted through gritted teeth.

"No? Are you sure? This," Wallace pulled out a sheet of paper, "is your statement to the police regarding Casey's murder. In it you claim to have gone back to your hotel that night around nine, and stayed there until the next morning."

"That's right."

"Then why did the hotel's security cameras catch you leaving through the back door twenty minutes after nine? Why did they catch you coming back into the hotel around one-thirty?" Two time-stamped photos were laid on the table before him. "Strange that you just happened to go out in the timeframe that Casey was murdered."

"Casey was killed when somebody broke into her apartment. Her neighbor called the cops," Floyd replied with a condescending sneer. "Or did you not read that report?"

"Yeah, the neighbor did see a man trying to kick the door in; scared him off, too. The thing is, the medical examiner puts her time of death before the neighbor's call, and her apartment was ransacked. Why would the killer kick in the door after she was dead?" Wallace pondered the question for a minute, lighting up as she snapped her fingers. "If Casey knew her killer, she would have let them into the apartment. That would have made her murder seem far less random, and have narrowed down the list of suspects, wouldn't it? Of course, you knew Casey."

"I didn't kill her," Floyd snarled. "You don't have anything to prove I did!"

"I don't? Then, isn't it interesting that your fingerprints match the ones we found all over Casey's ruined apartment? Which is funny," Wallace added, waving a finger. "Didn't you say you'd never been to her place?"

Floyd didn't answer, jaw clenched, deep furious breaths rattled in his chest as he tried to keep calm. Detective Wallace hummed, placed a clear evidence bag on the table, tapped it to draw his attention. Inside was a damaged gold ring with a moderately sized red stone. Fury mixed with longing. Floyd's hands twitched as he fought back the desire to snatch it off the table.

"Where did you get that?" he rasped.

"That's your mother's ring, isn't it? The one you've been looking for? Your mother didn't trust you, Floyd. Neither did Casey. She did leave a very interesting note for her parents. It told us about the ring, and it told us about you. Your mother asked Casey to protect it from you, and she did, by hiding it in the lining of her trench coat," Detective Wallace revealed. "It was within arm's reach of you off and on for years, and nobody had any idea. Your niece was something."

The look on Floyd's face said it wasn't something good. "She left a note telling her parents where the ring was?" He could feel a molar threatening to crack.

"Not exactly. It took me a little while after reading the note, but I had a hunch. I called the director of the funeral home and met him there with officers Hogan and Kennedy. Luckily, my instincts paid off. In her ashes the mortician had found a ring that matched the description she'd left in her note." Wallace gave a breathy chuckle. "It was a stroke of serendipity that minutes after we'd shut off the lights and were about to leave, you broke in from the side door."

Her smug look of superiority made his blood boil. Wallace took her sweet time putting things in the folder, letting him stew in his impotent rage. Deft fingers plucked the evidence bag from the table, dangling it in front of him. "Tell me, Floyd, what was so special about this ring that it was worth killing your niece over?"

He stared at the ruined piece of jewelry. Decades had been wasted trying to get that ring, first from his mother, then from Casey. Floyd let out a deep whoosh of breath, looked Wallace dead in the eye, and said, "I want a lawyer."

Nodding, she left the interrogation room. Dropping the folder on her desk, Wallace stared at the letter she'd left sitting there in her rush to get to the mortuary. It would have been nice to have met Casey when she was alive.

Dear Mom and Dad,

If you're reading this, I'm probably dead. Sorry for that. I don't know how it happened, but I'm sorry to put you through it. I'm also sorry for the reason I wrote this letter. Don't trust Uncle Floyd.

Years ago, Grammy gave me a ring that Uncle Floyd tried to steal from her. It's gold with a moderately sized red jewel. Maybe a garnet or ruby? I don't know. What matters is that she told me to hide it. I don't know why. She never explained. It was a secret she trusted me to guard with my life. All I know is that Uncle Floyd desperately wants this ring, and he absolutely must not have it.

Honestly, after I hid it, I forgot about it. Then a few months ago, after Grammy died, Uncle Floyd started asking questions about the ring. Maybe I'm just being paranoid, but he got kind of aggressive about it. I don't know if he knows that I have it. I hope I'm wrong about my suspicions, but I don't think I am. If something happens to me, especially when he's around, this might be why.

There are two very important things I need you to do for me.

First: Always. Always. Remember I love you.
Second: Bury me with my trench coat.

Catherine Berry lives in Michigan, sings with her dog, and loves potatoes. Her work has been published by Horror Tree, and in the anthologies *Trembling with Fear: Years 1 & 2.* Read more at www.caterinaberyl.blogspot.com.

The Missing Body Mystery

L. T. Waterson

Why did it always have to be the beach? Detective Sergeant James Steele shuddered and pulled his coat closer. The wind swirled and the coat flapped around his legs.

A city boy through and through, Steele did not understand the appeal of the beach. For a few weeks of the year it would be so crowded with people that you wouldn't be able to move and then the rest of the time it would be like this, cold and windswept and mostly deserted.

The PCSOs who had been sent in answer to the initial call had already established a perimeter, but from the description he had been given there wasn't actually much of a crime scene to protect.

Have to make the best of it, I suppose, and with a grimace, he ducked under the police tape.

In front of him, laid out across the large pebbles that made up the beach, a trench coat was stretched, empty arms akimbo.

The wind would have snatched it away but someone had thoughtfully placed several large stones around its edges.

"It was like this when you found it?" Steele called back over his shoulder, but from the look on their faces he guessed that the two women hadn't heard him.

Maintaining a careful distance from the coat Steele walked around the perimeter, frowning. Then he walked around again.

Perhaps I'm missing something here? Maybe if D.I. Hutchinson was here, she would have spotted what I can't see.

"Where's the body?" he muttered and then, deciding it was time to talk to the uniforms, turned towards the two women.

"Where's the body?"

They looked askance at him. *They obviously didn't expect me to ask them questions but really, what else was I supposed to do when a supposed murder scene was so obviously sans body?*

"That's it, sir," one woman replied. "When we got here there were a few gulls pecking at the coat. We chased them off."

Steele did his very best to hide the smile at the mental image of the two women running around chasing gulls.

"But was there any sign of an actual body?"

"No, sir."

"Then why am I here? All this for a coat?"

The women exchanged glances, glances which quite clearly said they considered the answer to that question to be above their pay grade. "Caller to 999 said there'd been a murder, evidence on the beach, they said."

Of course, it had to be him who had taken the call asking for CID. He had made the mistake of telling D.I. Hutchinson that he spent most of his weekends in bed. She'd taken it as a challenge.

284

The Trench Coat Chronicles

The trench coat was a mid-brown colour and it had obviously spent some time submerged in the sea. He wouldn't have admitted to this, but he could see the coat was good quality.

"Would have set someone back a fair few pounds," Steele muttered to himself.

He crouched down on the stones to take a closer look. There couldn't be much forensic evidence here for him to compromise. So, maybe if he was careful, he could get a look at the label. He was guessing Max Mara or Stella McCartney.

Steele frowned as he noticed something red and frond-like clinging to the edge of the coat. It brought to his mind a vivid description from *The War of the Worlds* but looking closer he realised it wasn't vegetation he was looking at.

Bile rose in his throat. *Could the frond-like tendrils be the remains of whoever had once worn this coat?*

Standing up, Steele backed slowly away. The body remnants must have been what had attracted the gulls. The coat was soaking and must have been in the sea for some time. *Did fish eat humans?*

Just getting their revenge. The thought made him chuckle and he glanced across to the PCSOs. *Had they heard?*

The sound of a falling rock made Steele look upwards and he saw a figure standing at the top of the cliff path. Whoever it was they were too far away for him to make out a face, but he could at least deduce they were young and male. Steele started forward, but it was too late, the figure was already gone.

"Where's forensics?" Steele raised his voice above the hiss of the wind. The two women exchanged glances. "I need them now, please." Of course, he could have made the call himself but where was the fun in that.

Having ascertained that the women were following orders, Steele turned back to his view of the coat. He had to admit that, having found at least some remnants of a body, he felt a little easier in his mind.

Questions nagged at him. First, was the person who had worn that coat a murder victim, and second, who had laid it out so neatly on the beach for the police to find?

The next morning Steele made sure to get into work nice and early. He could see from the lines wrinkling D.I. Hutchinson's forehead that the woman was less than enthusiastic to be taking on this case.

The room around him, despite the paucity of evidence, was buzzing with activity. The map pinned up on the large corkboard wasn't the usual checkerboard of fields and rivers which seemed to comprise over 95 percent of the land area of Devon and Cornwall. Instead, although a thin strip of land was marked, the majority of the area was taken up by a map of the sea. Steele had not previously realised that such things existed and he peered at it, trying to disguise the fact that he had no idea what he was looking at.

"So, the coat was discovered here." One of the D.C.s, who looked as though he was barely out of short trousers, drove a pin into the map at roughly the point where just the day before Steele had been standing.

286

"If we presume it was washed up nearby, then the most likely direction for it to have come from is here." Another pin. "You see how the prevailing current curves along the shoreline?"

Steele nodded and tried to look as if he understood what the D.C. was saying.

"Most of the detritus that washes up on that particular stretch of beach really hasn't had to come far at all."

"Ready to get to work?" The acid tone could only have come from Hutchinson, and Steele hurriedly shrugged his way out of his own trench coat.

My coat, Steele looked at it almost with surprise. It was a good deal poorer in quality than the one he had found and the manufacturer had skimped enough on the material to make the garment something of a snug fit, especially across the shoulders.

"What about the coat?" Steele asked, into a suddenly silent room.

If it were possible, Hutchinson's forehead wrinkled even more.

"It was expensive." Up until now Steele had always kept his interest in fashion under wraps, but sometimes even detectives had to suffer in the interests of solving a case.

"And you know this, how?"

Hutchinson believed him, but the woman had a sadistic side to her and he knew she would make him say it, right out in front of everyone.

"You just have to look at it." Steele shrugged. "Even after all that time in the water. The cut, the material, the ..." Steele paused. He was pretty sure that a couple of the D.C.s were sniggering behind their hands. "So ..."

"If we can identify where the coat came from, maybe we can identify the owner." That was Hutchinson, taking pity on him.

He smiled at her. "Exactly."

"Looks like you've got yourself a job, Sergeant." Hutchinson glanced around at the other people in the room. "Where's Brown? I need the list of evidence."

"He's on holiday, Skegness or Blackpool, somewhere like that. Only place he can afford after the missus walked out on him."

"I'm exhibits officer for this." A middle-aged woman, brown hair cropped short, raised a hand and gently waved a piece of paper at Hutchinson. "But it's not exactly a list." She handed the paper to Steele.

"Whatever you're going to find out, Sergeant, I need you to find it pronto. The Chief Constable is moaning about the budget, again, and we need to find some evidence that there was a crime, otherwise," Hutchinson said, gesturing around the room, "all of this is going to get shut down."

Steele nodded his understanding. "Where's the coat now?"

"Storage." The exhibits officer shrugged. "Body remnants, what there are of them, are with pathology."

It took him less than an hour and part of that was spent double-checking what he already knew to be the truth.

"Well?" Hutchinson had eschewed the delights of the incident room to slope back to her office. She always said she couldn't think clearly with too many people around.

"The coat was made for one person. An exclusive exclusive."

"Who?"

"Annie Lambert."

"The film actress?"

"She's filming right now, apparently, near Charlestown. Her latest film, *The Smuggler's Wife*, that's the working title, I think. Apparently, she wanted something warm to cover her when standing on a windy beach." Steele winced. "I spoke to the director."

Hutchinson waited without speaking and Steele placed the piece of paper he had been clutching down on the desk.

"She went missing two weeks ago."

"And we're only hearing about this now?"

"Nobody reported her disappearance. According to the director she does this at least once every shoot. Just disappears for no discernible reason. That's the artistic temperament I suppose."

"Convenient for the murderer."

"We don't know she's dead."

"We found her coat."

"She might have lent it to someone else."

A raised eyebrow. "You said you spoke to the director."

Steele glanced at the paper on the D.I.'s desk. "Yes, ma'am. Oscar Wythenshawe, apparently. Officially he's the director and producer of *The Smuggler's Wife*. Unofficially he and Annie Lambert were having an affair."

"She's married, isn't she? I'm sure I read that somewhere."

"She was."

"Two suspects then." Hutchinson's eyes gleamed. "The husband and the lover."

It was her; of course it was. Anyone who had known Annie Lambert even vaguely would have known that she would never have lent her coat to anyone.

"She were right fond of it." The owner of the bed and breakfast where the actress had been staying, told Steele. "Always had that coat on, even when the sun was blazin' away."

"You didn't find that odd?"

The woman shrugged. "I provide rooms for a lot of film stars and they all have their quirks. Although the way Miss Lambert clutched that coat sometimes, I think it was more like a security blanket than a garment."

"How did she seem to you?"

Another shrug. "Bit distracted. Always talking to herself. Suppose she were learning her lines."

"And you know that is what she was doing?"

The woman had frowned at them. "What else could it be? She were an actress after all."

"Actor," Steele had murmured, loud enough for the D.I. to hear. "They're all actors nowadays."

"I'm a busy man, you do realise that?"

"Of course, Mister Wythenshawe. This shouldn't take too long."

The detectives had tracked the director down to the Carlyon Bay Hotel and Steele had been instructed to bring him back to Exeter. The man complained the whole way and the sergeant hoped that he wouldn't be asked to drive him back again.

Steele stood back and let the film director precede him into the room, and at that moment the man's phone rang.

"Important call." He fished the phone from his pocket.

"I'm afraid it will have to wait." Hutchinson was firm. "Perhaps you could turn it off."

Steele was not surprised when this suggestion made the man grumble, but he did as requested.

"So, Mister Wythenshawe. Just to remind you that you're not under arrest and you are of course free to leave at any time."

"Helping you with your enquires?" The man smiled, a relaxed happy smile that Steele decided probably got him a lot of female attention. "I should take notes."

"It's us that will be taking notes, Mister Wythenshawe," D.I. Hutchinson replied.

The director gestured at them and with another flash of his big smile; he sat back in his chair.

"Why didn't you report Miss Lambert missing?"

"She does this all the time." Wythenshawe crossed his arms and stared down his nose at the two detectives. "Every film I've done with her she ups and vanishes for a few days, then she comes back. I always keep a few scenes that she's not in, so I don't waste the time."

"Really."

"So, this time when she left I had no reason to imagine it was any different."

"Where does Miss Lambert go on these jaunts of hers?"

"A hotel, normally. She'll book herself in under an assumed name."

"How do you know?"

"I keep tabs on her, and don't pretend you're surprised by that, my dear Inspector. Annie's a valuable asset. I have to keep track of her."

Steele glanced at Hutchinson but the D.I. was intent on Wythenshawe.

"You didn't do a very good job of that this time."

"Once I know she's safe, in whichever hotel she's chosen, I step back and turn my attention to other things. I can't afford to baby my actors."

"Not even the ones you're sleeping with?"

Wythenshawe looked up sharply at Steele's question, frowning.

"Annie and I have been a couple on and off since before she met her husband. It's all perfectly innocent."

"And her husband is?"

"Theodore Hamilton. Old money, old American money. He lives off his trust fund and Annie is his trophy wife."

"What does she get out of it?"

"Freedom to make the movies she wants to make. Being an actor is a hand-to-mouth existence, Inspector. Is that all?"

Wythenshawe half-rose and then dropped back down into his seat again. Steele tensed. *Here it comes.*

"I was hoping you might return her journal."

"Oh," Hutchinson said. "And why would we do that?"

"You must have been through it by now, and I can't believe there's anything useful in there. I'd like to have it."

"You'd be surprised what we can make use of." Hutchinson was all cool and calmness and Steele felt her press a piece of paper into his hand.

Steele excused himself from the interview room.

He drove along the A30 like a bat out of hell, being careful of course to obey all speed limits and road signs, back to the bed and breakfast where Annie had been staying.

Standing in her room Steele rotated through 360 degrees, looking for a clue as to the location of the journal.

"Would you like a cup of tea, Sergeant?"

"Please," Steele called back to the voice that had floated up the stairs. "Milk, no sugar." That would keep the owner at bay for a little while.

Had Wythenshawe actually been here yet? Steele didn't think so. The room looked no different from the way it had on their earlier visit, although someone had straightened one of the pictures on the wall. It was a wide panoramic photograph of a stony beach and had been decidedly crooked when he'd seen it last.

A crooked picture. Steele looked at it and rubbed a hand through his hair. The frame had been carefully wiped but Steele could see someone had left a finger mark on the polished surface that protected the photograph.

"Tea."

Steele turned to look at the woman and smiled his thanks. He gestured at the safe that had been hidden behind the framed photograph.

"Can you open it?"

"I could. I do have a spare key in case of emergencies."

"Not a usual feature of a bed and breakfast though, is it? A wall safe."

"A lot of film and telly people stay here. Seemed they were always askin' for a wall safe so I had one fitted."

Of course, once opened the safe proved to be empty.

"Do you know what Miss Lambert kept in here?"

"Saw her closing it once, very pretty notebook; she weren't 'appy that I saw it."

Steele was late the next morning and he was met at the door to the incident room by both Hutchinson and an excitable D.C.

"Excuse me, ma'am. We found a match to the finger mark D.S. Steele found on the picture. It belonged to a local, Samuel Trent. He was arrested last year, drunk and disorderly."

Steele nodded. "I remember that. The stepfather got involved and had all the charges dropped."

Hutchinson turned and looked at Steele.

"Samuel's mother is a former Miss World, Lisa Trent. No one knows who Samuel's biological father is, but she married Bart Agnew in 2007, one of the richest men this side of the M5. Samuel has learning difficulties, and that's why Mister Agnew managed to get the charges dropped last time."

Hutchinson grinned. "That's not going to work with murder."

✗ ✗ ✗ ✗ ✗

"*Murder?*"

Steele, watching closely as he always did, was sure the look of horror on Samuel's face was real.

"Now hang on a minute, Inspector. That's a bit much, don't you think?"

Hutchinson smiled. "Not really. We have numerous letters in which he declares his undying love to the victim and, more importantly, we found his prints in Miss Lambert's room."

"Circumstantial at best." The older man blustered. "Sam never knew the woman, did you?"

"It was Sam who alerted us to the presence of Miss Lambert's coat on the beach." Hutchinson pushed a photograph across the table. "CCTV caught him exiting a phone box just after the 999 call was made. And we have reason to believe it was your stepson who laid the coat out so carefully."

"Sam?" The bluff man turned his gaze on the boy.

"I did know Annie." Sam, whose gaze had been riveted on his hands, looked up. He glanced first at Hutchinson, then across to Steele, and then his gaze went back to his hands.

"She was in the very first film I saw at the cinema and I've been in love with her ever since."

"Sam." Mr. Agnew laid a meaty hand on his stepson's arm. "Perhaps we should wait for my solicitor."

Sam shook his head. "When I found out she'd be filming down here, I was so happy. I'd been writing to her for years. I went to the beach to watch the filming but I couldn't get close. Then the director asked for some extras."

"You volunteered?" Steele couldn't help but feel a pang of sympathy for the young man—he was sweet, and perhaps Annie Lambert had seen the same thing.

Sam nodded. "At the break Annie came to speak to me. She knew who I was." The boy beamed. "Then she asked me for a favour." Sam shifted in his seat and he crossed his arms. It wasn't so much a defensive pose, more of a self-comforting one. "She said I had to promise to do what she asked. I couldn't believe that Annie was actually talking to me, and she wanted my help. So, I promised."

Sam shook his head. "I wish I hadn't. She told me she was unhappy; she said she was tired of living." Sam's eyes were filled with tears. "I begged her to ask for help but she refused. I said I'd tell someone but she said no, that I had

296

promised and that bad things would happen to me if I broke that promise."

"She said she was going to end it all, fill her coat pockets with stones and walk out into the water. No one would miss her she said." Sam was crying freely now and Steele passed him a tissue.

"What did she need you for, Sam?"

His breath hitched and the young man rubbed his hands across his face. "At the end of the day, she were an actress."

Hutchinson nodded in understanding. "She wanted someone to witness her final performance."

"Only after I watched her go I was hopin' it all might have been a dream. I went down to the beach every day, and then I saw her coat. I know I promised to do what she said but I didn't think she'd mind if I laid her coat out. It were a lovely coat." Sam looked at Steele. "That was OK, wasn't it?"

"It was fine," Steele murmured. "You did the right thing."

"So why did you take her journal?"

Sam glanced towards his stepfather. "She asked me to." The young man gulped. "Gave me the combination, she said I could keep it." Sam looked at Hutchinson and then back at Steele. "I can keep it, can't I?"

"We'll need to see it first," Steele replied, as gently as he could. "But after that I don't see why not."

"I took this picture of her." Sam held out his phone and Steele took it. The image showed Annie Lambert wearing her trench coat and staring serenely out across the waves. "Took that two days before she ..."

Steele nodded in understanding and then he saw that the beach on which she was standing was the same one pictured in the photograph that had hung on her bedroom wall, and it was the same beach from which she had set out to take her own life.

L. T. Waterson lives in a house filled with books, halfway up a hill in Southampton, England. She has been a journalist and an archaeologist, and is now just generally curious. Her work has appeared in a number of different anthologies.

Who Profits?

Lee F. Patrick

Detective Marthan Krogal looked at the pile of folders on his desk, then at the older detective sitting at ease at the adjoining desk. "You drew the short straw, newbie," Jertyn Westrel said with an evil smile.

"Or the captain decided it was a case that would be good for me to take on. For the experience. Where's the crime scene? Unless someone else gave up on solving a cold case. Like you."

"It's recent, but not necessarily a murder. The scene is contained so you can go visit it later. Your task is to decide if it is."

"Oh. One of those." *Natural causes or not.* "How old was the deceased?"

"Seventy-two-year-old lady. Beati Somners. Widow who lived alone. It's all in the folders. Better start reading. The family wants this settled fast so they can start the probate and whatnot. Fair bit of money involved, I heard."

"And bury her, I guess." He stared at the pile, then took off his trench coat and hung it on the stand at the edge of their desks. He nearly patted the shoulder of his coat. Inherited from his father, dead in the line of duty ten years ago. *How would Dad handle this investigation? Only one answer at this point.* "Coffee first."

"Of course." Jertyn raised his own mug.

Marthan put the last folder on the completed pile and stretched. "Thoughts?" Jertyn asked, looking up from his computer. He'd been out for several hours on his own cases.

"No clear evidence, at least for now," Marthan replied. "Coroner hasn't found anything obvious, but it seems that toxicology isn't back yet. Heart failure is her main thought. Blood clot in the wrong place and she died quickly. Not necessarily painlessly. She'd been getting ready for bed from the pictures."

"That's possible for either."

"I know. Time it took for her to be found didn't make it better. Three days. A neighbour called in a wellness check since her mailbox was full. He went over to pick up the mail if she was away. It wasn't often, apparently."

"Anyone hate her?"

"Doesn't seem to be any big hate in the family. Not much information on who might covet her wealth outside the family. She didn't have any children. All of her siblings are dead, so their kids are her heirs. Nine of them, it seems." Marthan leaned back in his chair. "There is a slight complication. Barrat Trelner bought one of her properties two years ago. He'd been renting."

"Didn't see that bit. Why should we care, though? Old news."

"I heard about all the hysteria when he was thought to be involved in the huge market crash. And I know someone who knows the business world in town. Trelner's a big deal in the development projects here and elsewhere. Don't know if his company might be looking to expand their holdings here. Might need to talk with him, just to ask if they're interested in buying up the rest of her property."

"Killing the old lady since she wouldn't sell out to them?" Jertyn shook his head. "Not very likely, I think. But the heirs might be more willing to swap the buildings for some of that stock. Be very careful if you do talk to him. A buddy went to see him right after he moved here and Trelner's lawyers were in the colonel's office a half hour later. We were warned to stay away. Didn't your patrol captain give you the lecture? I'm sure every officer in town was warned. All the new hires get the same lecture before they're allowed out on patrol."

"She did. That's why I recognised the name. The financials folder showed the history of Mrs. Somners' holdings. He bought the office building just after his first year's lease ended."

"Don't see him unless you have to," Jertyn repeated. "Otherwise the colonel will be pissed."

"Hadn't really planned to. The management company rep doesn't have a statement that I've seen. The rep should have more of an idea on who might want Mrs. Somners' holdings and what she had planned for the future. The buildings are worth quite a bit now, and they're not likely to go down in value any time soon. The local economy has been in growth mode for over two years."

"Who else is on your list to see?"

"Mrs. Somners' lawyer. None of the potential heirs seems to have visited their aunt in the two weeks before her death, so I'd rule them out."

Jertyn shook his head. "Never rule out the family. Even if the estate gets divided between … how many heirs are there, again?"

"Nine. From four siblings, so the shares won't be even, depending on when her will was last updated. She was the youngest of her siblings. That's why I need to visit her lawyer and find out what's in the will." He flipped through a folder from near the bottom of the stack. "Some of the heirs have kids. They might need the cash. None are in serious financial trouble on a quick glance, and there are no big outlays or even the same amount coming out of all their accounts."

"You're thinking of an assassination? Really?"

"Gotta be on the list of how and who," Marthan said with a shrug. "Like the family."

"You've been watching the wrong drama programs again."

"Or the right ones. Some of the writers get interesting ideas."

Marthan checked his city map before leaving the station and decided to see the management company rep first. A three-story office building with at least four businesses in it—another law firm, a doctor's office on the main floor, and a café.

"I hope she's in," he muttered as he crossed the street. That was the problem with dropping in on witnesses. Especially busy ones.

He'd heard of detectives making appointments with

witnesses or suspects, arriving only to find that they'd left immediately after the call. Sometimes the detectives called while watching the person's vehicle, preventing the suspects or witnesses from attempting to leave the area.

Fortunately, she was in her office. What she told him about an alternate plan for her estate confused him. The possibility that someone wanted a quick payday increased the chances of this being a murder. She seemed to mourn the deceased as a person, not just a client. Trying to do her best for the people she represented.

However, since he came out more confused than when he went in, he headed for the lawyer's office next. He passed the building that held Trelner Consulting but wouldn't stop there. *Not now, maybe never.*

More complications from the lawyer, new to both the practice and to Mrs. Somners' file. Sionie Walthin truly wanted the will that she possessed to be the only one, so she'd profit from the various fees from settling the estate. Probably less likely to have committed other, more sinister machinations, he decided on his way home.

After he reread the files on his desk the next morning, he had a very oddball idea as he recalled a crime drama he'd watched a few weeks ago. "I wonder if there was an update to the will. Despite what the lawyer thinks."

"Didn't the lawyer have the will?"

"She had *a* will. Mrs. Somners had a notion to update her will courtesy of her management rep, however the lawyer seemed to have discouraged the idea of any changes. The sense I have of the deceased was that she didn't like it when people just dismissed her ideas with no rational arguments on the reason. Simply not liking the idea wasn't good enough."

"You think that someone else wrote her a new will? Why wouldn't they have come forward?"

"Depends on what that will says, if such a will exists. And who profits the most from it. Maybe there's a copy of it at the house."

"Finding anything at this point is going to be impossible," Jertyn opined. "Nothing had been found disturbed in the house. If someone had been searching for a specific piece of paper, it'll be long gone by now."

Marthan smiled and patted his computer monitor. Jertyn laughed, and toasted Marthan with his coffee as Marthan headed off to the crime scene in an attempt to find a piece of solid evidence that could justify his inclination to declare the death as murder, not a simple age-related illness.

He parked around the back of the house to cut down on watching eyes who might contact an interested party, and pulled on evidence gloves before opening the back door.

The last piece of his puzzle arrived with the coroner's full report.

Marthan walked past the law office's reception area toward the conference room. Two uniformed patrol officers strode just behind him, and his stomach was knotted beyond the ability for any chance of relaxation. All of his evidence was at best circumstantial and more likely a flight of fancy, but there was really no other way to shock the murderer into a spontaneous confession. Once he had that on the recorder in his trench coat's pocket, any judge would grant the warrant to send his quarry to the Interrogation Clinic for final confirmation of his guilt. Just putting the coat on to come here had helped his confidence, but the trip over here gave his mind far too much opportunity to think of ways that he had made a terrible decision to proceed. He touched the lapel with his free hand, imagining that his dad walked next to him. With action imminent, it did help to distract him from his worries.

"Officers? How may I help you?" The young man at the desk tried to move in front of Marthan but stopped in confusion when Marthan held up a folded document. It was a copy of the one that had given him the courage to attempt this confrontation. It wasn't the arrest warrant the young man assumed. But it could send someone, or someones, to prison. The man might have been working on his own. Or not.

Jertyn warned him what would happen if he'd guessed wrong when he first mentioned this idea. Sent back into a uniform and patrolling the nastiest districts in the city, if he was lucky. Tossed out of the force completely if he wasn't. So, the answer he'd come up with had to be right. He couldn't imagine any other scenario that fit all the available facts.

He opened the conference room door and quickly placed all of the heirs seated around the large table. No windows to this room, which eliminated one possible escape route. One officer closed the door once they were all inside, and stood in front of it. The other followed him to the lawyer's side. She stared at him with confusion at first, then anger. That she might lose control of the estate, or for some other reason didn't matter right now. She wasn't directly involved, but her actions had set another's plan into motion and resulted in an old woman's murder.

"I'm glad that all of you are here," he said as pleasantly as he could manage. Ancillary relatives sat in chairs set against the walls. His quarry was present. *One potential disaster averted.*

"Why are you here *again*, detective?" Sionie Walthin asked, a touch of venom in her tone. She hadn't been pleased when he'd brought up several notions in his interviews with her. That his notions would, or might, be vindicated here was a bonus for him.

"Because I have completed my investigation into the death of Mrs. Beati Somners. I wished for all the heirs to hear the results directly, so I was happy to learn that you had already gathered everyone with an interest in the estate here today. It certainly saved all of them time."

"So you just barged in, bringing your men to disrupt the reading of the will?" A sneer.

"Well, that's part of the problem, Ms. Walthin. I am convinced that Mrs. Somners was murdered, and that someone in this room is responsible. Any attempt to settle the estate has to wait until after my department can ensure that none of her other heirs are complicit in her murder."

Everyone started to mutter and talk at each other, some tones accusing, others just confused. Some stood to point fingers and glare at other heirs. No one was yelling. Yet. His quarry was shocked, and probably regretted coming along to witness their triumph.

"Please sit down and be quiet." Marthan projected all the confidence that he didn't have into his voice. Behaving as his father would have. The coat gave him the nerve to act. Once the civilians all sat down, staring at him, he smiled. "I'll explain, then I'll take the guilty person into custody and let the rest of you get on with your day."

Silence. Even Ms. Walthin sat down, taking the chair from the head of the table and moving it to the side. *Good. Another body in the way if my quarry tries to run.*

"Thank you. The coroner's office has determined that Mrs. Somners' death was directly caused by several blood clots, one of which blocked a major vein in her heart. There was also evidence of several earlier clots in minor blood vessels, none of which were successful at causing her death. Another, smaller one ended up in her brain, according to the coroner. If that had been the only one, she might have survived the attempt." A faint rustling of clothing from various people and a tiny squeak from a chair.

"One might think that those clots formed by natural causes. However, the amount of plaque and the number of small clots in her circulatory system were abnormally high. Too high, the coroner said. There would have been other, quite obvious signs if her condition had resulted from natural causes. That led her to find for a suspicious death and for me to look for a murder suspect. There are several drugs that can cause clotting consistent with the coroner's findings. Matrinal has been used by assassins in the past. Its presence can only be detected very soon after the death."

"But Aunt Beati died three days before anyone

found her, I was told," one of the heirs said. "Doesn't that ..."

"Make the drug responsible harder to detect? Very true. However, Mrs. Somners regularly took medication. Those capsules are easy to tamper with, replacing the contents of the opaque capsule with Matrinal, then placing the adulterated ones back into the bottle on a later visit. Eventually, she would take one with the drug in it and die, probably late that night."

"But," another heir started. Marthan didn't let him continue.

"The capsule, or capsules, could have been placed in the bottle at any time after it was opened," Marthan said. "So, none of you have an alibi or any way to prove that you did not conspire together."

"But who would know about that drug?" Ms. Walthin asked. "I doubt that it is commonly available."

"True. But those who watch crime dramas would have heard of it as a cause of death. In fact, one show I've seen had the exact method used in this case. A few early half-hearted attempts, mostly to establish that there was a problem with clots forming. Mrs. Somners' doctor, sadly, failed to correctly identify her symptoms as the result of heart problems, and instead decided that their cause was a stomach issue."

His quarry wasn't moving yet, but his eyes were. Looking for a way out and not finding an easy route to freedom. There wasn't one. Marthan repressed a smile. He'd solved the murder; now he just had to encourage the murderer to admit his guilt.

"Those capsules, or others, made an ideal choice to hide the drug. With a large bottle of pills, which Mrs. Somners bought to save money on the purchase, it would be easy for anyone visiting her to remove several pills, replace the contents, and return them to the bottle on their next visit. Since she took two capsules every night, eventually she would take one of the fatal doses."

"Did they find another one?" Ms. Walthin asked.

"No," Marthan admitted. The heirs looked at each other. "I believe that is how the earlier attacks were carried out. Several supplements she took also have opaque capsules. I believe the last dose was put into her supply of stomach medication, since the number of pills was very low. The murderer wanted her dead quickly, before she could tell anyone that she had made a new will. The drug might also have been inserted into some filled chocolates. There was evidence of them in her stomach contents, but no packaging was found in the house, as if the murderer had taken it away with them. The reason was that she signed another will *that night*. She had to die before she told anyone about it."

"You think it was about that stupid trust fund idea she had?" Ms. Walthin sneered. "I did *not* write that will. We're proceeding with this will, which sells all the property and divides the amount equally among the heirs." She held up the document she'd been holding all this time.

"This firm is not the only source of legal advice that Mrs. Somners had available to her." Marthan finally looked directly at his quarry. The young woman sitting in front of him turned around to look at her father once she realised who Marthan was watching. "She has known of Cargrin Regar since his daughter met and then married one of her nephews. Six years now, I believe."

"But ..." He was unsure who spoke.

"We found this document on Mrs Somners' computer," Marthan said, holding his document higher. Everyone stared at it now, including Regar. "While it is unsigned, there are margin notes suggesting that you, Mr. Regar, and she had several discussions on word choice. You should have done a better job of deleting the documents. We also found that the keyboard for her computer was remarkably clean for such a device. No fingerprints at all were found. What do you have to say, Mr. Regar? Were your daughter and son-in-law also complicit in your actions?"

"Daddy, what did you do? We don't really need the money from Aunt Beati. You ..."

"I, I did it for you, dear." Everyone stared at him slumping in his chair.

Marthan started to relax. It wasn't the greatest confession, but it would be enough. There were certainly enough physical witnesses if his recording wasn't sufficient.

"What did you do with the signed copy you removed from her home the same night you attempted to delete the computer files?" *Finding that would solve many other problems.*

"My office. The safe. I should have burned it. Or burned the whole house so nothing would be left."

"Cargrin Regar, you are now under arrest for the murder of Beati Somners." He nodded and the officer nearest Regar walked over to him and helped him stand, cuffed his hands behind him, and led him out. The man still looked shocked that he'd been caught. *At least he hadn't tried to fight.*

"What happens now?" Ms. Walthin asked once the door was closed again.

"We hope to clear the rest of the heirs of any complicity within the week, retrieve the signed will and then hold the trial." He paused. "Since Mr. Regar cannot act in regard to the will he wrote, the innocent heirs will need to choose a lawyer to do so." A flash of a smile on Ms. Walthin's face. She'd still earn all the fees and such from the probate and ongoing fees from the trust. Now, she'd cooperate fully with him.

"I'll leave this copy with you, Ms. Walthin," he said. "So that you can familiarise the family here today with the general provisions. Once we have the signed version of the new will, I will inform you of any changes that were made in regard to the notes Mrs. Somners made on that document."

"Good day." Marthan handed her the will, picked up his fedora and left the room, hearing the heirs muttering to each other. He closed the door. A deep breath. *I did it. Success. It feels good.*

The Interrogation Clinic would discover if anyone else had known of the plot, who had sold him the Matrinal, and when. Then, he'd finally celebrate.

But for at least the rest of today, and more likely the next two or three days, he had a lot of paperwork to do. As he left the building, he caught sight of his reflection in the window of his car. He blinked. He could have sworn he'd seen his father's face in the window instead of his own.

"Thanks, Dad," he murmured as Jertyn opened the passenger door from the inside.

Lee F. Patrick is a Calgary, Alberta writer of science fiction and fantasy, and sometimes poetry. Lee's fourth novel, *Always My Love*, will soon join *Alter Egos*, *The Alanyo Heir*, and *Lonely Together*. Lee's short stories can be found in *On Spec*, *Mythaxis*, and *Sirius Science Fiction*, among other wonderful magazines and anthologies including *The Twofer Compendium* and *The Trench Coat Chronicles*. All of Lee's books are available in print and eBook format from Amazon and Kobo.

The Heap of Cloth

Marian Powell

The trench coat lay crumpled in a heap. Torn and muddy, it had obviously been discarded on the dirt beside the seldom-used country road.

Time passed and either no one in the nearby small town drove down that road, or if they did, they didn't notice it or they ignored it.

All was quiet and peaceful in the small town. This was to the liking of the paunchy, grizzled sheriff. He had just settled in when the office door banged open.

"Sheriff! Come quick! Murder!" A lanky young man burst into the room shouting.

"What is it? What do you mean, murder?"

"Oh, it's awful, just awful. I was driving down Old Toll Road. You know the one. I don't usually go on that road, but I needed to call on an old friend who lives out that way. We was buddies together as boys though we've gone separate ways and ..."

"Is he the murder victim?"

"No. This was before I got to his house. You know where the railroad tracks cross the road?"

"Oh, so the victim was hit by a train?"

"What train? I said the tracks cross the road and then I drove another mile, well, probably it was more like half a mile, no, I think three-quarters of a mile."

"And that's where you found the body?"

"Oh no, that's where I turned off onto Green Street and that's where I saw it."

"It? You mean a body?"

"A pile of old clothes. At least I think it was. I didn't look too closely because, well, because, you know ..." His voice trailed off.

"You thought it was one of them. What's your name, son?" the sheriff asked.

"Jim Smith."

"You've been listening to the news about all the murder victims."

"I heard the last one was in the next county. That's getting too close for comfort."

"Jim, let's drive out there and you'll see it's nothing but what you said, a pile of old clothes."

"It wasn't really a pile. It was more like, like, I'm sorry, I can't say it."

"It was more like a coat, a trench coat, to be precise. That's what everyone is talking about. C'mon." The sheriff sighed as he stood up. Then, before leaving the office, he doublechecked that his pistol was loaded.

The drive was short and simple. In no time it seemed they drove up to the spot. Despite an outward appearance of calm, dread gathered inside the sheriff as he pulled up and parked. He made a quick decision to stay on the road and to leave the motor running. The abandoned coat or whatever it was looked harmless, like any piece of cloth that's been left out on the dirt too long. Still, he drew his gun.

"Sheriff, it looks like a, oh, I can't say it."

"Like a trench coat but it's hard to tell from here. Of course, we know if it's what we're both thinking, it wants us to walk up close enough to grab it. Now, don't get jumpy. From all I've been told, these are not intelligent. They are a mass of reflexes, like a Venus flytrap. That's a plant that lures flies so it can eat them. OK, here goes nothing."

As he spoke, the sheriff bent down, picked up a pebble and tossed it at the trench coat.

The cloth seemed to explode with eagerness, leaping up, grabbing the pebble, then collapsing back to the ground. The sheriff started shooting.

The trench coat seemed to writhe as it absorbed the six bullets.

"That was a waste of ammunition," the sheriff sighed. "C'mon, Jim. Get in the car. I'm locking the doors and pulling further away while I call for back up. And I'm sorry I didn't believe you. I thought you'd been listening to too many conspiracy theories. But the truth is bad enough. Two months ago, you told me flying saucers encircled the Earth."

"They weren't saucer-shaped."

"Don't interrupt. The alien ships dropped trench coats all across the world and they've been munching their way ever since. And they are getting clever on how to lure victims."

The sheriff had been focused on driving and re-parking a safe distance away after talking on his radio. Now he could finally relax. "It'll be at least an hour before reinforcements arrive, but we should be safe."

As he spoke, he turned toward his companion, saw that he was just a lump of battered old cloth, no longer human at all. He looked like a trench coat, abandoned and rumpled.

The sheriff leapt out of the car wishing he had time to radio the warning that the trench coats could imitate humans. Now, all he could do was run.

Marian has written since childhood and was first published at age 14. She earned two graduate degrees, traveled, worked a variety of jobs from counselor with the homeless mentally ill, to clerical, to picking crops and raising chickens. Eighteen of her short stories have been published.

Peanuts on the Half Shell

Willow Croft

I looked at the address I'd written down. *When did people stop putting the address numbers on their residences?* Luckily, there was a break in the traffic and I saw flashing blues-and-reds ahead. I slid in next to one of the squad cars and got out of my vehicle. I turned up the collar of my coat against the afternoon drizzle, but wet drops still managed to find their way in. A uniformed cop stood by the crime scene tape that looped across the entrance to the brownstone. I could smell the delicious aroma of his coffee as I approached.

"You know, Detective Carrera, you really should start using your lights." He slurped his coffee.

"Save me the lecture, Officer Sampson. You gonna let me in or what?" I nodded at the tape.

Officer Sampson held up the tape as I ducked under it. The rain was cold against the back of my neck. I shook the water off as best I could and opened the door. I was just about to step in when an arm swung out and smacked me in the chest.

"Whoa, hold on there, Detective."

I turned and glared at the person speaking.

"Hey, Miranda, it's me. Caroline. Sorry about that. But look." Officer Caroline Peters gestured with her outstretched hand.

If it hadn't been for her, I'd have stepped in the pool of blood seeping from the body sprawled across the floor. She still had her coat on; it looked like the young woman had just come home.

"Crime techs already been over the body, Officer Peters?"

She nodded. "Yep. They're going over the upstairs rooms. I'm waiting on the coroner."

"So, who is she?" I tugged a pair of nitrile gloves out of my pocket and put them on.

"Lexie Starr. Makes YouTube videos about, well, I don't know. Whatever kids like these days."

I looked around the foyer. It was lavishly decorated. I whistled. *Money. And lots of it.*

"So, what's her family do?" I crouched down to get a better look at Lexie.

"Uh, she doesn't have any. She's an orphan." Caroline knelt down next to me. She was chewing gum and it snapped loudly in my ear.

Poor girl. I moved some of the hair off her face. Pretty, but she lacked the glamour needed to live here. She had on a pair of black jogging pants, and her sneakers didn't look very expensive. They were scuffed and well-worn, and her sweatshirt had holes in it.

"What sort of work does she do, then?"

"I told you, she makes these YouTube videos," Caroline continued to snap her gum.

Something wasn't adding up. "But this is a restored brownstone. Right across from the park. They go for millions of dollars. So, where's the money come from?" I frowned.

"No mystery, there, Detective. Her videos went viral, and she makes tons of money off them. It's all kids want to be when they grow up. YouTube stars. Heck, it's hard to even get my son to do his homework. 'Why,' he says. Kid's got a good point, though." Caroline stood up.

I put Lexie's hair back to where it'd been before I disturbed it. Something fell out of her tangled strands and plopped onto the floor. I picked it up. It was a peanut, still in its shell.

"That's weird," I said. "You got an evidence bag on you?"

"Yep. Here you go." Caroline handed me the bag and I put the peanut in it and sealed it up.

"Let's get this to the techs. Then we'll go for drinks at McCrae's, OK?" Caroline didn't answer. I felt something wet press against my ear. I swiveled around.

I was looking straight into a mouthful of sharp teeth. Saliva dripped from the mouth. A dog. I yanked away from it and nearly fell onto the body. The mutt whined and then it started licking me, right in the face. I heard Caroline laughing. I wiped my face with the sleeve of my coat and stood up. An officer with slicked-back hair was holding the bulldog's leash. Its big brown eyes watched my every move.

"Oh, sorry, Detective," the officer said, trying to pull the dog away. "He seems to like you, though."

"Is the dog gonna be OK, Officer Steinberg?" Caroline asked.

"I think so. We found him hiding under the bed. Animal Services is on the way." Officer Steinberg patted the dog on the head. The dog's tail started thumping against the officer's leg.

I stared at the dog. "What on earth is it wearing?"

"It's a trench coat. Probably custom-made. Keeps the rain off him." Officer Steinberg said.

Caroline laughed again. "You and he have matching coats. I should ask the chief to make him a detective. Your new partner."

I glared at her. "Very funny. I gotta do my sweep of the upstairs rooms. Then we'll get out of here, OK?"

Caroline nodded and headed upstairs. I skirted the dog and hurried after her.

"So, it's a robbery, right? What was taken?" I asked her when we reached the landing.

Caroline shook her head. "Better if I show you." She went down the hall to a rear room.

As we neared, I heard a humming noise coming from inside. I stepped into the room, and was hit with a blast of hot air. The heat was coming from a line of computers along one wall. In the corner was a green screen and a small table with a microphone and a webcam.

"This is where she makes her videos," Caroline said.

"Funnily enough, I figured that out." I gazed around the room. This equipment had to be expensive. *So why hadn't the thief taken any of it?*

I met Caroline's eyes. "So, we're not looking at a simple break-in, are we?"

"'Fraid not. Unless they ran after they attacked Lexie. The front door didn't show any signs of damage. Whoever it was either surprised Lexie as she was unlocking her door, or it was someone she knew."

"Anything show up on camera?" I asked.

"Nope. Place didn't have cameras. Or a security system." Caroline sighed. "Maybe we'll get a match from the fingerprints they lifted."

"Or DNA from the peanut." *That was a phrase I'd never expected I'd say at a crime scene.*

"And we're back to waiting." Caroline stomped out of the room and down the stairs. I followed her. Downstairs, Officer Steinberg was still waiting. The dog was sprawled out on the floor, all four legs splayed out under its chunky body. His tail began to thump when he saw me. I tried not to look into those big brown eyes. They looked wet, as if he'd been crying.

Dogs can't cry, I told myself. *Mucus or something gross like that. Probably some weird dog disease.* The front door opened slightly and an animal control officer poked his head in.

"I'm Rick, here for the dog," he said, entering the house.

"Sure thing," Officer Steinberg said. He held out the leash to Rick.

"Whew, it's a bulldog," Rick said, taking the leash. "They're sweeties. And look how cute he is in his little trench coat. Good thing, buddy, it's raining hard out there." Rick gently tugged on the leash. But the dog didn't move.

"Come on, be a good boy. You're a too heavy for me to carry you." Rick bent over and got the dog on its feet. "Bulldogs are sweet, but lazy as all get out." The dog plodded to the door after the officer, but came to a halt when he saw the rain outside. He whined and looked back at me with those big, goopy, brown eyes.

"Wait," I said, quickly moving forward. "I'll take him."

"Uh, Miranda, what are you doing?" Caroline stared at me.

"He may be our only witness," I explained.

Rick looked from me to Caroline. She nodded to him.

"Well, one less animal stuck in the shelter," he said, handing the leash to me before bolting out the door.

I stared down at the dog. His tail was wagging and drool started to drip from his mouth. I sighed.

"Well, I guess we aren't going for drinks, now," Caroline said. "I'm headed home. Officer Steinberg, I'll leave you to wait for the coroner."

I walked out into the rain with the bulldog plodding along beside me. A couple of joggers slowed as we approached them.

"Look, they have matching coats. How perfectly adorable," one of the joggers commented as they let us pass.

I unlocked the door to my car. "Get in, you little bastard," I growled at the dog. I heard one of the joggers gasp as the bulldog scrambled up in the front seat, his tail still wagging. I started up the car and remembered to use the bubble light as I pulled out into traffic. I had a passenger to think of, now.

It was two days later, and I was still poring over the Lexie Starr file. The autopsy report listed blunt force trauma to the head as the cause of death. And the bulldog hadn't been any help. He was currently curled up at my feet, snuffling and drooling all over his custom-made trench coat. His presence was making it hard for me to concentrate on the case. Every time someone walked by, they would stop and pat him or talk to him. Even a few perps tried to stop and pet him on the way back to the booking cells. The dog didn't even bark at them; he just wagged his tail and drooled some more.

So much for my key witness. I spread Lexie's crime scene photos out on my desk but I'd been over them a million times and they still didn't reveal any new clues. And all of her friends had alibis for the time of the murder. There were no fingerprints recovered from the peanut at the crime scene, and the DNA report hadn't come in yet. I stared at the photos. *What did I know about YouTube videos and their makers? Absolutely nothing.* I gave up trying to think up new leads to chase down, and shoved the photos back into the case file. I checked my watch. Almost four o'clock. There was a chance Caroline was still here, filling out her shift reports. I wound my way through the crowded squad room and breathed a sigh of relief when I saw her still at her desk. Caroline was frowning at her computer. As I got closer, I heard her banging at the keys and cursing.

"Problems?" I asked.

"It's this new system. I've been here nearly an hour and I still can't figure out how it works. I swear, the chief needs to hire a bunch of fifth graders as IT consultants. Show us all how to work it."

My mouth dropped open. "Caroline, you're a genius."

She had a puzzled look.

"Grab your keys and let's go. I'll explain on the way."

It was nearing rush hour, so I had plenty of time to fill in Caroline on the way to her apartment.

"I'm not sure about this," she said, after I explained my plan to her. "This could stir up a whole lot of trouble. Not just for me, but for my son."

"Who's gonna know?" I grabbed the armrest as she zipped around a delivery truck.

"I forgot. You don't have kids. Kids talk to each other, on record these days. Via texts, instant messaging, social media posts—all of it can be recovered and used in a court of law." Caroline squeezed her car between two taxis.

"Well, what other fifth grader do you know that we can ask? Besides, your son may be instrumental in keeping a murderer from going free." I said, hanging onto the armrest for dear life.

She sighed and swung the car into a parking place in front of her apartment building.

"Are we there yet," I muttered under my breath as I opened the door.

"Did you say something?" She came around to my side of the car, glaring at me.

"No, Officer." I shook my head.

Luckily, Caroline was distracted by the arrival of the school bus. A few kids hopped off the bus. One of them, a boy with blue-dyed hair, walked down the sidewalk toward us. He never looked up from his phone, not even when Caroline ruffled his hair and asked him how his day was. We rode up the elevator in silence. Once inside Caroline's apartment, he dumped his backpack by the front door.

"Uh-uh, young man. Come here and pick up your bag." Caroline put her hands on her hips. "Besides, Sean, we need some help. Put your backpack in your room and bring out your laptop."

Sean turned around and rolled his eyes. "Like what kind of help? Turning on your computer? Logging into your email?" He yanked his backpack off the floor. His phone beeped and he looked down at it. Caroline reached over and snatched it from his hand.

"Hey," he yelled. "I was talking to someone."

Nice move, Mom, I thought, watching Caroline tuck Sean's phone into her pocket.

"Hey, nothing. We need to know if you can find someone online. Not their online profile, but their address. Where they live, private personal information, and things like that." Caroline lowered her voice. "Can you do it, well, legally?"

Sean looked from his mother to me. "Is this a trick? Am I going to be grounded? Because I haven't done anything. Well, nothing that all of my friends don't also do."

That didn't sound good. I felt Caroline stiffen next to me. I glanced over at her. She looked like she was about to launch into an entire Mom lecture. I laid my hand on her arm and whispered into her ear. "Later. Right now, we need his help. OK?"

"Help with what?" Sean asked.

"Sean, we need to find out if someone can be tracked down via the internet. This person makes videos online," I said.

"Oh. A YouTuber?" Sean opened his laptop and turned it on. "What's their name?"

"Lexie Starr," I said. "But we need her real name."

"Yeah, I know her. Give me a few minutes." Sean typed something on the keyboard and waited. "Yep, here she is. Name, address, phone number, even a map. And I didn't do anything illegal to get it. She's just out there for everyone to see." He shifted his eyes toward his mother.

Sure you didn't.

"Of course, you didn't, honey," Caroline finally answered. She ruffled his hair again.

I suddenly had a thought. "Can you tell me if she had any enemies? If anybody disliked her?"

"Yep. I just have to go to her video page and read the comments." He typed something and then began scrolling with the mouse. "Here's someone. SquirrelFriend546. They start off like any troll—making comments that can be taken as mean or nice depending on who's reading them. But then, here," he tapped the screen, "they start getting angry. Apparently, Lexie Starr quit responding to Squirrel's comments, so then they start making threats. Threats that sound like Squirrel plans to carry them out for real." Sean's voice sounded sad.

Almost like he knew from personal experience what that was like. What kind of a world is it out there for kids, these days, on the internet?

Caroline leaned forward to look at the screen. "Can you find out who this Squirrel person is, like you did Lexie?"

"I'm already trying, but nothing's come up. Squirrel's covered their tracks pretty well." Sean frowned at the screen. "I might try something else. ..." He typed in a few words.

"Yep, got it. It's their profile on ChatWorld. Still no real name, but look here." Sean hit a button titled "Photos" and started clicking through them.

"Wait," I yelled, causing Sean to jump. "Go back."

Sean went back to a photo of a squirrel. "Let me enlarge it."

The squirrel was sitting on a wall. It was eating a peanut. *A peanut.* Water splashed behind the squirrel. The photo had a caption. "Feeding my squirrel friends at my favorite spot." I took a closer look at the photo. I could see part of a statue in the background.

"It's a fountain," I breathed. "And I know right where it is. Great job, kid." I held up my hand to Sean for a high five. He stared at it.

"Right," I laughed, and lowered my hand. "Call it in, Caroline." But she was already on her phone, talking to someone in a low murmur. I waved to get her attention. "Tell 'em to meet us at the park. You know, the entrance across from Lexie's place." I didn't need to tell her to have her fellow officers go in quiet. After a few more minutes of low conversation, Caroline hung up her phone.

"We going?' I asked.

"We're going," Caroline strode toward the door, her keys jingling in her hand.

"But, Mom, what about my cellphone?" Sean asked.

"Later," she said, as she flung open the door. "Use the landline, and order pizza. And do your homework."

I followed her out the door, and down the elevator to Caroline's squad car.

When we neared Lexie's brownstone, Caroline slid in behind a delivery truck. We jumped out and ran toward the truck. The truck driver was unloading a dresser. Caroline flashed her badge and told him to stay put.

"Wait," I said as we peeked over the front of the truck. "It's a clear line of sight from here to the fountain. Let me go in. I'll wait around there and see if this Squirrel shows. Just watch for my signal."

"Hmm, what sort of signal?" Caroline asked.

"I'll, uh, pull my collar up."

Caroline gave me a look that reminded me of her son's, earlier. "Or, you could just text me."

"Uh, yes, I could do that." I muttered. I strolled to the park's entrance, and crossed over to the fountain. It had to be the same statue. I pulled a coin from my pocket and tossed it into the fountain, then sat down on a nearby bench. I checked my watch again. It was almost five-thirty, and probably too late for someone to come to the park to feed squirrels. *Too easy*, I thought, but I waited anyway. I was looking down at my phone when I felt someone sit down on the bench next to me. I stole a glance out of the corner of my eye at the young man who had sat down. He was wearing a black sweatshirt and his sneakers were scuffed. Messy blond hair hung down into his eyes. I would have bet money that they were the exact same brand of clothing that Lexie wore every time she jogged through the park. I heard the rustle of a paper bag.

"I love feeding the squirrels," the young man said. I glanced up, briefly, as he tossed a handful of peanuts toward the fountain. *Peanuts still in the shell*. He was our guy. I stood up and moved away from the bench. I texted Caroline. "Move in."

Within minutes, Caroline and three other cops surrounded the young man. He screamed and dropped his bag of peanuts. He started crying when Caroline took him to the ground and began searching him.

"I was just feeding the squirrels," he wailed. "I ain't done nothing wrong."

"Tell it to the courts," Caroline said, hauling the young man to his feet. He reminded me of the bulldog, big, sad, brown eyes.

I walked over to the bag of spilled peanuts. I snapped on a pair of gloves and picked them up, putting them into an evidence bag.

✗ ✗ ✗ ✗ ✗

A bag of peanuts was still only circumstantial evidence, but we had Judge Ramirez on our side and a district attorney looking to close a high-profile case before the upcoming election, and so Squirrel Boy went to jail.

Caroline and I went out for our usual "case closed" celebration after the trial.

Caroline and I were waiting for our drinks at McCrae's when her phone rang.

She picked it up right away. "Officer Peters here." She listened, and then hung up the phone.

"What is it?" I asked.

"That was the police chief. It's a murder. We gotta get down to the crime scene."

"Seriously?" I asked.

"No, I'm making it up." Caroline threw some bills on the table.

"Why the hurry? Or, better yet, why us?" I shrugged back into my coat.

"Because they found something next to the body." Caroline had her keys in her hand already, jingling them. "It's a peanut. A peanut still in its shell."

I sighed. "Funnily enough, I figured that out." *And, Caroline, let's arrest the right squirrel lover, this time.*

Willow Croft is a horror and speculative fiction writer who currently lives in the high desert but dreams of a home by a tumultuous ocean. When not writing, she cares for her rescued stray calico and two very fat TNR feral cats. Find her hiding out on her blog, https://willowcroft.blog, or on Twitter: @willowcroft16.

Out of Hiding

Trisha McKee

Lila showed Alex the band T-shirt, pleased that his mood had stayed steady throughout the day. He had been through hell and back the last six months, and the least she could do for her best friend was get him out of the house. Keep his mind off everything.

To her delight, Alex smiled. "Cool shirt, but not really my listening style."

"Do you really have to listen to the band to wear the shirt?"

Alex's mouth fell open and a short, hard laugh came out. "Yes, Lila! You can't wear the shirts of bands you don't listen to. That's so high school."

"Funny," she retorted as she hung the shirt back on the rack. "I was also going to say it doesn't matter because we're not in high school anymore."

"Yeah, great comeback."

Lila turned to respond but something caught her eye, and before she could guard her reaction, her mouth dropped open and a gasp fell out.

Alex narrowed his eyes, concern coloring his face and tone. "Lila? Wh-what is it?" He twisted his upper body to try to see what had caught her attention.

Immediately, she stepped in front of him. "I … nothing." When he gave her a quizzical look, she sighed and motioned. "That woman there is wearing a trench coat. A tan leather one with fur along the edges. … Like *she* used to wear. I'm sorry."

The color drained from his face as he caught sight of the woman. "No. It's OK."

"I mean, it's obviously not her. It isn't Rebekah. That woman has short blonde hair."

He shrugged. "Let's just go. Get out of here."

Lila wanted to kick herself for bringing him back to that dark place, reminding him of what he already remembered almost every minute of every day since that horrible time six months ago. When his mother and his girlfriend went missing. When his mother's body had been found in a river not ten miles away, a week after they'd gone missing.

People assumed the women had been kidnapped and murdered, although Rebekah's body had not been found. During this time, Lila was Alex's only support. His father was emotionally unavailable. He had always been a gruff man, always coming across as angry. Alex revealed that their relationship was even more strained during these strange days.

Lila started to pull Alex away from any reminders, but the blonde lady turned, and Lila gasped. There was no mistaking Rebekah's huge green eyes and her upturned nose.

"Alex," she managed to breathe out, and she wondered how he could turn back to her so slowly. She wanted him to look quickly, before Rebekah suddenly vanished.

Finally, he followed her gaze, his expression blank for a moment before it contorted into shock; he started to sway and she feared he might faint. "Oh, my God!" He charged past Lila, and she could only follow, although it occurred to her that they could be in danger. What if the person who kidnapped the women, and killed Alex's mother, was nearby? What if Rebekah was still under the person's control?

"Rebekah!" Alex reached out and clenched her upper arm, giving a slight tug. "What are you doing here?"

As soon as he spoke her name, the woman jumped, her eyes wide. Then she shook her head and whispered, "I'm sorry. You've mistaken me for someone else."

Alex leaned in and hissed, "Rebekah! What—" He glanced over his shoulder, meeting Lila's wide-eyed stare. And that was all it took for Rebekah to break from his grip and run. He ran after her, calling out, "Rebekah! I just need answers!"

Several minutes later, he returned, his shoulders drooping, his head down. "She ran off. I couldn't catch her."

Lila stooped down to catch his gaze. "Alex, what was that? Do you think she—could she have—"

"No!" His head snapped up, and Lila was taken aback by the intensity of his glare. "Don't even say it. She wouldn't do that. Something or someone has her. ... I don't know."

"We need to call the police!"

"No! If she's in danger and that person knows we called … no, please. Let's just … now I know she's alive. We have to wait until she can reach out to me."

"Alex, be reasonable. If she is in danger, we need to contact the police."

He rubbed his face and then stared at her, and she saw the panic in his eyes. "Please. The police have done nothing to help. I need you to trust me on this. I just need to get her to talk to me. No police."

"But … how are you even going to find her?"

"I know she's out there now. I'll find her." His jaw tightened.

Lila wanted to convince him that it made no sense. That this was dangerous, Rebekah's situation was dangerous, but she knew that look. She had known Alex most of her life, and she understood that when he had his mind set, there was no changing it.

They had been best friends through the divorce of Lila's parents when she was eight, and the death of Alex's little brother when Alex was eleven. She knew he was never the same after that. Little Brian had only been four when he had run out in front of a car. The brothers had been playing in the front yard, and Alex had been unable to stop him in time. Alex confessed to her that his parents had never forgiven him.

She was not sure he was right about that, but she knew they mourned their son to the point that nothing else penetrated that grief. Even their firstborn.

Lila had cried with him, had been his support, had let him comfort her through trials and heartbreaks. Now as adults, they were still friends, but she did not feel that closeness. She understood they were growing up and going in different directions. It was natural.

Now she wondered if she should keep his secret. This was about a murder. This was about a woman who was possibly in danger.

Lila had not trusted Rebekah when she first met her. She saw the beautiful woman flirting with a man at the bar when she thought no one was around. But they were young, and Rebekah was nothing but kind to her. And she made Alex deliriously happy.

But now something was off. Lila felt it in her bones, felt it in the sleepless night she had as she tried to decide what to do. Her boyfriend, Sean, finally gave up trying to sleep beside her as she tossed and turned, and went to make her hot chocolate.

"If you think something isn't right, then it probably isn't right," he lectured, and she admired his bare muscular chest, losing her train of thought. For years, she had harbored a secret crush on Alex, but when she went away to college and met Sean, she wondered how she could ever think Alex was right for her.

"But I don't know for sure."

Sean set the steaming mug down and then sat across from her. "The woman is thought to be missing, dead even. The police will want to question her if they know she is alive, if she is in public places. And if she is in danger, you don't want that hanging over your head, hun."

He was right. She could not have this weighing on her. She kept picturing that trench coat, and it struck her that Rebekah *wanted* to be seen. It was such a unique, such an exquisite coat, that it got noticed. It drew attention. She would not have worn her signature coat if she were trying to hide.

Lila went to Alex's place early the next morning, before he left for work. She started to knock on the front door but heard voices close by. Slowly, she made her way around the house to the backyard. The high fence blocked her view, but from there she recognized the voices, and, finding a gap between the boards, she peeked in, trying to stifle a gasp.

Alex was bent forward, his face close to Rebekah's, her shoulders hunched up, leaning back.

"You could have ruined everything! One year. I asked for one year of hiding."

"Alex, I needed to get out. I thought—"

"You didn't think! That damn trench coat! Why would you wear that coat? We had this planned, and it was working! We would have been in the clear—"

"I'm sorry!"

"Are you? Because this all seems a bit suspicious to me."

There was a pause as the couple glared at each other, and then Rebekah hissed, "As suspicious as it already is?"

Rebekah started to walk away toward the gate, and Lila fled to her car, managing to drive off before the sobs erupted. The mere implication of what her best friend was saying ... she could not fathom it. Sure, he had changed since his brother's death, but did he really have a hand in the death of his own mother?

Lila knew he resented his parents because they distanced themselves emotionally from him. He admitted to her that he felt they blamed him. *Could that have driven him to —*

Her phone beeped and a quick glance told her it was Alex. She dragged her focus back on the road, trying to calm down, trying to unravel her thoughts. Sean was right. She had to contact the authorities.

But she had not been home five minutes when there was a pounding at her door. She froze, trying to remember if she had parked in front of the house, if it was obvious that she was home.

"Lila! I need to talk to you. Please!"

Alex knew she was home. With a deep breath, she reminded herself that this was the guy who had carried her home after she had fallen out of a tree when they were ten. This was the guy who had read to her from her favorite book when she was sick. This was the guy who had left college and had driven straight to her when she was homesick and miserable. This was Alex.

She opened the door, and he brushed past her, pacing in her living room even before saying hello. "I think Rebekah … I think she's behind Mom's death."

This was not what Lila had expected him to say. She sank into the couch, her mouth open, no sound coming out.

Still not looking at her, his steps were determined, hard, as he paced. "There's some things I haven't been honest about."

"OK." The word popped out of Lila's mouth, and she jumped, as if surprised to hear her voice.

Before she could ask him to continue, Sean walked through the front door, stopping when he saw Alex. "Hey." His eyes sought out Lila and immediately, he frowned.

"What's going on?"

She straightened. "Alex was just about to tell me how he hasn't been honest with me." She turned to Alex. "I don't keep anything from Sean, so you might as well tell both of us. We have a right to know what's going on." She again was surprised at her words, her strength.

Sean remained standing, squaring his shoulders and staring right at Alex. "I think it's time you come clean, Alex."

He nodded, finally standing still. "Yeah. Ugh!" He rubbed his face. "I just … I—I told Mom and Dad that I was thinking of proposing to Rebekah, and Mom said she didn't even know her. So she planned a day with her. Shopping. Lunch. That type of thing. Halfway through the day, Rebekah and Mom stopped at a convenience store. Some small mom-and-pop place out of town. Rebekah went in to pay for gas and when she came out … Mom was gone."

Sean folded his arms. "Why wouldn't she just call the police?"

"She got scared. She drove off, looking for her. See, Rebekah has a past. When she was a teenager, she got into a bit of trouble. Hurt her stepfather pretty bad. He almost died. But listen, he had it coming. He was cruel to her. So she called me and told me she couldn't find Mom. And … we came up with a plan. That she would go into hiding until Mom showed up. I thought Mom would walk through the door with some story of running into a friend or even just leaving because she didn't like my girlfriend. When that didn't happen …"

"You expect us to believe this?"

Lila heard the fury in Sean's voice, but she motioned for him to wait. She wanted to hear this. "Alex, when that didn't happen, what?"

"I got scared. I told Rebekah to go into hiding. Mom was missing. Then, her body was found. It would look too suspicious if we tried to explain after all that. She had to stay in hiding. I told her after one year, I would join her, and we'd leave. Just … go somewhere."

Sean sighed; his eyes narrowed. "And you don't think she had something to do with your mom's death?"

"No! Rebekah wouldn't—I mean, what could she possibly have to gain by hurting my mom? It doesn't make sense."

"None of this makes sense," Sean snapped. "And I'm more than a little irate that my girlfriend was brought into this."

Alex whirled around, his eyes wide and jaw clenched. "Do you think I wanted Lila involved? I didn't bring her into this. We were shopping, and we saw Rebekah."

"Yeah," Lila cut in. "That's a little weird, isn't it? She was wearing the trench coat."

"So?"

"I mean … she was out in public in that trench coat. I think she wanted to be seen."

Alex stared at her, and for a moment, she worried she had said too much. But then he tilted his head in that way he did when he was considering something. "You think she was there for a devious purpose?"

"She wasn't exactly at a remote location wearing a disguise. I mean her hair was different but that trench coat. She said she had had that specially designed. One of a kind. And she was out wearing it?"

For a few moments, no one said anything. Then Alex sank into a chair, his hands tangled in his dark blond hair. "No. I don't think so. I mean, *why*?"

Sean sat beside Lila. "If what you're saying is true, and you don't have a part in this, I think you need to find out what's going on. The whole why question; start there. I mean, was she angry toward your mom?"

"No. She didn't even really know her. I mean, I complained about Mom. We weren't close, but she was better than Dad. If I'd want anyone gone, it would be that asshole."

"I'd watch my words if I were you," Sean advised. "You're not really in a place to joke about that stuff."

"I said *if* I wanted anyone gone. But I don't. I just … Mom was distant but Dad is a drunk ass. He told me it should have been me instead of Brian. He said he would never forgive me for letting my brother die."

Lila gasped. "Oh, Alex, that's horrible! I know you said you felt they blamed you, but I never knew he said that!"

"Not really something someone wants to share. He would get drunk and blame me, blame Mom, curse us and his life. He is just mean. But Mom … I think she was just … she lost her younger son. I understand the emotional shutdown. I was hurt by it, but I did understand. I'd never hurt her. I'd never have anyone hurt her. When she was gone, when Rebekah said she wasn't there, I actually thought maybe she just ran off to escape Dad."

Lila felt for her best friend. In her gut, she knew he had nothing to do with this. His only mistake was not going to the authorities immediately. He had protected his girlfriend, believing his mother might have disappeared to leave a bad marriage.

"You need to go to the police, Alex," Sean insisted, his expression softening only slightly. "This can't go on."

"Sure, yeah. But I should talk to Rebekah—"

Sean cursed. "So she can have a chance to run? Alex, she might be involved. You have to face that."

Before he could answer, his phone dinged. Checking, his expression fell. "It's Rebekah. She's at my place. I'm going to see what she wants." He caught their exasperated expressions. "I'm not going to let on that I'm suspicious. I mean, for all we know, she has nothing to do with any of this."

As soon as he was out the door, Sean shook his head. "You want to follow, don't you?"

"You know me so well."

"Let's take my car. I'm driving. Keeping you out of trouble."

On the ride there, Sean focused on keeping a safe distance behind to not be seen. As he concentrated, Lila blurted out, "You never liked Alex."

He swung his head toward her, his eyes wide, and then he turned his attention back to the road. "No. Not really."

"Why?"

"I've told you. He drains your energy. He takes advantage of you. Anytime he is upset or in trouble, he runs to you. And I just think you have to let go of the need to always fix him."

"He's my best friend."

"And me?"

She grew silent for a few moments, stunned with the realization that he was jealous. Finally, she said, "You're right. *You're* my best friend. You are the one who is always there for me. And you are the one I love. But I can't desert him."

He nodded and then parked a block down from Alex's car. He turned to Lila and admitted, "I get it. Just … I don't want you in danger."

They waited for several minutes until Lila sat up straight in her seat and pointed. "Look. That's Alex's dad. Where's his car? He's … why is he sneaking around the back?"

"That doesn't look good. Lila, stay here. Call the police. Tell them Rebekah is here, and you think there might be some trouble. Don't follow me."

Lila made the call quickly, and then she was out of the car, running to the house. She slowed down and tiptoed to the side of the house, where Sean was staring into the window. He saw her and cursed. When she was close enough, he whispered, "Dammit, Lila! He has a gun in there. Get away. Go wait for the cops. Please."

"Who has a gun?"

She peeked in and saw Alex's dad with a gun aimed right at Alex. Lila gasped, her heart leaping into her throat. The most shocking part of that sight was that Rebekah stood beside his dad with her arms crossed, an almost bored look on her otherwise flawless face.

"C'mon." Sean led her away from the house. "We need to wait here for the police. Just as he pulled out his phone to call again, police cars with lights flashing pulled into the yard.

Everything after that was a blur of activity. Lila was in shock as Sean explained to the police that Alex's father and Rebekah held Alex at gunpoint in the house. The police ushered Sean and Lila to a cop car down the street, out of danger. They watched as, in less than twenty minutes, Alex's father and Rebekah were led from the house in handcuffs. Lila and Sean rushed from the car when they saw Alex emerge.

He collapsed in their arms, his body trembling. "He was trying to kill me. He had a suicide note written up that basically had me saying I killed my mom."

"I don't understand," Lila cried, helping Sean hold up the young man. "Why?"

"He and Rebekah were having an affair. Mom found out, and on the day they went shopping together, Mom confronted her. She was going to leave Dad. He didn't want to lose all the money. So he and Rebekah were framing *me* for the murder."

Lila was at a loss for words, but it was Sean who held Alex up and spoke in a low, comforting tone. It was Sean who instructed him to go with the police and give his statement and they would be there to get him when he was done.

"That poor guy," Sean murmured. "He never even had a chance to mourn his mom. He wanted to protect the very woman who was responsible and scheming with his own dad to frame him. I don't— I don't understand it." He squeezed Lila's hand. "We'll be there for him."

She nodded before noticing Rebekah's trench coat visible in the window. And she made a mental note to burn it before Alex returned to his home.

Trisha McKee has resided in a small town in Pennsylvania after coming out of hiding. Since April 2019, her work has appeared in over 60 publications, including *The Oddville Press, Hybrid Fiction, Horror Magazine, Night to Dawn, Crab Fat Magazine,* several anthologies, and more. Her debut novel, *Beyond the Surface,* is available on Amazon. Her next novel, *Beyond the Dreams,* is scheduled for a fall 2020 release. You can find her work at www.trishamckee.com.

Family Secrets

Stephanie Scissom

Lightning flashed across an angry purple sky, and thunder shook the building as the automatic doors of the Mega-Mart slid open. I hurried inside as the first drops of rain pelted my back.

A woman in a red Mega-Mart vest shook a shopping cart free from the stack and shoved it toward me.

"Welcome to Mega-Mart." Her bloodshot gaze had already drifted to something over my shoulder.

A dazzling flash of lightning lit the darkened parking lot like a nuclear blast, and I heard a loud pop before the rumble of thunder drowned out everything else. The store lights flickered and died.

I hesitated with my hand on the cart. As the security lights winked on, I watched a gray-haired woman in a strangely bulging trench coat try to slip out. The greeter stepped in front of the doors.

"I'm sorry, ma'am, but the security system is electric. I can't let you leave until the lights come back on."

"You can't keep me here!" the old woman sputtered. "Why, I, um, I have a, um ... a roast in the oven!"

"Sorry, ma'am. It's store policy." The greeter looked tired, overworked. And she was definitely a cop. The way she stood, the way she talked. ...

Ah, Vinnie, I thought with amusement. *All this for me?*

A poster of Vinnie hung on the wall next to the doors. He looked serious and slightly ridiculous in a black fedora framed by the words,

Riganali Family Secrets: Shocking Tales of America's Most Violent Mob Family by Frankie Riganali's Right-Hand Man, Vincent Bagoli. Book Signing Today!

The fact that the little weasel had profited from dishing dirt on my family still galled me. Nobody crossed the Riganalis. Pops was dead and my brothers Tony and Viggo were in the joint. It was up to me, Sal Riganali, to get revenge for my family. After I'd sent word to Vinnie that I'd get him myself, Vinnie had disappeared, knowing Sal Riganali was a man of his word.

They'd looked for me for five years. The police must be getting desperate to dangle Vinnie out in front of me like a carrot.

I claimed a cart and threw my satchel in. Then I joined the other shoppers browsing shadowy aisles lit only by security lights. Didn't want to look too suspicious by running right up to Vinnie, even though I wasn't worried they'd crack my disguise.

After selecting a few items, I casually made my way to the book section. There sat Vinnie. He still looked like a hood, though his clothes were better now. He was flanked by two cops dressed in gangster garb. I was probably the only civilian in the place who knew the pieces they carried were real.

Nice.

I got in line behind a teenage boy and the old dame in the trench coat who'd tried to sneak out. The officers were really checking her out. The teenager got his autograph and turned to leave, jostling her.

A can fell from beneath her coat, sounding like a shotgun blast when it hit the floor. Vinnie jumped three feet in the air and both guards and the cashier at register eight reached for their pieces.

Security rushed in to grab her and pulled her away. My heart sank because Vinnie was on his feet, arguing with his detail. That old shoplifting bird might have cost me my best opportunity.

They must've appeased the little rat because he sat back down, and finally I stood before him, the man who'd betrayed my family. The cops eyeballed me as I lay my satchel on the table. One of them motioned for Vinnie to move.

"Let me get that for you." He ran some device over it and then opened it. He needn't have worried. Vinnie wasn't worth blowing myself up over. Besides, explosives were my brother Tony's bag, not mine.

Lifting my eyebrows, I reached inside for my copy of Vinnie's book. I opened it to the front cover where my pen was already stuck inside.

As expected, Vinnie picked up my expensive pen. It was a Parker, and a pretty snazzy one, at that.

"Sorry about that." He shrugged. "Security guys. Who do I make this out to?"

"Cecile," I said.

Vinnie frowned and for a moment I was afraid I'd said too much. Cecile was my mother's name, but Vinnie knew her as Cee-Cee.

"C-e-c-," he paused, giving me a perplexed look.

"I-l-e," I replied, doing a mental eye roll. Fame hadn't made him any smarter. He signed it with a flourish, handed me back my book, and pocketed the pen. Geez, the guy raked in three mil on the book and he still stole pens.

I thanked him, replaced the book in my satchel and snapped it shut. As I walked away, I spared a backward glance at Vinnie.

Dead man walking.

The lights flickered back on.

Although I'd have loved to stick around and see the show, I figured I'd better get out of there. In about another five minutes, Vinnie would feel the effects of the parathion poison I'd coated the pen with. Probably the cops would think he was having a heart attack, but I didn't want to take any chances. I wondered if the sweating had started yet, or the dizziness.

Easy enough, I thought, as I stood in line at the register.

Vinnie and the cops had never seen me coming. A lot of things had changed in the last five years.

I paid for my pantihose and adjusted the plastic rain bonnet over my auburn hair. I nodded at the greeter/cop before stepping out into the rain-soaked afternoon.

Sal Riganali was a changed man. These days, I went by Sally.

Good thing Vinnie hadn't known all the family secrets.

Stephanie hails from Tennessee, where she works nights in a tire factory and plots murder by day. She's published in romantic suspense and horror. You can stalk her at www.facebook.com/stephaniescissom2019.

The Trench Coat Murders

Andrew Sellors

It was a bright, blue morning, and I was horizontal on a brown leather recliner in the orangery, oiling my trench coat and reciting lines from a script that had landed with me when Smith, my butler, came in rather flustered. Smith is normally a rather level fellow whose impassivity makes all alarming situations that would spin the ordinary chapess on the Clapham Omnibus into a blind fumble, mere death rites. So, when a chapess sees such a fellow flushed, it is rather confounding.

'My Lady' he said.

'Goodness Smith, you seem rather agog.'

'Yes, My Lady, I believe that may be the impression one gives at this present moment.'

'Well, what is it muddling you?'

'Well …'

'Is it that clumsy coal man with the big red nose and dislike of non-coal-coloured carpets?' I now moved to an erect position on the recliner.

'No, My Lady.'

'It's not not-so poor kiddiwinkles collecting on behalf of poor kiddiwinkles is it? You know it's the eyes that get you?'

'No, My Lady.'

'No … it can't be …' I rose up in indignation. 'Mr Dewsbury-Hartwright formerly of my sleeping quarters, here at North House?'

'No, My Lady, it is neither merchants of fuel, espousers of emotive language for monetary gain, nor errant lovers, My Lady.'

'Well, what in the name of Simon is it?'

'A large baby-blue Daimler motor vehicle has just pulled outside the west porch, My Lady.'

'Oh,' I perfunctorily added, looking to an ugly green rug woven by an ancestor noted for his sobriety, in a contortion of thought. Who the Frank did I know who was vulgar enough to drive a baby-blue car? There was Freddie 'Ten Fingers' Mortimer-Harrington, whose presence at parties always led to the 'Tickle Game,' but he had died ten years ago, so it wasn't him. What about Major Kent owner of Irish Wolfhounds that came up to his shoulder? He was blind and deaf though, and as Smith hadn't indicated the car was in the privet hedge it probably wasn't him. Hmm … a very strange affair.

'Who is the driver, Smith?'

'As one was peeping through a net curtain lest one give away location to a collecting usurer, I, alas, got merely the touch of a view.'

'And?'

'A moustachioed gentleman in a large, felt trilby and off-the-peg suit, My Lady. The lower portion of him is merely circumspect.'

'Find out who he is Smith, and remember …'

The Trench Coat Chronicles

'If he is seeking monies, I am an actor merely purporting to stage the role of an incumbent servant on behalf of a film unit due at suppertime. Any enquires to Mr. Chaplin care of The London Film Studios.'

'Yes, very good. Oh, and tell them they can jolly well use the tradesmen's entrance, Smith.'

'Thank you, My Lady.'

Smith made his leave and I returned to a reclined state. I stared at the latticed ironwork of the roof of the orangery feeling rather bereft at an unsolicited gentlemen visitor in a vulgar motor vehicle. Realising I was still grasping my coat I made action to tuck it behind the pot of an ebullient Bougainvillea and reached for a Viennese finger from the table. Crunching the bikky, I pondered whether this unsolicited visitor had anything to do with the activities of last night; it would be awfully indiscreet on my part if that were the case. Suddenly I gasped and flashed up, dangling my legs over the side of the recliner. 'No, golly, no,' I uttered to myself, grabbing a pink wafer.

Before I could calculate any further Smith returned, looking rather more flustered than before.

'Oh, for the love of ...' I began, 'what is it now?'

'The unsolicited gentleman is refusing to use the tradesmen's entrance. To your instructions he said ...,' and at that this point Smith, who is a wonderful mimic, strode into a grating Yorkshire accent. "Do I bloody look like a butcher? Does the doctor use the tradesmen's entrance? Well, I'm a doctor of the dead so I'm using the front door. Now shift."'

'I say, what an indignant fellow! Striding into a chapess' abode and shouting the ones and twos about doors! Did he say what he wanted? Aside from to create an air of indignancy?'

It was at that moment that Old Moustachio eclipsed the light that had flooded in from the door of the orangery, his frame of such girth that slipping past him would have proved unfeasible.

'Are you Lady Worthington?' he verbally poked at me.

'Yes, at your pleasure, my good friend! Thank you, Smith.' Smith slid out of the orangery leaving me with just my non-tradesman visitor.

Uninvited, the visitor perched on a wooden bench, tongue planted firmly in cheek and hat placed to his left. Out popped a little red notebook, as if he were one of those jobbies who watch birds and I some rare hawfinch he wished to observe.

'My name is Inspector Harris,' he began. 'As you are no doubt aware from the papers, I am investigating a number of murders in the local town—four to be precise. Each victim was thirty- to forty-years-old and all were strangled near the Old Horse Public House.'

'Golly!' I rejoined.

'Yes, golly indeed. We have no motive, weapon, or killer. The only thing that links all four is an individual wearing a trench coat, seen in the vicinity of the Old Horse in the moments before each killing.'

'I do hope you catch the dastardly chap or chapess.'

'And that's what I shall do!' he emphasised.

'Awfully crude behaviour isn't it? Macaroon?' I said proffering a plate of delicacies.

'No, I don't think he's a Scottish fella,' he said engrossed with his notebook and not looking up.

I don't know whether these fellows are trained to play the ninnyhammer as decoy or they are just naturally blessed with ignorance, but even if he was lacking the white stuff, he did possess a bite. I decided it best to be a careful chapess here; men who deal with vagabonds and footpads for a living are liable to develop some rough edges over time.

'Well, it's awfully kind of you to visit me but I must ask what the George has any of this got to do with me?'

'Do you drive a silver Lagonda V12 with cream hide interior? Reg 14904KAF?'

'I do, and what a splendid machine it is! Do you know Sir Edin "Odd Socks" Hop-Freeman?'

'No.'

'Well, when we were a little on the chummy side ...'

'Has this got anything to do with my investigation?' he butted in.

'No. Tart?' I proffered a delicious slice.

'No, no none of that sort was involved,' he said, scribbling away. 'Look, let me cut to the chase here, Madam. Last night a silver Lagonda V12 with cream hide interior, Reg 14904KAF was seen driving away from the Old Horse Public House at nine o'clock in the direction of North House. And we have established that is your vehicle, is it not?'

'Yes, it's my rather splendid machine. Lovely leather seats. Cream hide interior.'

'Right, it's your vehicle. That naturally leads me to ask if you were driving. So, were you driving it?'

'Oh, yes I was indeed! I learnt during the summer of '19 when I moored up with the son of an admiral somewhere on a channel island. Parker was a terrible guzzler so in order to return to mooring without being tardy, one had to override the controls by herself …'

'So, you own the car and were driving away from the Old Horse Public House at nine o'clock at night in the direction of North House?'

'*Oui, oui!*'

'No thanks, I went before I got here. So, what was your purpose for being in the vicinity of the Old Horse Public House at nine o'clock at night?'

'Why it was Benny Boatlaker's card night! Whist for four guineas a hand! He and his pals are rather clumsy after drinkypoopoos so a sober chapess can easily clean up. …'

This officer of the law seemed rather taken aback by my anecdote, his brow a little sweaty. I offered him a handkerchief, which he declined. He looked rather quizzical too, as if the game was too easy.

'Did you know that Ben Boatlaker was strangled last night?'

'Oh, yes!' I said.

'How do you?'

'Because I did it!'

The Inspector jumped up, dropping his notebook. I noticed how his shirt had come out of his trousers exposing a lump of flabby belly and giving him the air of a drunk. Rubbing the sweat from his brow with a dirty brown hand, he glanced to the orangery door, whether to measure any escape I might pursue, or for him to utilize if this murderess got a little handy, I did not know.

'But … but … you're a Lady!'

'Yes, I am! Iced finger?' I offered.

'So, you murdered Judge Timpkin-Hortly?'

'Yes.'

'The Earl of Sheer House?'

'Yes.'

'Lady Freisiana Horton-Dimple-Jaspers?'

'Yes.'

'And Benny … Boatlaker?'

'Yes.'

'But the trench coat?'

'Oh, just here and freshly oiled!' I said whilst reaching behind the ebullient Bougainvillea to retrieve it.

'In that case, I'm arresting you for the murders of …' he positioned a pair of handcuffs over my person.

'Steady on, chap; that wasn't in the script.'

'The script?'

'Yes, the script!'

It was at this moment that Smith burst into the orangery looking most frightful, his hair oiled back and gathered at the back like a duck's tail. His garb consisted of a vulgar wide-awake suit in frightful yellow and white check, and horror of horrors … brown shoes! A little pink and black spotty bowtie added the icing to his vulgarity! I recognized this brazen tailoring from the wardrobe of one

Morty Carmichael, III, a loud, brash American who had made a permanent getaway through a drawing room window one evening after a drunk local player, having escaped from an earlier party and garbed up as a beadle, had been jumping around from room to room shouting "What's all this about?" Whilst my American friend did not return, even for a stiff one, he did leave a sordid collection of new money attire, some of which Smith was wearing in our present confrontation.

'Hey!' Smith announced with wide arms and spot-on with an American East Coast accent spookily similar to that of the suit's erstwhile Morty Carmichael, III. 'How is my little babbbbbyy … *baby*!' he added, kissing my forehead. 'So, what do you think, my friend?' Smith said, pinching the cheek of the Inspector, to which his British reserve sat open-mouthed. 'When I first saw this gal, I thought, *wow*! She *will* be the next big thing!' Looking down at the handcuffs, positioned mid-air he changed tone. 'Hey, what the hell are these?'

'They …' stammered the Inspector.

'Get em' off or I break your nose, ya' ball of lard. These wrists are for Gable; if you damage them …'

'STOP!' shouted the Inspector. Both Smith and I froze, looking at the Inspector icily stupefied. 'I am an officer of the law and this lady has just admitted to the murder of four innocents. Therefore, in the name of the King, it is my duty to arrest her. Let me remind you, her car was seen near each crime scene. Correct?' We both nodded. 'The killer was wearing a trench coat and that item of clothing is here. Correct?' We both nodded again. 'And finally, you confessed.'

'A jumbled confession can only receive a jumbled absolution,' offered Smith.

'Look, I've had it with you two ...'

'Flapjack?' I offered.

'He's nothing to do with it! This lady is coming with me into custody on charges of the murder of Judge Timpkin-Hortly, the Earl of Sheer House, Lady Freisiana Horton-Dimple-Jaspers, and Benny ... Boatlaker. Now, you tell me why she isn't the Trench Coat Murderer.'

'He doesn't think, does he?' asked Smith in a confused tone.

'I think he does ... darling.'

Smith picked up a bundle of papers from a side table and threw it underarm to the Inspector, who was deceptively sprite at catching. 'Take a look my friend.'

The Inspector leafed through the script, and then with an indignant tone read aloud, '"The Trench Coat Murders: The Script." You're bloody actors!'

'That's right, my friend,' I said. 'You didn't think he thought I was being serious, did you ... darling?' I directed at Smith.

'I think he thought you were being serious ... *baby*.'

'We aren't the *real* Trench Coat Murderers. You see, Louis Sackerville, Jr. here is one of the leading lights in American motion picture direction. Some evenings ago, I was having a little gathering in the drawing room and doing the Charleston when one Commodore Halfpenny introduced me to his American friend here. Having been so aghast at the Trench Coat Murders from having read about them in an American newspaper, he boarded the first steamer out of Long Island with one focus …'

'To make "The Motion Picture: The Trench Coat Murders,"' said Smith, using air quotes. 'And you know what … baby? I was on the line to Goldwyn Mayer himself *today*, and he said, "Sonny, I'm gonna pour so much money into this movie it's gonna hurt, but you gotta have a real, and I mean real, mean cop in there, and YOU are gonna find him," and you know what … baby?'

'What … baby?' I retorted.

'I think we found him!'

'Oh, I would be humbled!' interjected the Inspector.

'Inspector James!'

'WHAT!' bellowed Inspector Harris. 'But what about *me*?'

'What about you! Hah!' Smith teased. 'Get outta here! Ya' loser!'

It was at that moment I believe Inspector Harris began to shed a tear; he realized the movie career he had built in the previous few minutes was now over. Then he did a curious series of gestures, a kind of mixture of waving and pugilism, from which no sound but a tinny wail emitted. Taking a large gasp of breath, he folded away his notebook into a jacket pocket, plonked his hat back on his head and stomped out with handcuffs dangling from his hip. Once his frame filled the orangery door again, he fired a parting shot. 'Bloody timewaster! You know I could have you done for this! All I can say is … let's hope you never encounter whatever monster is out there killing these people! And you, sir!' he pointed at Smith. 'It's just some *Sunday Lark* to you!'

'Toodl-oo!' I said.

'With my diabetes?' he growled before stomping off. A half-minute later we heard the sound of wheels on gravel as our acquaintance hurried off in search of more priggers and jackrollers.

Obsequiously, Smith took his leave from the orangery. He returned several minutes later minus the ablepsy-inducing attire of the sometime Morty Carmichael, III.

'My Lady,' he offered.

'Say, that was rather flagrant, wasn't it?'

'One would agree with your use of "flagrant" in the sense of the aforementioned situation.'

'It does make one feel rather giddy, though.'

'Would you wish me fetch a Brain Salt?'

'Oh no, turn over the old Lagonda; we are going on a little excursion, Smith.'

'Oh, of course My Lady.'

'And pass me that trench coat. We aren't going to let a silly little man stop our fun, are we, Smith?'

Andrew Sellors is an English teacher and writer from Belper, England. Andrew's work has appeared in the *Tyranny of Bacon* anthology as well as treadbikely.com and voiceclub.org. His story, *Causa Mortis,* has been nominated for 2020's Ouen Prize. Andrew lives with his wife and soon-to-be-born son.

THANK YOU!

Thanks for buying *The Trench Coat Chronicles*.

We hope you've enjoyed reading this anthology as much as we enjoyed compiling it. If you did love it, please consider writing a review for it on Amazon and Goodreads.

Check out our website geminiwordsmiths.com/publishing for our future submission calls and publications.

And like us on Facebook at Celestial Echo Press and Gemini Wordsmiths, along with all of our fabulous authors!

Also by Celestial Echo Press ...

The Twofer Compendium, an anthology with 36 stories based on the theme of twins, available in eBook and paperback at Amazon and Barnes & Noble.

About Gemini Wordsmiths

Gemini Wordsmiths, LLC, a woman-owned editing, copywriting, and proofreading business, was founded in 2011 in Abington, Pennsylvania. As karma would have it, Ruth, Ann, and Gemini Wordsmiths were all born under the astrological sign of Gemini.

Every project is given the same intense review, regardless of whether it is a one-page document or a 100,000-word novel. And instead of getting one editor for their dollars, our clients receive a second set of eyes at the same cost, as both editors review each project separately and then collaboratively. For more information call 215-605-5231 or visit geminiwordsmiths.com.

About Celestial Echo Press

A few years ago, Gemini Wordsmiths' partner, Ruth Littner, had a crazy idea to expand into publishing. That crazy idea came to be in June 2019 when we formed Celestial Echo Press. Our first anthology, *The Twofer Compendium*, contains 36 stories based on the theme of twins, penned by 34 international authors. *The Trench Coat Chronicles* is our second anthology. We are deep in thought about where we go from here. …

Thanks for joining us in our adventure!